The Sentinels

The Sentinels

Derek Smith

FREDERIC C. BEIL

SAVANNAH

Copyright © 2001 by Derek Smith

Published in the United States by
Frederic C. Beil, Publisher, Inc.
609 Whitaker Street
Savannah, Ga. 31401
http://www.beil.com

LIBRARY OF CONGRESS CATALOGING-IN-PUBLICATION DATA
Smith, Derek, 1956 Nov. 3–
The sentinels / Derek Smith
p. cm.
ISBN 1-929490-13-5 (alk. paper)
1. Charleston (S.C.)—Fiction. 2. Underwater archaeology—Fiction.
3. Hunley (Submarine)—Fiction. 4. Submarines—Fiction.
5. Shipwrecks—Fiction. I. Title.

PS3619.M58 S45 2001
813'.6—dc21

2001025820

This book was set in the Galliard typeface by SkidType, Savannah, Georgia;
printed on acid-free paper; and sewn in signatures.

Printed in the United States of America

The Sentinels

I

1994

"NOTHING BUT CLASSIC rock and roll without the talk!"

The VHF-band radio static was suddenly cut by a disc jockey's canned spiel.

"Leave it there, at least we can hear some decent music and maybe a weather report."

Raising her arms above her head, Majorie Wagner stretched like a contented house cat as she groggily stepped up to the yacht's main deck. The movement made her abruptly aware of her new sunburn.

"Over did it, damn I'm hurting," she said aloud to herself, gently patting her stomach to determine how burned she was. "When will I ever learn?"

At the helm, Sherman Wagner fired up another cigar to fend off the waves of mosquitoes and gnats relentlessly attacking them since they had reached the Carolina coast. He paid no attention to Majorie's complaints.

In front of him the Intracoastal Waterway was a writhing ebony ribbon of water unraveling to the south. Over the dark tree line to Wagner's right, the sky was illuminated by a city's metropolitan sprawl. Probably Charleston.

Watching the lights play off the scattered clouds, Wagner imagined that aliens had landed in the Southern swamps and that he was sailing in to meet their huge-headed generalissimo. Negotiate a treaty to save the Earth and promote galactic harmony. Around the next stand of mossy cypress he would be awed by the splendor of their mothership.

Magellan meets the Martians? Nah, he'd have to do better.

In reality he already had. Copernicus Press had just agreed to publish the fourth in his series of science fiction novels. Public response had been good to his previous efforts, and Copernicus had offered him a generous contract. The talk-show people were calling again.

To celebrate, he and Majorie had stocked their forty-seven-foot Chris Craft Commander with a galley full of gourmet delicacies and Canadian beer for a quick Dixie excursion to Key West from Perth Amboy.

In a cloaking New Jersey fog, they had embarked three days earlier in the *H. G. Wells*. Wagner had christened his boat in honor of the famous Englishman who wrote *The War of the Worlds*.

The trip had been soothing but boring to this point, the throaty drone of the twin-diesel Cummins engines a fitting soundtrack for the trek.

"How far are we out of Wilmington or Charleston or wherever?" Majorie broke into his unearthly vision.

"I think we're getting close to Charleston. We passed Wilmington while you were zonked out. And we passed Georgetown. Remember the smell from that damn paper mill?"

Majorie retrieved her tumbler of Chivas from a deck chair where she had been sunbathing earlier. Its ice long dissolved, she downed the watery drink in three quick gulps.

Gingerly she reached over her shoulder and felt her back, probing around her bikini bra strap to determine the sun's napalm damage. Her skin tingled and chilled on account of the baking.

"I'm a frigging lobster, Sherman, how could you let me do this to myself?"

"We'll tie up at the Charleston marina, get some Southern

fried seafood, and then hit the water again in the A.M.," Wagner said, keeping his eye on a flashing navigational buoy coming up to starboard. "Isle of Palms should be next, then Sullivan's Island and Charleston. Heck, Savannah isn't that far."

Wagner checked the instrument panel that gave everything in the cockpit a faint greenish hue. All was in order—fuel levels, direction finder, radar, compass, and speedometer.

"Why don't we spend a day or so in Charleston or Savannah? Remember when I spent your first book's royalties at Radley's?"

They had ducked in to the boutique on King Street in downtown Charleston during a summer rainstorm in 1987, and Majorie had played a buccaneer princess in looting the place of its posh Fifth Avenue fashions and Italian designer jewelry.

"If nothing else we should hit the bars on River Street and City Market in Savannah. Remember that Saint Patrick's Day a couple of years ago?"

"Not much, and I know you don't either. You were too busy running out to kiss those Army Rangers in the parade and flashing the crowd. What was the name of that square we ducked in for a quickie in the azalea bushes?"

A hard and sudden jolt against the side of the hull interrupted everything—conversation, thought, and motion.

"What the hell did we hit?" Majorie asked, momentarily being thrown off balance. She steadied herself against the cabin wall.

There was no time for Wagner to form an answer.

Within milliseconds a vesuvian blast wrung the Chris Craft in an explosion of mind-numbing noise, white-hot light, and flying debris.

The *Wells* was splintered like a balsa airplane in a child's fist. A miasma of wood, water, fiberglass, flesh, and metal burst into the sky and slowly plummeted downward, thousands of splashes violating the creek.

Briefly hurled about on the water, the United States flag that had been attached to the *Wells*'s stern was among the last flotsam to be swallowed by the roiling waves.

Infinity

Humans have been seafood for the underwater world in and around Charleston for many centuries. Rotten, freshly dead, and from any racial origin, man has been a main course for the ocean dwellers that have savored the taste of people for some time.

Occasionally the meal came from a Catawba or other red man who lost his footing while wading in the shallows and never reached land again. Other feedings came from whites that settled about Charlestown Landing on the Ashley River and died of disease or were hurled overboard from ships during storms.

Hurricanes left bodies draped in trees or washed into tidal creeks. Whether the dinner was a Huguenot farmer, Broad Street socialite, or "homeboy" wearing the wrong gang colors, the soft-shelled legions and finned browsers cared less when shopping the harbor floor.

By far, the best feasts came after shipwrecks and during wars. Trillions were served when a British fleet was shot to pieces trying to capture Charleston and Fort Moultrie in 1776.

With proper ceremony the Englishmen dumped their mangled dead into the ocean and sailed away, their admiral nursing an ass full of lead.

The War Between the States killed generations of sea turtles and dolphin with man-made weapons like underwater torpedoes and huge naval gun shells that ripped the water with gargantuan explosions.

But again, everyone ate well. While the Rebels in Charleston nearly starved on a diet of mule-tail soup and collards, their salt-water neighbors enjoyed the dead fruit of "Southern rights" and "the Union forever."

Unlike the humans' surface navies, no allegiances extended to the offshore regions. Yankee corpses, including a smorgasbord of slain U.S. Colored Troops, tumbled in and out with the tide after the 54th Massachusetts' bravely vain attack on Battery Wagner in July 1863.

The killed Rebels were a bony lot in comparison to the better-fed and plumper Federals. Sixty-two Union boys went to the deep with the sinking of the monitor *Patapsco* in January 1865, and it was clean-up in aisle five for the denizens of the depths.

Whatever happened, the ocean scavengers instinctively knew to follow the black mass. They sensed it did not belong among them, and most kept their distance when it emerged from the fathoms. Yet their appetites drove them to stay relatively close.

By the millions they congregated, waiting for the food to appear in the murk. Like a large school of fish shadowing the water, the dark shape always traveled close to the surface. And it always left a harvest of dead humans in its wake.

February 17, 1914

The Model T's headlights sliced the night as John Quincy "Iceman" Turner steered the Ford along the coastal road on Sullivan's Island. The stiff wind whipping off Charleston Harbor seemed to cut into all of the automobile's rivets, swirling up through the wooden floorboard.

"Ocean's mighty upset tonight," Turner said, turning to watch the whitecaps and to catch an eyeful of his passenger. "Devil must be tap dancin' on the bottom."

Turner had earned his nickname for coolness under fire as a corporal in the U.S. 10th Cavalry during the Spanish-American War. The 10th was a crack outfit of black troopers who fought to glory at Kettle and San Juan hills in Cuba. Teddy Roosevelt's Rough Riders took all the headlines, but the 10th went up the slopes, bled, and died with the best of them.

Iceman liked to tell the story of how a young lieutenant named John Pershing, who had since risen among the Army elite, once complimented him for his marksmanship in dropping a Spanish artillery officer.

There was more to the event, always left untold. Turner never talked about how he and his men clambered up the hill to find a white captain from another outfit sawing away at the dead man's wrist with a dull bayonet to retrieve a gold identification bracelet.

Pershing's pat on the head was good, but the sight of that dusty brown corpse would always jerk back and forth in his mind.

"You niggers want a button off his blouse?" the officer shouted, squinting up at Turner's platoon from beneath his slouch hat.

Clenching his carbine with both hands, Iceman glared at the captain for a few seconds and then silently led his men on up the slope to clean out another pocket of Spaniards.

Turner returned to Charleston to a less-than-jubilant welcome after the war. Desperate for a job, he turned to his piano experience to land work at several downtown bars.

Turner knew the keyboard like the business end of a straight razor. His mother was a gospel pianist who played on a circuit of black churches on Edisto Island when he was young. During the week she was a washwoman for the well-to-do white folk.

Iceman could remember driving her down those narrow, rutted island trails in a one-horse buggy while she held an umbrella over her with one hand and worked a wooden-handled fan from some funeral parlor with the other.

As a child, he had often filled in when the fever took her and the sweating, swaying congregation was waiting. Banging out the rousing old-time hymns on endless Sundays had been a great primer for the smoky honky-tonk of Charleston's steaming nights.

Working as a stevedore on the docks during the day and playing the bars after dark, Turner had been able to save some money and lead a comfortable life. His piano finesse attracted such attention that he was able to give up his dockfront job and concentrate on performing at the Mimosa Club on Prioleau Street.

"Why don't we try to take a little walk on the beach. I got an old quilt in the back in case you get cold. This ought to warm you up too." Turner passed a flask of brandy to his companion.

"Why, Mr. Turner, what is a girl to do with you?" Ella Solomon accepted the flask and took a swallow, the brandy burning her throat and making her eyes water.

Two weeks into her eighteenth year, she had been working at the Mimosa as a singer for the past five months. She and Turner had been out many times with a group of other blacks that

worked the downtown clubs, whether their friends were perform-
ers or kitchen help. Iceman finally had summoned the nerve to
ask her out the night before. Ella enjoyed the flirtation game she
carried on with Iceman, but was unsure whether she totally
trusted his intentions. They had left the Mimosa well after midnight, driving through the city streets before heading north for
the island across the Cooper River. Iceman had awakened a
ferryman and bribed him to take them over the river.

If Iceman was a piano wonder, Ella's soprano renditions like-
wise mesmerized the bar regulars who were as much taken by her
songs as by her light complexion and slit skirts. She too had
grown up in Lowcountry churches, singing in choirs where her
voice flowered.

Ella came from a family of sharecroppers whose history was
rooted in the fields around Beaufort. Her grandmother had done
mending for various units of United States Colored Troops
stationed in the Port Royal area during the Civil War. She had
never traveled much, but had gone to Charleston when she
turned seventeen. Staying with an aunt on Nassau Street, Ella had
landed a job at the Mimosa. Always with her were the painful
memories of her farm-calloused palms and the surprised expression
of the Mimosa's manager when they shook hands at her audition.

Iceman parked in a lane between sand dunes near Fort Moultrie, and they got out of the car, Ella with the quilt draped over
her shoulders.

"Ain't this a pretty sight," he said, waving an arm toward the
lights of Charleston sparkling in the distance. They walked a
short distance down the beach. "Here, why don't we plop down
here for a minute and get some more refreshment?" Turner
patted the flask in his coat pocket.

"I'm not sure this was such a wondrous idea," Ella said, "but
that brandy might help break this chill."

They spread the quilt on the sand and Turner gave Ella his
jacket, sliding close to her.

"Miz Ella, I do believe you are one of the finest ladies ever to
grace the streets of this old town," Iceman said, using the opportunity to slip an arm around Ella.

7

They matched swigs from the flask and cuddled on the quilt. "Did I ever tell you the story about Shiloh Brown? He was an old mule driver from somewhere down around Darien, Georgia, who showed up with two señoritas while we was in Cuba. We was bivouacked outside this little village when he rode up with these two women on these donkeys and . . ."

Iceman stopped talking. His eye caught several dark forms trudging toward them. When it appeared obvious that they were heading in their direction, he got up to see what they wanted.

Four men, he could see by the moonlight, all slightly built and wearing hats and what appeared to be overcoats or capes. Silently they walked up the beach until they were within a few yards of the couple.

One of the interlopers stepped forward as the others hung back, and Turner caught the glint of something near the leader's waist.

"Somethin' I can do for you gentlemen?" Turner uneasily shifted into his step-and-fetch mode, wanting no trouble. Hell, these could be some of those Klan bastards who had a noose waiting for him although he couldn't imagine why.

The man crunched forward across the sand and got in Turner's face. "What y'all doin' here, nigger? You lookin' to make a few dollars by spyin' on us and telling the Yanks?"

His confronter's evil breath made Turner wince and turn his head. This cracker hadn't brushed his teeth for a while.

"Excuse me, sir, but me and my lady friend are just out here enjoyin' the evening. We didn't mean to disturb you or your friends. I play the piano down at the Mimosa Club and just got off a few minutes ago."

"You better have some pass or proof of ownership. And I'm only gonna ask you one more time what you're doin' out here."

Turner glanced to the side and saw that Ella had gathered the quilt about her and was crouching, rocking back and forth in obvious fear.

"Boy, I don't think you're worth killin', but I can't take a risk that you have a loose tongue. The bluebellies are everywhere and our mission is too important. Simpkins, send this fella to hell and then we'll decide how to handle his whore."

The nonchalant order caught Turner by surprise as one of the other men deftly moved forward and closed with him.

"Man, are you crazy? Y'all still fightin' the war or something? That's been over for a long time!"

The shriek of metal on metal and the quick gleam of a burnished blade were the last visions to register in Turner's brain. Instinctively he raised his arms in defense, but the sword bore in low, tangling briefly with his pocket watch chain before gliding smoothly into his abdomen.

Ella was petrified by the nightmare of Turner's blood spattering across her face and blouse and the sight of the blade point spearing through the back of his jacket. Yet the blood actually revived her to the reality that she would be next to taste the cold steel.

Iceman slowly sank to one knee, clutching his stomach. With his death gurgles ringing in her ears to linger there forever, Ella leaped to her feet in a primeval dash for survival.

Flinging the quilt and a clinging cloud of sand toward the killers, she turned and ran. The beach seemed to mire her every frenzied step as if she were running through marsh mud.

The satans who murdered Iceman seemed to be sucking at her legs, pulling her to the same fate. A vile hot breath singed the back of her neck. The gore-draped sword had to be close behind, the red-dripping blade about to impale her at any second.

Suddenly her feet hit solid sand and she dug hard, stretching for distance, gathering her dress above her knees to gain speed. Her nostrils and throat wildly clawed for air.

Chancing a look behind her, she saw there was no pursuit. The executioners stood in a hushed pack with Iceman's prone body heaped before them.

Ella didn't break her stride and darted down the beach. Gasping for breath, she trudged up through the sand dunes toward a clapboard, two-story cottage. A horseless carriage of some type was parked in the yard.

Ella had used all of her might to escape the death scene. Now she climbed the eight steps to the porch on all fours, staggered to her feet, and pounded on the screen door. Her fists beat through

9

the wire, and her arms became entangled in the strips of metal mesh. For the first time she screamed as the tattered strands bloodied her forearms in the grasp of unseen demons.

A yellow light wavered at one of the windows, and Ella felt the vibrations of feet on the wooden floor. She heard voices inside the house, but could not distinguish words.

"By Jehovah, who's out there?" someone called from within as the light and footsteps came closer.

Ella managed to fight free of the screen door and reeled backwards, stepping on one of her shoes.

"They killed him! They stabbed him right out there on the beach! Lord God Almighty, Jesus please help me!"

A wave of dizziness, exhaustion, and nausea suddenly engulfed her. Her eyes fluttered, trying to focus on a spinning sky as she collapsed on the porch.

Two days later the Charleston *Orpheus* ran a story about the killing:

Negro piano player John Quincy "Iceman" Turner was killed early Tuesday morning on the Sullivan's Island beach. The circumstances of his death border on the mysterious although police Detective G. D. Wiley stated that Turner's demise might be attributed to a dispute about a woman. Turner was fatally knifed about 3:30 A.M. on the island's south end strand near Fort Moultrie. Turner was a performer at the Mimosa Club on Prioleau Street. His companion, a Negress identified as Ella Solomon, told officers that she and the victim were out for a walk on the beach when they were approached by several men whom they did not know. An argument ensued and Turner was stabbed at least once in the stomach with what Wiley described as a long-bladed weapon of unknown variety. She also told constables that the men appeared to be clothed as Confederate soldiers, a notion the police have attributed to her panic and possible temporary insanity as a result of the crime. The Solomon woman, who is a singer at the Mimosa, stated that she fled the bloody scene and eventually made her way to the seaside home of

A. F. Selig of Charleston. In her hysteria, the woman stated that Turner's murderers made several references about the old Confederacy. Detective Wiley reports that he has found no substance to the woman's description of the Negro's killers which he attributed to her immense agitation and excitement at the time of her questioning. The police presently have no suspects and the case remains unsolved.

In the same edition an *Orpheus* columnist also had some fun at the expense of Turner:

"Iceman" Turner, who was a keyboard wizard at the Mimosa, met an untimely demise the other night on a local beach. The police tell us that a lady friend who was with him at the time stated that the men who killed Turner were dressed in Rebel gray and made statements related to the late Southern republic. This writer has inquired at the homes of several aging veterans who fought for the Confederacy during the "late unpleasantness" and found that all were soundly asleep at the time of the incident (had been for several hours after a rousing round of warm milk!). Perhaps this reporter's investigation will lead the police in another direction!"

February 17, 1964

Berkeley County sheriff's Deputy H. W. Frye was having a Monday to forget. His ex-wife had accused him of skimping on child-support payments. During a happy hour bar call, he had jammed his left index finger separating a pair of battling rednecks at the Pelican Bar and Grill. Now he had to respond to a report of a suspicious vessel on the beach.

God knows he hated to walk on the sand and have to stay late and vacuum the floorboards to get it out of his patrol car.

Someone who lived on the ocean had phoned about a bunch of rowdies and an occasional obscenity heard on the strand. They also said there was some type of nondescript boat riding low in the surf near where the disturbance occurred. Frye knew he had to check it out.

He wheeled his Dodge into the paved parking lot adjacent to the bridge linking Sullivan's Island with the Isle of Palms, both just to the north of Charleston across the Cooper River, which was the boundary between Charleston and Berkeley counties.

"Probably the Rubins' kids and that snot from Pine Woods Academy," he said to himself as he trudged down the sandy track to the beach.

The low tide waters of Breach Inlet softly lapped at both islands, creating a watery gulf of about two hundred yards between them. Frye's eyes adjusted to the darkness, and his flashlight's beam washed the underside of the bridge. Nothing. He walked about fifty yards down the beach, playing the light from the dunes to the water.

"Whoever was here must've gone home," Frye muttered, groping for a pack of Newports in his breast pocket as he clicked off the flashlight. "Probably one of those jumpy old-timers who always used to call about Nazi U-boat crews coming ashore back during the war. Like there was anything here to invade."

He fired a cigarette—and through the match's flame saw a knot of people on the shore in the distance. Frye adjusted his belt, his hand gripping the Smith and Wesson revolver to make sure it was snug but ready in its holster. A hard wind blustered off the harbor as he walked within earshot of the group.

"I jest can't understand why we don't hear some war news bein' so close to Charleston," Frye heard one of them say.

"We ain't seen a bloody monitor in a coon's age."

"What're you boys doin' out here," Frye called, squinting to make out some details about them in the darkness. "I got a complaint about somebody cussin' out here. Would that be y'all? I don't want no trouble from any of you."

His words were met by silence from the group standing like statues on the beach.

"Well would you look at this fancy pants," one of the men finally said after a few moments. "Some of Abe's boys must have new uniforms. Yank, I'd kill you where you stand, but we have more important work to do and I just don't have the time." His comrades laughed and snorted under their breaths.

"Friends, as I said, I'm not out for trouble, but y'all don't need to push your luck. Let me get a look at you. How much have y'all had to drink tonight?"

Frye reached for his flashlight, holding his ground about ten yards from the strangers. His gaze shifted to the sea, but he saw no signs of any vessel. The flashlight's opaque beam speared the night as he aimed it in their direction. To his surprise, the light found an empty strand. Frye swung the flashlight from the waves to the sand dunes—nothing.

"Hell, they must have skedaddled," he thought to himself. "Sure were damn quick and quiet."

He had almost reached his patrol car when the eastern horizon melted into an orange glow several miles out to sea and he heard a distant boom. Watching the tiny flame, Frye radioed his dispatcher.

"Headquarters, this is unit six. Nothing to report on the Signal 27 on the beach, but it looks like there's been some kind of explosion just outside the harbor mouth. Might want to call the Coast Guard boys."

For days after the blast Frye had seen, the local papers, radio, and TV were filled with reports about the tragic end of the *Sea Lynx* and the ten of the eleven people aboard her. The New York-based, seventy-one-foot ketch had been en route home from Jacksonville when an explosion "of suspicious origin," as the investigators put it, had blown her out of the water off Charleston.

Investment banker Thackeray Bishop of Long Island was the only person found alive, clinging to a fractured hatch frame with his left leg ripped off above the knee. Coast Guard Commander Ian Gould headed the investigation and personally recovered dozens of pieces of debris from the *Sea Lynx* scattered across the water or washed ashore. Unfortunately there was not enough left of the boat to determine how she met her fate. Gould had even sent a charred, foot-long mast section to a friend who worked in the FBI laboratory in Washington. But a battery of tests was inconclusive.

What would stay with Gould to the last of his days were

memories of his hospital visits to see Thackeray, who died a week after being rescued. Sitting beside Thackeray's bed in the intensive care unit for hours on end, Gould patiently tried to coax the slightest information from the dying man, but Thackeray was semicomatose, rarely waking, and then for usually less than a minute at a time.

Thackeray did not slide peacefully into the arms of angels. His momentary returns to reality were fitful rides of sweaty delirium and bedeviled thoughts, ending every voyage with weak mutterings of one word: "Carlson."

Over and over the banker said it, his mutilated body thrashing so much in the first days that the staff had to bring in restraining straps. As the week deepened and Thackeray began to shut down, the restraints were no longer needed. Yet even into the last hour of his life he whispered the name, or whatever it was. No one among the *Sea Lynx* victims was named Carlson, and Gould could find nothing in Thackeray's background or business dealings related to the word.

Even after his retirement some twenty years later, Gould always kept the piece of the *Sea Lynx*'s mast on his desk as a constant reminder of the mystery and of the eleven lost souls whose deaths he could not decipher.

2

1994

"WE GOT A REPORT of an explosion of unknown type on the Intracoastal from some guy in a johnboat. Said his name was McCutchen and sounded like he'd had a few pops."

Communications specialist Stan Jenkins of Coast Guard Station Charleston figured the caller had been drinking on account of his slurred speech heard over the telephone. Probably some Lowcountry shitkicker whose brain had been pickled by years of cheap beer and South Carolina's furnace summers.

Even so, the report of an explosion warranted informing the officer of the day. Jenkins paged Petty Officer Mike Green, who appeared in the communications center in less than two minutes.

"What else do you know, Stan?" Green was insistent and calmly efficient.

"The incident location is near McClellanville, and the call came in at 11:36 P.M. The only vessel I have currently logged in that area is a southbound forty-seven-footer out of New Jersey. No radar contact. Do we want to send up a chopper?"

Small craft advisories had been broadcast all day because of a slowly lifting fog. And Green knew the helicopter boys would give him hell if he got them up for anything less than a legitimate rescue. He also had the option of dispatching one of the station's four forty-one-foot utility boats. A UTB would likely be better than the helo with the weather such as it was.

"Have you been able to raise the skipper?" Green asked. He was scheduled to go off duty at midnight and had planned to head downtown and have a beer with a few buddies.

"No, sir." Jenkins swiveled in his chair to face Green. "Mike, I got one call from this New Jersey craft about 9:45 P.M., and the guy asked about traffic volume in the harbor. That's all. They didn't file a navigational plan, and I haven't heard from them since. This dude in the bass boat sounded half crocked, but there was something in his voice that made me think he saw something."

"No confirmation on the explosion and no report of anyone in distress," Green mulled aloud. "We haven't heard anything from the sheriff's department or highway patrol? I'd expect them to get some calls from people living in the area if there was something to it. Don't you think somebody else would have seen or heard something?"

"Haven't heard a word from a soul other than this fisherman. That's a pretty tough fog out there. Said he was hunkered down in an inlet when he saw something blow to hell about three-quarters of a mile away. Took him about twenty minutes to get to a telephone at some bait shop and he called us. He was babbling pretty bad and then he hung up."

Green weighed the information he had and made a decision.

"I can't see sending anybody out based on what we know now. Hang with it, Stan, and keep me posted, at least until Kazlow relieves me, which is in about ten minutes."

"I'll do it, Mike. Hey, have a good time downtown. I gotta stay here and work on a term paper." Jenkins turned back to the communications console, which had been quiet, other than ship-to-ship traffic, for about two hours.

As he started to fill out log information about the call, Jenkins remembered something else the drunken fisherman had said, but which he had not told Green. In his ramblings McCutchen slurred that moments after the explosion he heard someone shout, "There's another one for . . ."—the name was foreign.

"Who's that?" Jenkins had tried to ask, but his answer was a dial tone.

"Heck, I can't even spell it, but I'll put it in the report. B.O.R.Y.G.U.A.R.D."

The salt sea air flooded in through the sunroof as Eric Ashby sped down U.S. Highway 17 toward Charleston. The old coast road had, at one time or another, been used by pirates, pioneers, and British troops, the latter chasing the wily "Swamp Fox" Francis Marion in the American Revolution.

Ashby's eyes shifted from the highway to take in the scenery. A collage of pine woods, cinder-block churches, and mobile homes whizzed past the Mazda's windows. At some of the bridges spanning moss-cloaked swamps, old black men hunched on buckets while they fished in the inky backwaters.

Ashby had hit the road from Wilmington, North Carolina, that April morning and was looking forward to his new assignment with the Coast Guard in Charleston. As a lieutenant junior grade, he would serve as the station's public information officer, among other duties.

Ashby needed the change and had requested the transfer when he heard about the opening in Charleston. Wilmington was a beautiful city, and he had enjoyed most of his two years there. Like Charleston, it had a rich history, which he relished, and the beach, which he also loved.

The town had gotten a lot smaller, however, when he broke off a six-month romance with one of the reporters from the local newspaper. After the breakup it seemed Monica turned up everywhere he went—there was a limited number of bars and other places where singles could hang out in Wilmington. The opportunity to head south could not have come at a better time.

Through his mother's intense interest in genealogy, Ashby knew that he already had a Charleston connection. One of his ancestors had served as a gunner on the USS *Nahant*, a Union monitor in the U.S. blockading squadron that had unsuccessfully tried to take Confederate-held Charleston during the Civil War.

Growing up in the suburbs of Frederick, Maryland, Ashby had acquired a passing interest in the war. He and his friends plowed their dirt bikes through woods and valleys where Yanks and Rebs marched and fought in Robert E. Lee's 1862 campaign into Maryland. On camping trips in the hills, he had occasionally kicked up a minié ball fired more than a century earlier. His most prized relic, however, was a U.S. belt buckle. What made the buckle unique was that it had been ripped by a musket slug, indicating that its wearer probably did not live very long.

After high school he had earned a few credits at a community college, but soon realized that he did not fit in the world of higher education. His dad in particular had been disappointed when he joined the Coast Guard instead of trying to enroll at one of the larger Eastern schools. He had hoped his nineteen-year-old son would follow up on his all-state lacrosse skills by trying to make a team at the collegiate level.

Ashby enjoyed the competition of lacrosse and the popularity it brought him in high school. He had received some offers from coaches at several universities. But the calls stopped after he twisted a knee in a pick-up basketball game after his junior year. The injury required surgery to repair torn cartilage. Still, his dad had wanted him to at least go out for a team as a walk-on without benefit of an athletics scholarship.

Life didn't flow in that direction, and Ashby found himself in the Coast Guard by 1987. He had always loved the sea, and the USCG offered him the chance to learn more about it while he decided what to do with his career.

The leadership skills honed on the lacrosse fields served him well in the Coast Guard and he advanced rapidly. His promotions, as well as his stature within the ranks, had been accelerated after an incident during his rookie base assignment at Baltimore.

A single-mast sailboat had been caught in a flash thunderstorm off Hooper Island near the mouth of Chesapeake Bay, causing the two people aboard—a man and his ten-year-old granddaughter—to radio for help. Ashby was an ensign assigned to UTB-44, the *Saracen*, which was dispatched to the scene.

Ashby never believed he had done anything worthy of accolades, but the Coast Guard brass thought otherwise. Indeed, his perception of that day was of sadness and a mission that he could never complete.

Arriving astride the stricken vessel after a forty-minute whipping by the tormented sea, he and the other *Saracen* crewmen were horrified to see a wave shove the craft onto its starboard side, the pair aboard spilling into the bay. Without thought or orders, Ashby had gone over the side. He surfaced to find himself battling the snarling water to reach the victims.

The fast-moving storm seemed to hover over all, intent on exacting some toll on humankind before it roiled up the Chesapeake to drench Baltimore. Glimpses of flailing arms and the lemon yellow life jackets some sixty-five yards distant were all that Ashby had to guide him through the salty torrent.

The wind-slung swells ripped at his eyes and pulled his arms toward the depths as he tried to swim, but somehow he made it, coughing brine and gulping for breath. Ashby found himself in the face of a panicky seventy-year-old man whose few snatches of silver hair were matted to his head. Embracing the man in a virtual death lock around his neck was the girl, her eyes set in terror. The squall had flushed them well away from their swamped sailboat.

On seeing their nearly exhausted rescuer, the man and girl simultaneously broke apart and splashed toward him. There were no words; the battle to stay alive and afloat left no energy for it.

To the end of his days Ashby would always remember the hands. Clutching, clawing, dragging him down, the child's tiny pink fingernails scratching his face. The combined weight of the two thrust him under, and his life-saving effort had suddenly become a fight for his own survival.

Struggling to break their grasps, Ashby managed to free himself and stroke upward with the last of his waning strength. Choking and sputtering, he emerged and saw the girl pop to the surface about five feet away. Where the hell was the *Saracen*?

Ashby grabbed the coughing child by the collar of her life preserver and pivoted in the direction he believed the UTB would be waiting. Out of the corner of his eye as he swam he saw the older man bobbing in the distance. He appeared to be semi-conscious and feebly raised an arm—his last plea for help. There was no way Ashby could do more for him and not risk the girl's life, as well as his own.

Pummeled by the bay and pelted by the rain, he turned away, hoping that she did not see the big wave that pulled her grandfather to his death. Five minutes later they were fished to safety by Ashby's shipmates. Wrapped in blankets and drinking hot chocolate with the child still clinging to him, sobbing quietly, he felt no triumph in the rescue. The ocean and the storm had beaten him, and a man was dead because of his failure. At that moment he decided that never again would he let the sea take a soul on his watch.

The Coast Guard overlooked his impetuous dive from the *Saracen* and presented him with a commendation for saving the girl. He knew her only as Simone until a deluge of calls from reporters interested in "such an exciting and touchy feely story," as one of them put it. The rescue was great copy, and Ashby found himself the Baltimore media's hottest item for a few days. He didn't enjoy the hype, preferring to privately critique his actions to help the drowned man. The body was never found, and Ashby had attended a memorial service, where he held hands with Simone during a prayer. An alert photographer snapped the somber moment, which was page one for several major A.M. dailies the next morning.

Ashby's heroism and the trove of wonderful publicity for the service resulted in the ensign being assigned to the Coast Guard Academy at New London, Connecticut, for courses to supplement his experience.

Ashby spent three months at the academy, studying subjects in the Government major and answering questions from underclassmen eager to learn about the real world from a real hero. The younger guys all were on four-year scholarships and destined to enter the Guard with ensign commissions, committed to serving five years of active duty. Already ahead of the pack, Ashby sensed some animosity and standoffishness from a handful of the cadets.

But his experience at the academy had been great for the most part. The friends he made in his classes and on the playing fields above the Thames River would always be with him.

Among the courses he took at the academy were several in public relations and in handling the media. Ashby's smoothness in answering the bombardment of journalists' questions about the rescue had impressed the higher-ups, and he had been encouraged to take these subjects at the academy. It also resulted in his assuming duties as spokesman for the Baltimore station in any dealings with the media unless the commander wanted the spotlight.

At twenty-three he had made lieutenant j.g., and was transferred from Baltimore to Wilmington in June 1992, a cocksure young officer bent on conquering all the local belles. When not on duty or carousing in Wilmington's hot spots, Ashby absorbed the area's history, including the siege and eventual fall of Confederate Fort Fisher in 1865.

Many times he and his buddies had skimmed down the Cape Fear River on their wave runners. Fort Fisher had guarded the river's mouth in the Civil War, but most of the massive bastion had long ago been washed into the sea. The remains of other Rebel batteries lined the waterway that linked Wilmington with the Atlantic during a time when the city was a vital port for the Confederacy.

Ashby would always remember exploring one of these earthworks with a pretty Wake Forest junior he met at a friend's birthday party. They had taken a moonlit boat ride down the Brunswick River and ended up making love among the rifle pits of the overgrown battery long reclaimed by nature.

Ashby took the bypass around the Charleston suburb of Mount Pleasant and soon saw the lofty Cooper River bridges and Charleston in the hazy distance. To his left, the Atlantic Ocean shimmered in its vast majesty, flooding around the dagger peninsula occupied by the old city.

Ascending the southbound bridge, Ashby looked down on the USS *Yorktown*, a World War II aircraft carrier that was the main attraction of Patriots Point, a maritime museum in Mount Pleasant. His gaze settled on a small brick structure at the harbor's mouth several miles distant—Fort Sumter. In April 1861 the eyes of a nation were focused on this little stronghold. Its bombardment by Confederate artillery rimming the harbor ignited the Civil War. During four years of conflict, the fort would be virtually pounded into a mountain of brick rubble, but the Southerners never surrendered it.

Ashby looked at his city map and some directions he had scrawled on the back of an envelope to help him find the Coast Guard station. Since he wasn't officially due to report until the next day, he decided to take a quick driving tour. Coming off the bridge, he headed downtown on Bay Street, passing the gray marble Customs House and a waterfront park lined by palmetto trees overlooking the Cooper.

Charleston seemed to embrace the courtly elegance of its verdant history and the vibrancy of a thriving seaport. Navigating the narrow streets, Ashby admired the massive antebellum mansions with their expansive verandas and immaculate gardens guarded by gurgling fountains. Plush ivy cascaded over courtyard walls, and elaborate wrought-iron grillwork crowned gates and shuttered windows.

Every street and lane offered a bounty of flowering pulchritude, as Charleston's spring debutante ball of nature blossomed in fragrant grandeur. Honeysuckle sweetened the breeze, while dogwoods, azaleas, wisteria, and yellow jasmine competed with others in a pageant of floral royalty.

Veering around tour buses and horse-drawn carriages, Ashby pulled over at White Point Gardens, better known to the locals as "The Battery."

Squadrons of pigeons wheeled in the sky or challenged squirrels for tidbits of food found in the tree-shaded park. Joggers and sightseers plodded along the railed sidewalk where the Ashley River poured into Charleston Harbor. Gulls and pelicans skimmed low over the water, searching for fishy treats.

The Battery offered Ashby another view of Fort Sumter although he was no closer now than when he saw it from the bridge.

A double-deck, white tour boat bound for the fort was sluggishly making its way out of the Ashley and into the harbor channel.

Ashby had retrieved his binoculars from the car and was focusing on Sumter when an attractive young woman wearing a College of Charleston sweatshirt and briskly walking a Boston terrier distracted him.

"Monica who?" he smiled to himself.

Late that afternoon Ashby turned off Tradd Street and drove through the main gate of Coast Guard Station Charleston. As he parked near the base administration building, he could see three white and orange cutters moored at a dock with the Ashley as their backdrop. The admin complex was a three-story structure that Ashby later learned had been a rice mill storehouse in the mid-1800's. Like many other buildings he had seen in Charleston, Ashby noticed what appeared to be iron rods protruding from the exterior brick walls.

After asking a passing ensign where to find the base commander, Ashby inquired about the curious shafts.

"Oh, those are earthquake rods," the ensign cheerfully explained. "I'm from Kansas, you know, the tornado capital of the world, but from what I'm told there was a mother of an earthquake in Charleston in 1886, I think. Afterwards they ran these long support irons through the floors and walls along the window levels to help bolster them in case of another shake."

Ashby grinned at him. "You're a walking history lesson. Thanks for the tour."

"No problem, sir. Welcome to Charleston." The ensign hesitated. "And lieutenant, I am the man in the know about any of the local stripper bars."

Ashby made his way into the "Rice Mill" administration building and found the office of Captain Rodrigo Starnes, the station commander.

Starnes rose from his chair as Ashby entered and walked around his desk to greet him.

"I'm Lieutenant Eric Ashby reporting for duty," Ashby barked, saluting stiffly, intent on making a first impression as a squared away Guardsman.

"Welcome to Charleston, lieutenant," Starnes said, casually returning the salute and extending his hand. "You can rest easy."

The captain appeared to be in his early thirties, his molded physique and crew-cut black hair making him appear more a Marine than a Coast Guardsman.

Starnes's gritsy drawl marked him as a native of the Gulf delta country, raised, as Ashby later learned, from the stock of Mississippi's first settlers. His handshake was as if Ashby had put his hand into a bear trap. Ashby tried not to wince.

"No need to be so formal, Lieutenant Ashby. This ain't boot camp and we're not at war. Have a seat."

"Thank you, sir."

Starnes motioned toward a chair and Ashby relaxed, settling into it.

"Just wanted to look good, captain. New assignment and all."

"I know, I know. I'll keep a rein on you like everybody else here. All you have to remember is to follow regulations and we'll get along just fine."

"Not a problem."

"So you're from Maryland. Isn't that just basically a suburb of Washington?"

"Not exactly, sir. The western part of the state is beautiful country. Lots of hills and farmland. Pretty rural. That's the area I'm from."

"You're not saying you screw around with barnyard animals are you?" Starnes laughed.

"Not unless you count one of the Petrovsky sisters from the next block," Ashby replied, trying to keep a straight face.

"Seriously, I am strict about the basics and ensuring that everyone in this command adheres to the book. I like to have a good time like the next guy, but we have to maintain discipline through neatness, promptness, and a total sense of duty. I'm not a big stickler on all this saluting protocol, but I guess we have to do it once in a while just to keep the rust off. Especially when 'Grizzly' is around."

"Grizzly, sir?"

"Uh, that would be Commander Hugh Vandencomp. He is over Coast Guard Group Charleston which, I'm sure you know, includes not only this station, but the base at Tybee Island, Georgia, near Savannah, the air stations here and in Savannah, and our station at Georgetown. He is my superior officer and certainly yours, Mr. Ashby."

Starnes was back in his desk chair and toying with a cigarette lighter that resembled a hand grenade. He pulled the pin and a little flame shot out.

"Fortunately for all, Commander Grizzly lets us handle most of the day-to-day tasks here while he concentrates on his bigger picture. Plus he's getting up in years and is damned close to retirement I would think. Anyway, you let me handle Grizzly."

"Does Grizzly—I mean, Commander Vandencomp—want to give his prior approval to news releases or statements or any other contact we have with the media?"

"I'll make the call based on the individual situation, but I do want to have that courtesy extended to me. Nothing goes out without my okay."

"Understood, captain."

"Vandencomp has his own liaison to handle his press matters. You'll meet Lieutenant Kapowski at some point. Do you have any questions or concerns?"

Ashby was about to reply when a strong rap at the door interrupted him. On Starnes's order Stan Jenkins stepped into the office and saluted them. Starnes introduced them, and Ashby saw that Jenkins was instantly relieved to have the new PR guy on board.

"Hey, lieutenant, I'm sure glad you're here. We've gotten some calls from reporters in New Jersey . . ." he stopped in mid-sentence, realizing he had overstepped. "Captain, with your permission I would like to give Mr. Ashby an update on the missing-persons case."

Starnes nodded for him to proceed.

"As I was saying, sir, we've gotten some calls from newsmen in New Jersey about a missing boat from two days ago. Apparently the guy on board had written a couple of books, and it looks like he might have disappeared somewhere around Charleston. I told them someone would call them back."

"Eric, about the only thing we had going on that might have anything to do with this was an unconfirmed report of an explosion on the Intracoastal," Starnes told Ashby.

"Some unidentified fisherman phoned it in and said it was in the McClellanville area, which is about thirty miles south of here. About two hours earlier, we had one radio call from a guy who said he was sailing south from Perth Amboy, New Jersey. He inquired about harbor traffic and that was about it. Stands to reason that he is the missing person."

"He wasn't exactly sure where he was on the Intracoastal, but we guess he had to be somewhere between Cape Romain and Capers Inlet . . ."

"Which puts him in the general vicinity of where the explosion was reported," Starnes interrupted.

"What's the name of the missing boater?" Ashby asked.

"We didn't have it before one of the reporters identified him as Sherman Wagner. Said he wrote some science fiction books. Foley, one of the reservists, told us he had read some of Wagner's stuff."

"Anyone else supposedly on the boat with him?"

"Again, the reporters are telling us he was accompanied by his wife. I don't recall her name, but I've got it written down somewhere."

"What kind of vessel were they supposed to be on? Better yet, can I see the report about the explosion?"

"Sure, it's right here."

Jenkins sifted through a folder and brought out the two-page document. Ashby read it, his eyes fixing on the last word of the narrative—Boryguard.

"Hey, Jenkins, what's this word here, is this the spelling the fisherman gave you?"

"No, sir. He hung up before I got any more information. I spelled it like it sounded to me."

Was it French? Maybe some Latin phrase that Jenkins had

misunderstood? Ashby turned the word over and over in his mind, but nothing registered.

"Captain, has there been any type of search mounted for this boat?" he asked Starnes.

"The Air Station sent one of its Dolphins over the area yesterday morning, but they didn't see anything. Their choppers routinely fly down the Intracoastal. Nobody has turned up a trace of this craft or any debris."

With nothing much to say, Ashby returned the phone calls from the New Jersey journalists, all of whom were from Perth Amboy and all frustrated with the lack of response they had received to this point from the Charleston base. No, he didn't have any new information about the Wagners. Was an active search underway? He knew better, but told them that the Coast Guard was doing all it could to aid in finding the missing couple.

"Check back with me in a day or so," he said before hanging up with each of them. "Maybe we'll have some developments by then."

Ashby also was interviewed by Charleston's media and gave them basically the same answers. All they had to go on was a telephone call from some redneck who claimed he had seen an explosion of some sort. Still, a couple of people and a boat were missing, but they could have anchored or gone ashore at any one of countless points along the Intracoastal's creeks and inlets. If the vessel had been destroyed, surely something would surface—a body, wreckage—anything.

Starnes felt the case would give his new lieutenant a good chance to acclimate himself with the Charleston region. Ashby thus spent several days riding the backroads, stopping at country stores and trailer parks to find anyone who might have seen or heard something about the Wagners' disappearance. Because no flotsam had been discovered and there was no other physical evidence that the Wagners' yacht sank near Charleston, no formal investigation was launched.

After a week of eating pickled eggs and Vienna sausages at countless bait shops and convenience stores, he had turned up nothing. It wasn't as though people were trying to hide information; for all he could determine, no one had the least idea about what he was trying to uncover.

Nobody seemed to know the fisherman who had phoned in the report. And the caller was lying low or was so drunk that he woke up the next morning having forgotten the incident entirely. Or maybe it was a prank call. Ashby's instincts told him otherwise.

"There's all kind of spirits out in that water, mister," a stooped black woman had told him at a roadside stop. She and several others were weaving sawgrass baskets in the shade of an old peach stand by U.S. 17.

"Some bless you with a good catch, some take you out of dis world. The sea feeds us aplenty, like the Bible says. And they is good things and bad things out there. I'm thinkin' the folk you is lookin' for—well, it was just their time."

The disappearance of the Wagners and the *H. G. Wells* was mentioned daily in news reports for almost a week, but the media calls dwindled with each day passing and no new leads.

Ashby found a rumpled New York tabloid someone left on his bunk. The 48-point front-page headline glared that Wagner was abducted by some of the same aliens he wrote about in his books.

On a Saturday morning five weeks after his arrival in Charleston, Ashby was startled awake by a pillow smacking him across the face.

"Get your ass up! This Wagner case hit you in the kisser when you walked in the door. We're gonna have some fun today!"

Ashby groggily turned away to defend himself, glimpsing the 9:34 A.M. on his clock and Starnes stalking away with a pillow in hand.

"We're hittin' the beach in forty-five minutes!"

By 10:15 Starnes and Ashby, along with John Crawford and

Cliff Okai, two pilots from the Air Station, were heading for Folly Beach south of the city. The sky was cloudless, and the warm air swept through Starnes's black Jeep Cherokee as Charleston disappeared behind them.

"It's gonna be the perfect day for bikini babes, rays, and a few brewskis," Crawford shouted over the wind and the clamor of Lynyrd Skynyrd blaring from Starnes's compact disc player.

"Rod, when are you going to get some new music? That band's been outta here for a long time."

"Naw, man," Starnes replied, in his Biloxi twang. "This group was big when their plane crashed back in the late 1970's, and they're still around. And nothin' beats 'Sweet Home Alabama.' That's my theme song."

They arrived on the beach at low tide, just as Starnes had planned, so that there was plenty of sand to spread out, toss the football, and ogle the girls.

Okai managed to get a phone number from one of a trio of bronzed young women from Summerville after he promised to take her on a "good will" flight aboard his Dolphin.

Five hours later Ashby and his buddies were sweaty, sandy, sunburned, and loose after drinking most of the beer in Crawford's big cooler. They headed back to the city, at times inching along in the homeward-bound beach traffic.

When they got back to the base, many of the other Guardsmen were out on the volleyball court behind one of the residence halls. Fueled by the beer, Ashby raced to his room, slipped on a brace to protect his damaged knee, and returned to the action.

"Hey, Ashby! This ain't lacrosse, but maybe you could hit the ball better if you had one of those funny sticks with the basket on the end," Starnes yelled at him from a sideline lawn chair. Ashby laughed and flipped him the bird before turning his attention to the game. Without a second thought he had just made an obscene gesture to his commanding officer, but Starnes's laid-back manner and their burgeoning friendship made the horseplay all the more natural.

Ashby had just spiked the ball out of bounds when he noticed an older man wearing a bleached orange Coast Guard T-shirt and baggy khakis walking toward the court. Several of the men ran over, slapping him on the back or pumping his hand.

"Hey, Snapper!" Okai shouted. The man turned toward him and waved. Between points, Ashby judged the visitor to be in his late sixties. He obviously knew just about everyone at the base.

During a break, Ashby plopped into a folding chair next to Okai.

"Cliff, who's that guy?"

"He's Snapper Gould. He was the base commander for about twenty years or more. He's a great guy, and some of these older dudes served under him for a year or two. He's pretty much a legend around here."

"Why do they call him Snapper?"

"Ah, something about when he was investigating a ship going down with about a dozen people sometime in the 1960's. He wasn't able to find out what happened, but he never gave up. You know, kinda stubborn like a snapping turtle."

"I get the picture."

Ashby remembered seeing a photo of Gould in the headquarters' main hall, but the Wagner case had left him little time to find out anything about old Coast Guardsmen. Gould was tanned the color of caramel, and his close-cropped hair would have made any boot camp drill instructor proud. He was not physically imposing, but hands on hips and meeting everyone with a steady eye, he had the air of a man who feared nothing mortal. The hushed aura of a leader bespoke his presence.

Gould was talking with McIntosh, one of the machinists, when Ashby saw McIntosh nod and point in his direction. Gould strode toward him and gave a crisp salute as Ashby swayed to his feet.

"Lieutenant, I'm retired Commander Ian Gould. A belated welcome to Charleston."

"Thank you, sir." Ashby returned the salute as some of his comrades snickered at the formality. "You must be very proud of everything you accomplished here."

"Well, we had some good people to work with, but that's all history. These days I live on the ass end of Edisto Island and spend most of my time crabbing or fishing off my dock. I particularly wanted to meet you. Everybody says you've been the most active in trying to solve the disappearance of the Wagners, the fancy-pants couple from up North."

"I don't know about that, but it's a strange case and I'm not buying the alien abduction theory," Ashby laughed.

Gould looked puzzled.

"A New York paper said they were kidnapped by aliens."

Gould ignored the comment, and Ashby could tell that he didn't know what he was talking about.

"From what the boys here are telling me and from what I read in the papers, this case is a lot similar to one I had back in 1964," Gould said, watching the volleyball match. "A boat named the *Sea Lynx* exploded and killed eleven people. We never found out what happened. I still have some of the debris squirreled away. Always thought it was funny that it happened about the same time of year as the old *Hunley.*"

"The *Hunley?*"

"Yeah, the Confederate submarine that was the first in history to sink an enemy warship. It happened near Charleston during the Civil War. Sent a Union blockader to the bottom."

"My mom tells me I had an ancestor who was a seaman aboard the Union monitor *Nahant.* I'm from Maryland. Guess I've got some Yankee blood in my veins."

"No matter. Listen, Ashby, if there's anything I can do to help you with the Wagners' case, let me know. Just about anybody here knows how to reach me."

"Thanks, commander."

"Son, that rank is long gone in the books. Everybody knows me as Snapper. I'll be seeing you."

Gould wheeled and walked away. Moments later he was sharing a tall tale with a knot of Guardsmen gathered and guffawing around him. ❦

Two weeks later Ashby was returning from delivering some documents to the Ports Authority. It was just after noon, and he decided to grab a bite to eat in downtown Charleston. Even though it was early June, the day was mild and he enjoyed a walk past the shops, cafés, and offices on Broad Street in the city's heart. Ducking into a deli, he emerged with his lunch and headed toward a shady park near City Hall.

Biting into his pastrami on rye, Ashby took in the sights around him from a wooden bench sheltered by a cluster of dogwoods. The small park was bustling with smartly dressed businessmen and women and groups of tourists. Gray squirrels were doing their frantic frolic up and down the trees and in a furry foot race through the grass. He was feeling more and more comfortable in his new assignment and was enjoying Charleston. All of his fellow Guardsmen seemed to like and respect him. The story of his Chesapeake Bay rescue had made the rounds, but he always tried to downplay it, not wanting to stand out from any of his comrades. His modesty only endeared him more to Starnes, Okai, and the others.

The Wagner case had gone stone cold, as had the media focus it attracted, and Ashby had been able to join the crew of the cutter *Iroquois* for training maneuvers off Bull Island. It had been months since he had been at sea, and the excitement of assisting green reservists in learning shipboard duties was an elixir for him.

The mission had not been without incident. The *Iroquois* was returning to base when a lookout spotted a fifteen-foot commercial fishing boat that appeared to be dead in the water. Edging close to the vessel, Ashby could see the lone shrimper on board waving to them.

"Hey, everything's okay. Just had a little engine trouble and was taking on some water," the boater yelled in reply to the *Iroquois* skipper's bullhorn inquiry. "Had to dump a few pounds of shrimp and some mullet overboard just now to help stabilize my ballast, but at least I got the leak plugged."

Ashby squinted into the sky and then surveyed the ocean around the other craft. A fishing boat dumping almost anything, especially shrimp and fish, would be ground zero for dolphin and an air armada of wheeling seagulls eager for free eats.

"You draw any gulls when you pitched that shrimp?" he shouted over to the fisherman.

"Oh, hell yeah. There must've been a thousand of them

varmints. I'll tell you they about blocked out the sun, there was so many of them flying around."

On the bridge Ashby borrowed a pair of binoculars from an officer and honed in on the boat's deck and the shrimper's shoes. The deck looked clean and the man's tennis shoes were dry. In fact, he was remarkably slime free for someone who had single-handedly netted and dumped a haul of shrimp.

"Possible drug runner," Ashby had whispered to the cutter's captain, Pete "Doc" Holliday.

"He is pretty clean looking for a fisherman. Anything else?"

"Yeah. If he had a thousand gulls hovering over him, there'd be at least some bird crap either on him or the deck or somewhere. I don't see any, do you?"

"No kidding."

Minutes later Holliday and Ashby led an armed boarding party of three other Guardsmen aboard the fishing boat. The shrimper had given a verbal consent to search, and two of the sailors stayed with him in the stern of the craft while Holliday paused at a plywood door leading to the hold.

"You want the honors, lieutenant?" he said to Ashby, who was just behind him. In answer Ashby pulled and cocked his 45-caliber Colt, sidling next to Holliday. Maybe there was nothing on the other side of the door other than hundreds of dead or dying shrimp. And then maybe there were a couple of guys with automatic weapons guarding a big stash of primo cocaine.

Ashby looked back at the fisherman, but the man divulged nothing by his body language or demeanor. The guy was sweating like a neighbor in hell, but they all were; the sun was intense and the faint wind had died down.

With his foot Ashby pushed open the whining door and pointed his pistol into the blackness while his eyes adjusted to the dark hold. In a crouch he crept inside. Slowly, agonizingly, he regained his sight, relieved that in that blind moment of vulnerability he had not been pumped full of buckshot or other slugs.

In the dim close quarters of the hold he had immediately noticed the absence of a fishy smell. There were no shrimp or mullet in the hold, but there was plenty else.

Wrapped in thick-ply layers of plastic, masking tape, and brown paper were two 200-pound bales of marijuana. It was "Mexican dirt weed," as the dealers and users called it, but regardless of the cheap grade the *Iroquois* had made a drug intervention bust and arrest.

At a news conference the next day, the reefer bales and two Chinese-made AK-47 assault rifles discovered on the boat were displayed for the Charleston media. Crews from each of the three local television affiliates showed up along with a reporter from the Charleston *Herald*.

It was at this event that Ashby first saw "Grizzly" Vandencomp. The group commander stood with his aide, Lieutenant Nicholas Kapowski, along a side wall of the conference room.

Vandencomp cut a striking figure scissored from the same cloth as Ian Gould, Ashby thought. Pushing six feet, he had the lean bow-legged look of an old-time Texas wrangler and stood as if he had a machete strapped to his spine. Unsmiling, he seemed all but oblivious to everything going on around him, dismissing the *Herald* reporter's questions with a pointed finger to Kapowski. The latter officer was not nearly as impressive.

Kapowski was a well-known kiss-ass and would do anything to better ingratiate himself with Vandencomp, most of the Guardsmen who knew him believed. Why Grizzly tolerated such a waste of jellyfish was a frequently asked question in barracks circles. The standing joke was that Kapowski had his head so far up Grizzly's butt that he was considered a brown bear cub.

Ashby had met with Kapowski shortly after arriving in Charleston and basically had listened to "No Nad Nick" try to impress him as the group commander's spokesman compared to Ashby's lesser role.

Kapowski came across more like a used-car salesman hyping a Pacer than anything else, but Ashby let him speak his mind. This jerk had seniority and clout, and Ashby didn't want to rock the boat too early in his Charleston voyage.

Ashby stood with Holliday and the *Iroquois* crew while the journalists inspected the marijuana haul. Behind him Starnes whispered, "Check out that Channel 4 babe." Ashby had needed no prodding. Melanie Potemkin was hot beyond belief, and every guy in the room, other than Grizzly and his yes-man, was probably salivating on his dress whites.

"A direct order, lieutenant. I want to meet that young lady."

"Aye aye, captain," Ashby replied. He complied by introducing Starnes to Potemkin, but she was in a hurry to get to another story, something about a surfboarding cat, and did not have time for chitchat or flattery.

"We'll catch her next time, captain. You got my word on it."

Ashby smiled to himself, remembering the look on Starnes's face as he melted and gushed over the reporter. He had to find a way to see if she would be interested in having dinner with Rod. He'd have to contact one of her cohorts to see if she was available and interested.

Ashby watched a walking tour group, accompanied by a guide dressed in a Confederate uniform, approach a granite monument situated along a brick wall near his bench.

"This marker honors Confederate General P. G. T. Beauregard for his defense of Charleston," the guide began. "Beauregard was in command here when the firing on Fort Sumter opened the conflict. His war fortunes were mixed, but he was able to keep the Federals from capturing the city. For that, many Charlestonians of that time owed him an eternal debt of gratitude."

Beauregard. Ashby knew he had heard the name before, but where? The tourists moved on, and he got up to read the monument himself. On the back of a mustard-stained napkin he jotted down some information from the inscription.

The ragged lightning of thought then made the connection. Of course! Beauregard was the name mentioned in Jenkins' report about the *Wells*'s explosion.

Ashby found a pay phone and made a call to Starnes, saying that he was taking the afternoon to continue the *Wells* investigation. He then headed to the public library to see what he could find out about Beauregard.

In the Civil War section he found a musty biography of the general and leafed through its yellowing pages. Other books also had information about him.

A Louisiana Creole. Ordered the firing on Fort Sumter. Flamboyant and vain commander who was often described as the "Gray Napoleon." Fought at First Bull Run and Shiloh before returning to Charleston, where he deftly directed the city's defense.

There was nothing to indicate any link between the general's name and the suspected loss of the *Wells*. After the war Beauregard was a railroad president and lottery official before dying in New Orleans in 1893. The vessel's namesake, Herbert George Wells, wasn't born until 1866 in England and lingered until 1946, he learned from an encyclopedia.

"It was a long shot anyway," Ashby said to himself. He was about to close one book about the war when his eyes lodged on a particular segment. Something about a Rebel submarine named the *Hunley*. He glanced through several more pages, but was tired of reading and making notes after four hours. Besides, he vaguely remembered that Snapper Gould was familiar with the *Hunley* if he wanted to know more.

Back at the base that night, he got Gould's telephone number from Cliff Okai and called Snapper.

"We never released this to the public, Snapper, but did you know that the fisherman who phoned in the report of the supposed *Wells*'s explosion stated something like 'There's another one for Beauregard?' Pretty uncommon name."

"Where are you going with this, Ashby? The only Beauregard I know of was a Confederate general—a real dandy, but one hell of a defensive engineer."

"I know all about him. I've been in the library most of the day reading about him."

"So let me guess. Now you're theorizing that a group of white supremacist militiamen in hoods blew up a pleasure boat on the Intracoastal? And all in the name of General Beauregard? Eric, I'm glad you spent some time in the library, probably sniffing around some reference babe with horn-rimmed glasses, of course, but in the library nonetheless.

"Once when I—"

"Commander, don't go down memory lane with me right now," Ashby spat. "Just hear me out for a second. I'm trying to resolve a disappearance, and I'm looking for some guidance or advice—anything to pull this thing together. If you are too drunk to help me or could care less, just say so. You told me at the volleyball game that I could call on you, and that's what I'm doing. Apparently there is a problem, so, good night."

"Calm your ass down, Ashby. We're both tired and I've had a little too much gin. Get Starnes to give you the morning off tomorrow and come see me. Rod can give you directions." There was a steadiness in Gould's voice that quelled Ashby's anger and reassured him that Snapper was a man he could trust.

"I'll see you by eight, if that's not too early."

"Son, you gotta be kidding. Me and the lovely Rita will have consummated our relationship for the umpteenth time, and I'll be back with a catch for blue crab omelets before you get here."

"The lovely Rita?"

"See you in the A.M., Maryland." Snapper hung up before Ashby could answer.

3

THE SUN WAS just crawling from the sea when Ashby headed south on the Savannah highway. Beside him on the Mazda's passenger seat were directions to Gould's bungalow he had scrawled after he called Starnes around midnight. Without any questions Rod had given him permission to go see Gould as part of the *Wells* investigation, but Ashby sensed he was starting to push his luck.

He and Starnes had hit it off as friends from the beginning, but the *Wells* case was going nowhere. With no certainty that the Wagners had disappeared near Charleston, Ashby knew that Starnes was becoming increasingly irritated about the amount of time he was spending in his search for leads. At least to this point, however, Starnes had given him free rein.

Some twenty-five miles south of Charleston, Ashby turned off the main road, bound for Edisto Island and feeling as if he had reached the end of the world. The narrow two-lane funneled through bands of gnarled live oak garnished with necklaces of Spanish moss. Trashed and rusting cars and farm equipment stood sentinel in weeds and tall grass beside dilapidated houses and mobile homes. Dogs sleeping in the road ahead seemed little more than bothered that he would run over them if they did not amble out of the way.

The dirt lane leading to Gould's place was blocked by a scurrying flock of dirty-white geese who sent up a chorus of alarmed honks at the approaching car.

He pulled up and stopped in front of a tin-roofed two-story building that had the words "Edisto Cannery" written in faded painted letters on the side nearest a rickety dock that seemed almost to sway on sight toward a salt creek.

Climbing out of his car, Ashby cursed silently as he squished into a slime of goose dung near the front door. In frustration, he kicked at a fat gander that seemed angered at the invasion of his domain.

The honking must have alerted Gould because the door swung open and Ashby was face to face with Snapper, hoping he had not seen him taking a kick at the bird.

"Crazy goose tried to attack me," he said with a half-laugh.

"Hell, that's just old Ozzie. He's my attack gander! Damn, about time you got here, boy. We've been looking for you for about two hours. You hungry?"

"Hey, Snapper, I'm sorry I'm late but this ain't exactly a Stuckey's with a lot of signs posted on the road."

"Son, if you want South of the Border, follow the Pedro billboards up the interstate. Park your butt there. He pointed to an old kitchen chair with one leg shorter than the other three. Ashby immediately was annoyed by the unsteadiness, but ignored it.

Gould was wearing a frayed rat-gray bathrobe and an Oakland Athletics baseball cap that appeared to have been bleached by countless days spent under the sea sun.

"You don't exactly look like you were up at dawn trolling for your breakfast," Ashby asked. "Rough night or did you just decide to dive for pearls later?"

"Smart ass. Eric, I told you I would be up early to show my manhood to the lovely Rita and to catch a basketful of crabs, and old Snapper never lies unless it's to his immediate benefit."

Snapper curled into the womb of an ancient Barca Lounger,

and Ashby turned away as the movement revealed that Gould was wearing nothing beneath the robe.

"So just where is the lovely Rita?" Ashby asked.

"Want to feast your eyes, eh? Can't blame you." Snapper turned and called, "Princess, you got time to come out here a minute and meet one of the fresh fish?"

A dark-complexioned woman wearing a multicolored bandanna on her head emerged from another room. A flowered sarong surrounded her ample middle and wound up over one shoulder. To Ashby she appeared to be about fifty and was much larger than either Snapper or him. Without a word she slowly walked into the den where they sat and gave Ashby a smile that reminded him of the ivories on a baby grand.

"Rita, this is Lieutenant Eric Ashby from the Coast Guard Station in Charleston. He is quite a whipper-snapper, and we might be seeing some more of him around here if he knows what he's doing."

"You are welcome anytime, lieutenant," Rita said softly, her chocolate-brown eyes meeting his without the least flinch. Immediately she swiveled and left the den.

"Me and Rita've been together for many a moon," Gould said admiringly. She was born somewhere up near Pocotaligo, where her daddy was a moonshine king in the Combahee River swamps back in the thirties. Don't think she ever even knew her ma."

"Seems like a fine lady, Snapper."

"You damn right about that, Ashby. But heck, I'm wasting your time and you mine. Let's talk business."

After Ashby wolfed down one of Rita's blue crab omelets, the men spent several hours comparing notes on what little was known about the *H. G. Wells* case and Gould's theories as to its vanishing.

Sitting on Snapper's dock while he tied chicken necks to the wire of a crab trap to use as bait, they also discussed the exhaustive investigation that Gould had conducted into the *Sea Lynx*'s demise.

Gould told him of his bedside vigil with Thackeray, the FBI testing and his checks about "Carlson," all of which had led him down a dead-end street. Just like Ashby's, his search had even taken him to the library, where he had searched the microfilm for any newspaper articles about Thackeray. Like everything else he had tried, this too was fruitless.

"I did save something off microfilm that you might be interested in. Just for the hell of it, I checked around the fiftieth anniversary of the *Hunley*'s attack just to see if there was any commemoration or whatever. I'm kind of interested in that stuff. Civil War buff from way back. There wasn't any mention of it, but I did turn up this newspaper clipping from 1914." Gould handed Ashby a photocopy of the Charleston *Orpheus* article about Iceman Turner's murder.

"I understand from a friend of mine who is in the local NAACP chapter that this lady mentioned in the article is still alive and living downtown somewhere. She's gotta be around a hundred or more. Hell, I didn't know she was still around until about a year ago. Saw her name in one of the black newspapers as being the matron saint of the year or some such nonsense at a church out in the boonies. You know Rita gets those things in the mail and I read everything."

"So what's your point?"

"My point, cretin, is that this killing happened on the *Hunley*'s anniversary."

"The *Hunley* submarine. Yeah, I saw something about it when I was reading about Beauregard."

"He was the commander in Charleston when the *Hunley* made its last voyage."

Gould glared hard into Ashby's eyes. "The *Sea Lynx* also went down on one of the *Hunley*'s anniversaries of her last attack. The one-hundredth, to be exact. Damned queer coincidence, don't you think?"

Gould checked the rope securing the crab trap to a spar on the end of the deck and pitched the chicken-wire cage into the water. It splashed and sank rapidly in the mirror reflecting the green marsh grass and a bottomless rowboat decaying in the reeds and mud.

Gould saw Ashby looking at the boat. "That damned little

piece of crap almost killed me and my brother about ten years ago. I had just bought her from this retired Marine colonel who lives down around Bear Island. Crazy mother, I tell you. He commanded a rifle company that a whole VC regiment came down on somewhere near Khe Sanh. Hill something or other, some number, you know. His boys fucked 'em up pretty bad, but Charlie had the numbers. He ended up blowing a Claymore to take out a VC mortar squad, knowing when he cranked the switch that two of his wounded who had taken hits nearby would buy it too. Damned sad, but he saved the rest of his men. Never was the same, but still made colonel and came home."

Ashby was staring over the marsh, and Gould couldn't tell if he was listening to the story.

"Well anyway, I buys this rowboat from the colonel just so me and Hank can tool around and check out an oyster bank here and there or get us a mess of crabs. We take her out the first day, and the thing starts leaking like Moby Dick rams Noah's Ark! Just incredible. We bailed and bailed to get back to Edisto and dropped her right there where you see her, but I never said nothing to the colonel. Didn't have the guts, I guess."

Soccer-style, Ashby kicked a sun-shriveled fish head off the dock.

"Snapper, didn't you mention that the *Hunley* sank a Union warship off Charleston? What happened to it then?"

"Hell, nobody knows, it never resurfaced."

Detective Jeremy Lord had a bizarre homicide on his hands. A midnight shift security officer stationed aboard the USS *Yorktown* had been found run all the way through his body with some type of edged weapon. Lord had been awakened by a phone call from his chief about 6 A.M. and told to get to the scene.

Paramedics had rushed the guard to a Charleston hospital, but he did not live to make it to emergency surgery.

Murder was rare in Mount Pleasant. Lord and the other two investigators on the thirty-man force spent most of their time looking for burglars and car thieves. Like the spray paint graffiti

and cherry bombs in mailboxes, most of these crimes were eventually traced to kids who lived in the area. All pretty tame stuff
compared to this.

Driving to the aircraft carrier, Lord tried to focus on the
homicide investigation courses he had taken at the State Law
Enforcement Academy in Columbia. Remember, the pattern of
the blood splatters is real important, he told himself. Physical
evidence and witnesses. Motive.

Hell, what did he know about solving a murder? The only time
he had been involved in a homicide probe was back in 1984,
when he and old H. W. Frye were assigned to a case. Lord had
grown up on the Charleston islands and joined the Mount Pleasant department as a patrol officer when he finished high school.
Frye had been with the sheriff's department before becoming
Mount Pleasant's first detective. Eventually Lord became his
apprentice.

They had worked the case of a convenience-store clerk who
had taken a shotgun blast during a robbery. Couple of punk
runaways in a stolen Ford from West Virginia had knocked over
the place and got away with the king's ransom of $32. A state
trooper had surprised them a few hours later sleeping in the car
off an interstate exit. One of the kids had the Ithaca pump murder weapon tucked between his legs.

Lord couldn't forget the sight of Frye at the store, helping
himself to a mustard-dipped corn dog while surveying the bloody
carnage behind the checkout counter. When Frye retired in
1989, Lord had been promoted to chief investigator.

The humidity and the rising sun already were baking shadows
on the *Yorktown*'s flight deck when Lord scaled the ship's gang-
plank. There was little doubt where the crime had occurred.
Behind yellow crime-scene tape, Lord saw a blackened pool of
coagulated blood soaking the tarmac. The officer's hat lay nearby, and the medical debris of the paramedics' attempt to save his
life—red-stained gauze, syringe caps, and packaging—fluttered
and rolled about the deck.

"The Lord is with us!"

The detective had heard this greeting many times before, and it always irritated him. He turned to see a uniformed police sergeant walking toward him.

"You got anything, Loomis, or do you just want a dog biscuit?"

"Come on, Jer, this is your big chance to make the chief happy. You solve this one and you might make chief yourself."

Lord and Hugh Loomis despised each other, their dislike percolating since the days when their rival high schools tussled on the football field. The annual war between Shem Creek and Dunovant High, which Lord attended, was one of the biggest sports traditions in Charleston and Berkeley counties. Loomis had been a fullback for "the Creek" from 1971 to '73 while Lord was the middle linebacker for Dunovant. The pair had crashed into each other for three years in the big game, and Loomis never let Lord forget that Shem Creek won two of them. Lord's only solace was that his team won in 1973, spoiling the Creek's chances at a state championship.

The head knocking had continued over the years since both went from graduation to badges with Mount Pleasant's finest.

"Victim's name is Charles Hoyle, age forty-five," Loomis said, flipping through a tiny notebook. "Worked for Jim Shirley's security outfit based on Johns Island. Hoyle was working the midnight-to-seven shift, just walking the deck basically. A maintenance guy found him about 5:45 hooked in the stomach like a mackerel. No sign of any weapon on the premises. Wallet with about $50 was still on him as was his wristwatch and a couple of rings. Don't appear robbery was a motive. He wasn't armed either. I got his address and everything if you need it. The wife's been notified."

Loomis snapped his notebook shut, obviously pleased with his report. He stared at Lord, waiting for a compliment.

"Somebody gutted this poor sucker like an extra in an Errol Flynn movie."

"Thanks, Hugh, now put your bullet back in your pocket. Looks like your boys have got the deck taped off pretty well." Lord was trying to appear confident, but Loomis knew better.

"Yeah, boy, a homicide. Think you can handle it, Jer? Too bad ol' Hal Frye ain't here to hold your hand. You Dunovant pussies never could handle the pressure!"

"Get out of my sight, Loomis! I'm in charge now. Go find a donut to stuff in your face."

Loomis stalked away, trying to stare down Lord. "I'm goin,' Jer. Why don't you and me meet up sometime after work and settle this thing."

"You'll always be a jerk-off in the book of life, Loomis. "Kiss your ass good-bye if you try me."

"Hey, Jeremy?"

Lord wheeled away from Loomis and was face to face with a policeman holding something in a plastic bag.

"Yeah, Pritchard, whatcha' got?"

"Well, Loomis might not have mentioned this to you, but we found some physical evidence, at least I think that's what it is. The EMT's told me that this fell out of the security guard's hand when they were putting him in the ambulance."

Pritchard held up a small plastic bag, and Lord squinted to see the gold-colored object inside. It was a button with a face depicting a rope-entwined anchor with two crossed cannon in the background. At the bottom was "CSN" in capital letters.

"Uh, we've already contaminated this evidence," Pritchard said, dropping his head. "Some of the boys wanted to take a look at it. They took it before I could stop them."

Lord could feel the anger welling in his head. "So y'all just passed it around like a Pawley's Island whore, is that what you're telling me?"

"Yea, sergeant, but we also got a guy for you to question. Loomis let the janitor who found the victim go home because he was sleepy, but we located a possible suspect who we think was crashing on the beach when everything happened."

"If he was crashing on the beach when everything happened, then he's a possible witness, not a suspect, Pritchard." Lord was steaming. "Where is he?"

"We're holding him below deck in the old brig. Jer, I can't believe how well built this ship is. It—"

"Boy, just get this guy up here in front of me right now!"

As Pritchard scurried away, Lord inspected the death scene more closely. He found nothing to help him.

Lord was examining the coin-size bloodstains on Hoyle's cap when Pritchard emerged on deck with his catch.

Lord immediately recognized him as a transient who had bussed tables at several area seafood restaurants, but who spent most of his time panhandling. A sudden whiff of wind smothered Lord with the stench of bad wine, sweat, and human filth.

"Isn't your name Will Work For Food? Where's your cardboard sign, brother? I hear you spit-wash plates, you know about that?"

"I don't know shit about any of that, buddy," the man answered. "I've been through enough tonight to make me want to catch the next bus outta here."

"Well, I don't think the chamber of commerce would consider you a loss," Lord said sharply. "What's your name and what were you doing on the beach?"

"Mister, I ain't lookin' for no run-in with y'all. Name's Bobby Windrow. I been here about six months. Seen you in a couple of the restaurants where I worked. The best place . . ."

"Okay, okay. Just tell me what you were doing down here overnight. You kill this boy?"

"Friend, I ain't never seen him, much less killed him, but there was some wild shit goin' down out here last night."

"I'm listening."

"Well see, I was sleeping on the beach last night 'cause the shelter was full, and I heard some people talking about blowing up this boat. They sounded damn serious about it."

"Wait a second," Lord interrupted. "Are you talking about the *Yorktown*? This aircraft carrier?"

"I guess so, officer. I mean, I was curled up on a blanket in the dunes, but I seen about five of 'em standing with the waves a-sloshing up around their boots."

"Boots. Did you get a good look at these guys?"

"Not really. I was about fifty yards away from them, and it must have been after midnight, but I seen one of them pointing toward this boat. What I could see was that they were dressed kind of funny, with coats that came down around their knees. Most of 'em had some sort of hat, but I couldn't make them out. Looked like they had their pants tucked inside their boots, at least a couple of 'em."

"Alright. I'll tell you what. I wanna talk to you some more, so why don't we get one of the boys to run you down to the detention center, get you cleaned up and fed, and I'll see you in a few hours."

Lord called one of the patrol officers, who escorted Windrow to a police van in the Patriots Point parking lot. The June sun was beginning to bear down, and Lord could see a line of tourist cars blocked by a patrol cruiser parked sideways across the entrance drive. A uniformed officer was trying to explain to a fat man wearing Bermuda shorts, sandals, and black socks why the *Yorktown* was temporarily closed.

Lord didn't figure Windrow was a suspect based on his brief interview and the fact that the guard wasn't robbed. Still, they would hold him a little longer for questioning and a check on the national crime computer linkup.

Just as a precaution, he would notify the Coast Guard about the incident, since Windrow had reported the threat of the *Yorktown* being blown up.

Fishing into his coat pocket, he retrieved the button in the bag. He rolled it between his fingers and then noticed some tiny lettering on the back.

Squinting in the sunlight, Lord read: "Courtney & Tennent/ Charleston/S.C."

❦

Two days after Hoyle's murder, Eric Ashby made his way through the hallways of the Mount Pleasant Police Department and found the closet-like office of Jeremy Lord.

Rod Starnes had taken the detective's call earlier in the day and decided to send Ashby out to handle the matter. Maybe it would take his mind off the missing Wagners.

It had been three weeks since Ashby had visited Snapper Gould. Since then, Ashby had immersed himself not only in finding out everything he could about the *Sea Lynx*, but about the *Hunley*. He spent hours in the local libraries, poring over old newspaper microfilm and reading long-forgotten manuscripts, diaries, and letters related to the war. He also talked to local Civil War enthusiasts and scholars. Most of his research had to be done at night and on weekends. Starnes had cracked down hard on him, all but ordering him to put the Wagner case in the active but unsolved file—to basically bury it.

Ashby wasn't even sure himself why he was digging: four incidents, all probably coincidental, which had occurred over the span of more than a century.

Sure, "Iceman" Turner had been killed on the fiftieth anniversary of the *Hunley*'s final cruise. And the *Sea Lynx* had blown up one hundred years to the day that the submarine sank the U.S. warship *Housatonic*. But the *H. G. Wells* had disappeared in April 1994, and while the Turner slaying and the *Sea Lynx* were tied to Charleston, there was no physical evidence that the *Wells* had sunk in area waters. Still, there was that statement from Jenkins' report: "There's another one for Boryguard."

"Morning, lieutenant, I'm Sergeant Lord."

"Yes, sir, how're you doing?"

The men shook hands, and Ashby took a seat in a creaky wooden chair in front of Lord's desk.

"Be with you in just a second. Just have to dig out some paperwork for the chief."

The detective looked tired and rightly so. He had had little rest since the Hoyle killing. Mount Pleasant was in an uproar over the murder; and the sensational angle that the guard had been killed on the *Yorktown*, possibly run through by some type of spear or sword, had the media in a feeding frenzy. An immense green-glass ashtray on the desk was a virtual garden of unfiltered Camels.

On the wall of the office were a few framed commendations and graduation certificates. There was also a yellowing photo of a plainclothes police officer wearing a badge on his belt.

Ashby read the penned inscription in the right-hand corner: "To Officer Jeremy Lord—Best Wishes, H. W. Frye."

Ashby had kept up with the slaying case through the papers and TV reports, but Lord gave him a quick rundown of the investigation, including details not released to the media. The detective also supplied him with a copy of Windrow's statement and the police report.

"Man, I've been swamped with calls from these reporters," Lord said, rubbing his face and stretching. His movements reminded Ashby of an old neighborhood beagle who liked to sleep on the front porch, warming in the sun. "Lucky for me, the chief's handling most of them. He loves this public relations stuff."

"Sergeant, do you really think someone intended to, or intends to, blow up the *Yorktown*? Is there anything, other than Windrow's statement, that leads in that direction?"

"Not really. We just called you boys as a precaution, that's all. We let that damn vagrant go as soon as we questioned him. Hell, he would have robbed that poor guy blind if he was the one who wasted him.

"It's just plain strange," Lord continued, "there wasn't nothing missing from the body—wallet, rings, watch, nothing. I mean, this guy played bingo at the American Legion on his nights off. He didn't screw around with anybody that we've found out about. No enemies. Find me a motive and I'll pop the killer."

A lady secretary appeared at the door. "Jer, uh, Sergeant Lord, we just got a packet back from Columbia you'll be real interested in."

"Thanks, Margaret, bring it on in here. Must be some of the autopsy and preliminary forensics test results."

Ashby watched as Lord tore into the package and fished out a report.

"'Victim died of penetrating trauma to the abdomen . . . numerous organs perforated or damaged . . . ,'" Lord read aloud and smirked. "Hell, I could have told you that."

"'No residue found from weapon, which appears to be a sword, about three feet in blade length and approximately one and one-half inches in width. Exit wound punctured left kidney . . .'"

"Sounds like they didn't tell you much that you didn't already know," Ashby said. Lord scrounged through the envelope.

"And to top everything off, my dumb-ass assistant forgot to

send in the only physical evidence we have. I mean, Hoyle had this in his hand when we found him!"

Lord literally backhanded the bagged button at Ashby before storming out of the office.

"Corporal Collins! Didn't I tell you to put everything from the murder scene in the mail to Columbia?"

Ashby examined the golden button through the clear plastic. CSN. It had to be a reproduction. From the cannon and anchor he knew it represented the Confederate States Navy. Too new looking to be authentic. He saw the writing on the back and wrote it down on a notepad sheet from Lord's desk, stuffing the paper in his pocket.

A chill zigzagged sharply down his spine as he pressed his forefinger across the button's face, feeling the impressions and workmanship. "Damn, the air conditioning has finally kicked in," he said to himself. But the cold was unlike any he had ever experienced, numbing his hand like he had thrust it into a deep freezer. The iciness darted up his arm.

As Ashby watched in horrid amazement, frost formed on his wrist and forearm. He could hear Lord and another police officer talking in the hallway a short distance away. Ashby tried to yell for help, but fear paralyzed his every instinct. The button and its bag were glazed in ice by this time. Unable to grasp it, he let the plastic and its contents fall to the floor and disintegrate in a haze of crystalline fragments.

The tinkling of the flying ice skittering across the floor lasted no more than a second. As the sound faded, so did the malaise afflicting Ashby. In an instant he was bathed in sweat, slumped in the chair, exhausted and petrified by what had occurred.

Lord reappeared. "I was just telling Collins that this button might hold the key to the whole shebang. The stupid idiot, he . . . Jesus, boy, what's wrong with you? Are you having a heart attack?"

Ashby's mind was racing in a thousand directions, his sanity balanced on a frayed edge.

"The button! I, I was holding it and everything got real cold and I tried to yell, but I couldn't!" he blurted. "It was freezing my arm and I dropped it and it shattered all over the floor. Then there was nothing left. I, I don't know what happened."

"Margaret, bring this boy some water, please. Son, you mean to tell me you destroyed that button, the only physical evidence I had on this case?"

"No, it turned into ice and fell on the floor and broke all apart."

Lord looked at the dirty white linoleum. It was dry. He went down on his hands and knees to peer under the desk and chairs. Nothing.

"Lieutenant, I don't know what you're trying to pull, but I'm going to have to search you. That button did not just disappear."

"Whatever," Ashby said wearily. "I'm telling you the truth."

Two officers searched Ashby, but found no trace of the button.

"You don't collect swords, do you, Ashby?"

Suddenly Lord had a new suspect in his murder case. "I mean, why else would you come out here and destroy evidence. Did you know Hoyle? Ever meet him somewhere? Y'all have something dirty and deep going on?" Lord leaned forward from his chair to within a few inches of Ashby's face.

By this time Ashby had been frisked thoroughly enough to regain his wits. He was rattled by the button's destruction, but knew he had nothing to do with the killing.

"Listen, you shit-for-brains," he spat at Lord. "I've got about eighteen witnesses and taped radio transmissions with my voice that will prove that I was on duty as officer of the day when this guy died. As to your precious, damned button, well, I don't have an answer. I'm damned sorry about whatever happened to it, and I'll help you in any way I can to solve this case. But right now, I just wanna get outta here."

"Yeah, yeah, get outta my sight, homo." Lord gave him a dismissive wave. "Just you bet your sweet ass that I will be talking to the district attorney about some tampering-with-evidence charge or something against you."

Ashby walked unsteadily out the front door of the police department and got into his car. He drove over the southbound

Cooper River bridge, and descended in downtown Charleston, steering through the close streets for several hours, trying to bring some order to the disorder. With no answers he headed back to base just after dusk.

Rod Starnes was waiting for him when he hit the gate, stopping him in front of the Rice Mill.

"Ashby, what the hell have you done? I've gotten about twelve calls from the Mount Pleasant police chief, who is chewing my ear off! He told me that you went out there and either stole or destroyed a piece of vital evidence in their murder investigation!"

Starnes was leaning on the driver's side door, and Ashby was peering straight ahead through the windshield.

"Hey, man, don't you have anything to say? This is serious stuff, we're talkin' here! They were going to put out an all-points bulletin for you as a fugitive suspect, but I asked them for a little more time. You readin' me?"

"Rod, they know I'm not a suspect, I was here that night. So why would I monkey with their evidence?" Ashby's gaze was fixed on the common in front of the admin complex, but he spoke calmly. "Something happened that I can't explain and you wouldn't believe if I tried to. I was holding this button and it basically turned to ice."

Ashby related the incident at the police station as best he could remember. He glanced at Rod for any semblance of understanding, but found none in Starnes's incredulous look.

"Rod, all I can tell you right now is that the missing Wagners might be a bigger deal than any of us have ever imagined."

Starnes's mouth dropped and he rolled his eyes. This was the same old song and dance he had been hearing from Ashby for months.

"Eric, I'm gonna give you a few days off to get your act together. God knows you need it. We're gonna have a long hard talk about your future when you get back. Is this sinking in?"

"I know you think I'm a nut case, Rod." Ashby avoided Starnes's stare, fiddling with the car's air conditioner controls. "Just understand that I'm not taking it lightly that someone might be intending to blow up the *Yorktown* and maybe a whole lot of tourists with it. I'm looking into any and every possibility whether you believe it or not."

"So, Eric, what are you gonna do?" Starnes's voice was soothing as he shifted into the role of the peacemaker.

"Well, for one thing, I'm taking you up on your offer of some time off. Maybe I'm not cut out for the Coast Guard. For another, I'm gonna go see a woman who's gotta be more than a hundred years old. I think she knows something about all this."

Ashby did not give Starnes a chance to reply. He stepped on the gas and sped toward his quarters.

Several men were playing pool and watching television in the lounge when he walked into the barracks. Wordlessly he waved and headed directly to his room. Falling onto his bed, Ashby dialed Snapper Gould, but there was no answer. Almost immediately he was lost in sleep, barely able to return the telephone to its cradle. He had no idea what had happened to him that afternoon in Lord's office. Still rattled, he was awakened once by the dreamy vision of the button bursting apart on the floor. Otherwise, he was too exhausted to fight off his slumber.

Quite suddenly his world had spun off its axis and into a reality where madness held sway like a rampant, purging fever cloaking a city.

Ashby didn't doubt his rationality, even though the button incident was unsettling, to say the least. But he was running on empty in intelligent explanations for everything he had encountered since his arrival.

Finding and talking to Ella Solomon about Iceman Turner's murder was a shot in the dark, but what else did he have to do? He had found her address in the telephone directory. Maybe she could add something—anything—to expose the phantoms that seemingly swirled about Charleston.

Awakening around noon, Ashby set out to find Ella Solomon at her home on Nassau Street. In the shadow of the Cooper River bridges, he stopped in front of her little frame house, the starkness of its unpainted gray wood brightened by a bevy of morning glories waving from two front window boxes.

He knocked on the front door and heard someone moving inside. The door opened slightly and Ella Solomon peered at him.

"Yes?"

"Ms. Solomon? I'm Lieutenant Eric Ashby from the Coast Guard station in Charleston. I'm working on a history project, and I'd like to talk to you for a minute if it's not too much trouble."

"What kind of history?"

"Oh, you know, old Charleston's been around for a long time, and a lady like yourself has seen a lot of what's gone on here over the years. I promise I won't take up much of your time. I'll even pay you a few dollars if that would help."

"I don't want your money. I just have to be careful who I let in my house, an old woman living alone, you know."

"Yes, ma'am, I do and I promise you this won't take long. I just want to talk to you a minute about the Mimosa Club."

"I guess that would be okay," Ella said wearily, unlatching the screen door for Ashby. He followed her into the living room, where a color console TV blared "Wheel of Fortune."

Ella moved across the room with a stooped and brittle grace, looking as fragile as delicate china. She was a little woman with hair the color of mercury and pulled in a bun. She wore an off-white dress and matching heels. On a side table near the front door Ashby saw a pair of cotton white gloves and a glossy black purse. She looked to be ready for Sunday morning services.

"Miss Ella, are you sure I didn't catch you on your way out?"

"The way out? Mister, the way out for me is just to be called to kneel down at the throne of our Heavenly Father."

She eased into a worn recliner and Ashby sat on a sofa. He watched the game show for a minute, deciding how to broach the subject of Iceman's death.

"I hear you were a pretty fancy singer in the old days."

"Old days of what?"

"I mean, you sang at the Mimosa Club back when Iceman was there."

"I still sing when people want me to—at least when I feel like it."

They both turned their attention back to the television, where the game-show contestants were buying vowels.

"Miss Ella, I'm sorry to bring up something unpleasant, but I'm trying to figure out Iceman's killing."

"Boy, ain't nothin' to figure out. You talkin' 'bout something that happened a long time ago and nobody cares about no more."

"I've read what the newspapers said; tell me about the men who came up on you and Iceman. Did they say anything? What did they look like?"

"He didn't have no chance. That Vanna is one skinny white girl. Them devils come down on him like they sprung from Revelations and that's a fact."

"Miss Ella, do you remember what they were wearing or anything else about them?"

"Some things are best left alone and this is one of them." Ella's voice rose above the audio clatter. "This is a cross I have had to bear for a long, long time. Iceman didn't deserve what he got. Those Rebel crackers killed him for no reason."

"Why do you say Rebels?"

"Boy, I know enough about my roots to know the Rebels wore gray suits. Who is that with Vanna?"

Ashby realized he likely had obtained all the information he could gather. He rose to leave.

"Ma'am, I appreciate you taking the time to talk to me. Is there anything I can do for you?"

Ella sat motionless in her chair, staring at the screen as the colors of the bonus round danced on her glasses. She didn't speak as he left.

The screen door sprang shut behind him, and he squinted in the wash of afternoon sunshine. Children squealed and dodged between parked cars on the street.

"Talk to Mr. Frye from the police department." Ella, who had tottered to the door, startled Ashby. "We used to talk some about it. When I worked the Star Haze. You know, the motel."

"Mr. Frye? Who are you talking about, Ms. Ella?"

"He saw them too. Used to work out on Mount Pleasant.

White man like you. Good evenin', now." She shut the inside wooden door, leaving him alone on the porch.

Frye.

Ashby pondered what he had learned and eased his car into the street, barely missing a youngster who had scampered out to retrieve a careening baseball. Ashby was headed for Mount Pleasant.

Framed by a narrow gap between the houses across Nassau, he could see the USS *Yorktown* at its mooring at Patriots Point.

"What the hell are you doin' back here," Jeremy Lord yelled. "Margaret, why'd you let this psycho back in here?"

"I, I was on the phone and he went right by me!"

"Easy, sergeant, she didn't have a chance. I know I have to explain what happened yesterday, but I'm still looking for answers myself."

Ashby faced Lord in the reception area of the Mount Pleasant Police Department.

"You ain't gonna find that button in here. But I likely might just beat your skull in!"

"I know I was a blubbering fool when everything broke loose yesterday, and I want to help with this case."

Lord swerved around a secretary's desk to reach him.

"In fact, I came here to find out anything I can about an Officer Frye."

Lord hesitated long enough for Detective Collins to move between him and Ashby.

"Come on, Jer. We can find him if we want him, you know that. At least *hear* him out before you take him out."

"All I know is that I saw his photo on your wall. Do you want to interfere with a Coast Guard investigation of a threatened terrorist attack on a national landmark? I'm talkin' the *Yorktown*, Lord."

"What the hell makes you think Hal Frye has anything to do with the *Yorktown*, dumb ass? And why would any terrorists want to blow her up? That's just pure donkey crap."

"I'll ask the questions when I find him. Hey, he's not a suspect, I just want to pick his brain about a couple of things."

"Ease off, Jer, it's not like Hal's name ain't in the phone book." Margaret smiled slyly at Ashby. "And besides, the Gold Bug Bar ain't that hard to find. You know as well as I do that old Hal didn't have nothin' to do with this."

"Woman, the chief's gonna hear about your big mouth! I oughtta—"

"Yeah, yeah, Jer," Margaret said, coolly inspecting her cuticles. "I'm just real afraid the chief will fire me for cooperating with the Coast Guard."

"Thanks." Ashby hit the front door, winking at Margaret as he exited. "I owe you a drink."

"I still want my friggin' button!" Lord yelled after him.

4

THE GOLD BUG BAR was a watering hole on the main drag of Sullivan's Island about three miles across the salt marshes from Mount Pleasant. A narrow blacktop with a drawbridge over the Intracoastal connected Sullivan's with the rest of the world.

Fort Moultrie was the island's main claim to fame. From there (Fort Sullivan as it was called at the time) Carolinians had fought off a British naval assault against Charleston in 1776. It would be four years before the Redcoats finally captured the seaport.

Eight decades later Rebel gunners at Moultrie had taken aim at Fort Sumter less than a mile away across Charleston Harbor. During the ensuing century the island saw the rise of a few con-dominium complexes and a bevy of summer homes for Charles-tonians. Despite this growth, it retained its low-key charm and motorists on the two-lane spine running its length had to slow for an occasional dog staggering sleepily across the road.

The island had been hammered by Hurricane Hugo in 1989, but like the rest of the Charleston area, had rebounded with vigor.

An iridescent orange sun was sinking into the sea by the time Ashby parked in front of the Gold Bug, a low-slung, unpainted building, where a rented sign on a trailer advertised "2 4 1 Happy Hour—Toples Dancers." Ashby kicked at the missing "s" lying in the dirt. The lot was packed with pickups of every make and description and several chrome-heavy motorcycles.

He entered the lounge, squinting to adjust his eyes from the sunlight to the smoke-filled dimness. An Aerosmith cut blasted from a jukebox. The air hung heavy with cigarette exhales mixed with the smell of beer, farts, and long-gone seafood.

A rough cut of men bent over drinks around tables or at the bar. Bathed in indigo and white light, a svelte blonde wearing a thong and pasties on her breasts gyrated on a small stage. "Jesus, we're talking Cadillac bumper bullets," Ashby said to himself, staring at the dancer and almost walking up the back of a mammoth biker.

Ashby was glad he was in civilian clothes. His ice-cream Coast Guard uniform would have made him a trouble magnet in this place. He wedged his way to the bar and ordered a Molson. "What the hell is a gold bug?" Ashby asked the bartender when he returned with the beer. The man curtly waved his arm toward a framed picture hanging near one of the cash registers.

"That's Edgar Allan Poe. You know, the famous writer who wrote horror stories? He was in the army and stationed at Fort Moultrie for a while. He wrote the story 'The Gold Bug' and wrote how it all happened on Sullivan's Island. It's a story about pirates and buried treasure."

Ashby could tell that the bartender's jaded tale had been told many times to tourists who stumbled into the joint.

"You know a guy named Hal Frye? Is he here?" Ashby asked. "Why?"

"I just know Frye used to be a Mount Pleasant cop and I know some of his friends."

"Okay, okay. That's Hal down there." The barkeep pointed to an older man hunched on a barstool near the stage.

Ashby approached Frye, who was gently tucking a dollar bill into the stripper's pink lace garter.

"Gwen, you know you've got my heart on a chain. Come on home with me, darlin'." Frye's attention was totally focused on the girl, who shook her tits near his face and gave him an up-close look at the elaborate thorny rose tattooed high on her tanned left thigh.

"Someday, sugar," she cooed, briefly stroking the gray stubble around his chin. "You just keep comin' to see me."

The dancer spun off in a wild flurry as a Van Halen number erupted from the jukebox.

"How ya doin,' Hal. I'm Eric Ashby."

Frye glanced at him and shook his hand. "Grab a seat, friend. I'm in love with Gwen, here."

"She's a looker, all right."

Frye looked to be in his mid-to-late sixties with a beer gut made all the more prominent by his wiry frame. His grayish curly hair was short, but looked as though it hadn't been combed in weeks.

Both of them watched the stripper promenade before a cluster of bikers at a nearby table.

"Hey, Hal, I need to talk to you about an old case you handled," Ashby almost shouted above the music. "I've been talking to Ella Solomon and she mentioned your name."

"Old Ella's a fine woman, no doubt about that," Frye replied, his gaze trained on the dancer. "Haven't seen her in a while."

"Well, I saw her today and she seemed to be doin' fine. She said you and her talked once in a while about stuff y'all had in common."

Finally Frye turned toward him. "Tell you what, buddy. Give me time to have a coupla' more beers and get home after happy hour, and we'll shoot the breeze for a few minutes. You're not some reporter or something are you?"

"No. But I am with the Coast Guard. You remember a guy named Snapper Gould?"

"Course I do," Frye snorted in indignation. "We worked together on one of the biggest cases I ever had. Didn't solve it, but it wasn't for a lack of effort."

"The *Sea Lynx*?"

"Yea, boy." Frye now was staring hard at Ashby. "So you and Jeremy Lord are bosom buddies?"

Ashby nodded. "You could say so. I had an experience in his office yesterday that you might find real interesting. Say, how did you know I'd seen Lord and . . ."

"See you in a little while, buddy."

Ashby met Frye at his mobile home in the Rest Eaz-Zee Trailer Park about an hour later. Over a liter bottle of malt liquor, he told his story about the button. From a raggedy easy chair, Frye listened without changing expression.

"You might think I'm crazy, but I was stone-cold sober. Lord thinks I'm a mental case."

"Boy, I don't think you're crazy at all," Frye said, staggering to the bathroom. To this point he had not shared any details with Ashby about his involvement in the *Sea Lynx* probe or his relationship with Ella Solomon.

"Can you tell me anything?" Ashby asked when he returned.

"I can tell you a lot, old buddy," Frye answered wearily, falling into his chair. "That button story is pretty far out. I bet ol' Jeremy pretty much lost it."

"You could say that he did," Ashby laughed, reaching for his glass. "He basically wants my head for a hood ornament."

"Lord can get pretty excited. Sounds like he had a reason to this time. I mean, you lost his frigging button or it blew up or something, as you say! You sure you wasn't smoking some of that wacky weed?"

"Tell me about Ella Solomon."

"Oh, I've been knowing Miss Ella for a mighty long time," Frye said, shifting in his seat. "She used to work some light house-keeping duty at this motel on 17."

"The Star Haze?"

"Yeah, that was it, but she was up in years pretty much by that time, and they let her make a few bucks taking a shift as the desk clerk. When I was a deputy with the sheriff's office, I used to get by there a few times now and then just to hassle this one whore who used to work that stretch of the road. We called her, the whore I mean, Diamond Lilly because she . . ."

"Hal, you need a refill. Let me get it. So you and Ella knew each other because you checked on the motel on your patrol?"

"There was a little more to it than that. Mount Pleasant is a small town and word got around that me and her was cut from the same cloth you could say. That is, we both went through something on the beach, many years apart, that neither of us could explain. She brought it up one night."

Frye paused to take a long pull from his mug. "We were talking on a Sunday evening—not much was happening on my beat—and we got around to romance. You know, talking about love and that kinda stuff. We're both standing out by my patrol car enjoyin' the warm weather even though it was still real early spring.

"She was telling me about the only man she ever truly loved— Iceman Turner—and how he got killed on the beach back in 1914. Well, she swore up and down it was done by Confederate soldiers! Hell, the war had been over for a whale of a long time by then. She even showed me an old newspaper article about the killing. Now you know how an old person's mind can wander, but Ella has always been sharp as a tack."

Ashby was listening intently, not wanting to interrupt and possibly break Frye's train of thought.

"What made everything so freaky for me was that I had had a similar experience on the beach about two weeks earlier. We're talking just a few miles from where ole Iceman met his maker.

"The strangest thing about the whole wax ball was that it happened exactly fifty years after Turner's murder. It was 1964 and the same night that the *Sea Lynx* went up like some Roman candle."

"What did you see, Hal?"

"Well, it started when I got a call of some kind of disturbance down on the beach. I got down there and there were these boys talking about the war. There must have been five or six of 'em standing together with the waves breaking around their boots. I'll never forget they were wearing calf-high boots. I tried to get a light on them, but they were gone in a flash."

"The war. You mean Vietnam?"

"No, man, these guys were talking about the Civil War, the War Between the States. It was as if they were fighting it and were lost. They called me a Yankee who had on a fancy uniform and said something about 'Abe's boys.' To be honest, I didn't feel like I was in any immediate danger, even though one of them threatened to kill me. It all happened in about a minute. I was far enough away to draw my revolver if I needed to. By the time I raised the flashlight, they were gone."

"And the *Sea Lynx* exploded sometime after that?"

"Shoot, it couldn't have been two minutes before I saw it go up. 'Course I didn't know what it was at the time, but I was watching eleven souls go up in smoke and flaming diesel. Everybody was out searching the ocean for survivors the next morning, but it was one of those tour boats heading out to Fort Sumter that found this pot-bellied banker floating across a chunk of her wreckage. Some fucking tourist from Ohio or somewhere fished him out and noticed that one of his legs had been taken off at the knee," Frye laughed.

"Highlight of his vacation, eh? I know that old Snapper talked to him a few times in the hospital before he died."

The wind seemed to be picking up outside, and a welcome breeze softly brushed the blinds of Frye's open windows. Both men sat silently for a few moments, relishing the cool air and reflecting on Frye's revelations.

"Number one, I never thought Ella was crazy," Frye said finally. "She went through some kind of hell that stuck with her for a mighty long time. After I told her my story we developed some kind of bond—I can't explain it."

The wind's rush intensified to send creaks through Frye's home when someone banged at the trailer door. Small tree limbs and pinecones battered the roof.

"Now who the hell is that?" Frye said, clambering out of his chair. He opened the door, which was flung backwards by the wind, slamming into the side of the trailer.

Before him stood a blonde with mascara-laced tears spilling in black rivulets down her cheeks.

"Gwen!"

"Hey, Hal. You said I could come see you anytime I wanted," the dancer sobbed. "I had a big damn fight with my boyfriend tonight. He's my manager too, and I don't have a place to stay."

"You come on in here, honey pie," Frye said, throwing an arm around her shoulders. "I'll take care of you."

Ashby took this as his cue to leave as Frye helped Gwen up the steps. "Now don't you fret none, baby. You can stay here as long as you need to. It's just me and that damn cat who shows up to get fed every now and again. Heck, she stays knocked up half the time anyway."

"I'll be in touch, Hal." Ashby extended his hand. "I appreciate the information and hospitality."

"Sit right here on the couch, honey. Hey, it's no problem, son. I enjoyed talkin' to ya. Oh, one last thing about your button."

Ashby stopped in the doorway, heat lightning silently illuminating the swaying pines in the yard.

"Old Lord asked me to take that button and let a friend of mine take a look at it. This guy deals in Civil War relics and artifacts. Really knows his shit, I mean, goes to shows all over the place buyin' and tradin' the stuff.

"Well, this old boy gave it the once-over with one of them jewelry glasses, went through a bunch of books, and made some calls to some of his expert buddies."

"Hal, I'm cold." The girl was shoehorned into a corner of the couch, her legs drawn up under her chin. Her cutoff jeans did not contain the black panties spilling out around her ass.

"I'll be with you in just a minute, baby. There's a bottle of Jack Daniels in that cabinet over the kitchen sink. Help yourself."

Both men were distracted as Gwen deliberately unfolded from her seat, tugging at her thin T-shirt, and sidled into the kitchen.

She was playing for an audience of two as she stood on tiptoes and reached into the cabinet, slowly retrieving the bottle. Ashby and Frye both savored the vista of her coltish brown legs and shapely bottom.

"Uh, as I was sayin,'" Frye broke the spell. "My buddy tells me that this button was put out by a company that made Confederate equipment in Charleston during the war. It was a Rebel navy button. He also said that from all indications it was the real McCoy."

"Which means?"

"That it was original, not some reproduction made last year to sell to tourists. He checked with his friends, and they all agreed it was made during the war. Said it was the most well-preserved button of its kind he'd ever seen, almost like new, and wanted to buy it from me, but I told him it was evidence in a murder case."

"He didn't say who or what kind of sailors would have worn it, did he?"

"No, just that it could have been from any of the men serving on the Confederate gunboats or other vessels around Charleston at that time. Or that it could have been manufactured and later lost at the factory without ever being sewn on a uniform. He was mighty interested in where we got it and said it was worth a lot to collectors."

"Hal! Why don't you and your good-looking friend come join me?" Gwen was stretched back on the couch with a glass of bourbon in one hand and a cigarette in the other. She caught Ashby's eye and blew a series of smoke rings into the air.

"Very talented. I'll have to catch your next show," he said meeting her gaze.

"Baby, you could be in it." With her Marlboro hand, she briefly flicked up her shirt, exposing her breasts and their silver-dollar-size nipples.

Ashby took in the view over Frye's shoulder. "Maybe later," he said, feeling like he had stolen a line from a Mickey Spillane novel. "I'll be seeing you, Hal. Oh, by the way, how did you know I had seen Jeremy Lord?"

"Thought you'd forgotten about that, son. Margaret called me at the bar to warn me that you were on the way. Known her for a long time. She still looks out for old Hal."

Ashby stepped outside into the South Carolina night. The wind suddenly had died down, and the shrill concerto of katydids and crickets filled the hot, unmoving air.

How could a button made for the Confederate navy end up in the hand of a dead security guard on the *Yorktown*?

5

ASHBY SPENT HIS spare time over the next several weeks studying maritime charts, Confederate military reports, wartime newspaper accounts, and history books—any and everything he could find in Charleston's libraries and local archives about the *Hunley*.

He didn't really believe that a banshee boat from the past was still on the prowl, but there had to be some kind of bond based on all the evidence he had gathered. It was beginning to look as if someone or some group was committing copycat crimes based on the submarine's actions and exploits. If so, a blueprint for their next move might be as simple as discovering a long-forgotten battle account that might give some clue how and where the next strike would occur.

The key would be to find if the death of the *Yorktown* guard and the vanished *H. G. Wells* were in any way related. In itself this did not seem likely, but Ashby had to add in the history factor. Iceman Turner's slaughter and Miss Ella's lasting vision of that bloody night, Hal Frye's encounter on the beach, the destruction of the *Sea Lynx*, and the coincidences about the dates coinciding with the *Hunley's* anniversaries were too much to ignore.

Obviously what unraveled him most was the button incident. He could still feel it in his hand, the sticky tingling sensation of holding an ice cube fresh from the refrigerator freezer. The button's loss gnawed at his logic. He tried to bar it from his mind, but it was too unsettling; no other mortal would have had any better luck.

Also food for poisoned thought was the vagrant's claim that some men were plotting to blow up the *Yorktown*. How much credence did he or the police place in such information from a bum? And how would they all live with themselves if the carrier exploded while packed with tourists?

Starnes noticed the purplish circles under his eyes and the hollowness of his cheeks. Ashby went about his on-duty chores like a "Night of the Living Dead" movie extra, but, as always, performed with precision and efficiency. He virtually cut his social ties with everyone, preferring to ensconce himself with piles of old books and musty documents. On rare occasions he would join some of the others for an off-duty drink, but his mind was always adrift. There would be no return to normalcy until he had his answers. Starnes held off saying anything to him or recommending any action, but scrutinized him from a distance. Give the boy time and see what happens. Pounce and slice the jugular if you have to.

Ashby went to the *Yorktown* once or twice a week, walking her decks and corridors, always wary of anything that looked out of the ordinary. But the "Fighting Lady," as the carrier had been nicknamed by World War II sailors, was in fine shape, tourists climbing all over her even as the cool of autumn settled over Charleston.

Through classified ads in the newspaper, he bought a used Dodge pickup truck from a farmer near Ladson and a used fifteen-foot aluminum johnboat with trailer from a retired plumber in Goose Creek. He picked up a rebuilt Evinced outboard motor from one of Okai's helicopter mechanics.

As best he could from the sparse records, he plotted the *Hunley*'s location and operations on the dates of two sinkings in which she had carried her own crews to their deaths while making practice dives off Charleston.

The Confederates had salvaged and refitted her after each disaster. He also tried to piece together details and coordinates of her last mission, the February 17, 1864, attack on the sloop-of-war USS *Housatonic*. The Union warship was sunk, but the *Hunley* never returned. Most histories speculated that the sub went down after she successfully torpedoed the *Housatonic*, but was entangled in her foe's wreckage and also sank. Over the decades a number of searches to find her hulk were fruitless.

Weather permitting, Ashby used much of his off-time buzzing about the harbor mouth, exploring the intimate natural intricacies of its inlets, creeks, islands, and tides. Night and day he was on the water, the throaty roar of the outboard and the sea spray slapping his face becoming second nature to him.

What exactly was he searching for? He didn't know. Perhaps he expected some sign from the depths. Like Moses' burning bush, it would reveal some prophecy or manifestation to answer all. Ashby embarked from various boat landings around Charleston to explore different areas of the harbor and its features.

He spoke to his parents by telephone about every two weeks or so and assured them that everything was going well. They asked when he might get leave to come home, but he put them off, saying that at least for the short term he was too busy. They knew nothing of his turmoil; and when they talked of possibly coming to Charleston for a few days, he tried to discourage them. He knew it was only a matter of time before they came down and he would have to introduce them to some of his friends.

This had the potential for catastrophe. Only Starnes and Okai knew about the button incident. They supported him, but Ashby could tell they were a jury of two still mulling a verdict on his common sense. The other Guardsmen in his circle were casting him as pretty much a loner who liked to spend most of his downtime on the water or engrossed in history books.

The weeks stretched through the December holidays and into January. While most of the station's contingent rang in 1995 at various Charleston nightspots, Ashby spent the evening studying charts on tidal currents in and around the harbor. On a mild and clear Friday night in January's third week, he set out again in his boat. This time he put in at Jacobs' Landing on Wappoo Creek near the south bank of the Ashley River.

A pumpkin crescent moon rode low over the ocean, its tangerine playing on the waves. The water was calm, and the evening felt more like late spring in the Carolinas when the sauna of summer was nearing. It would be colder offshore, and as usual he crammed a heavy jacket, gloves, emergency flares, binoculars, flashlight, and a Thermos of hot chocolate into his backpack. Also in the bag was a bottle of Canadian Mist that he had been carrying since the first, but had yet to open. He figured the whiskey might help to break the chill on his outings, but as yet he had not needed it.

Ashby motored past Albermarle Point and out into the Ashley with Charleston gleaming about a half-mile over the water to his left. He cruised east along the shoreline, passing Plum Island and the mouth of James Island Creek, heading for the harbor entrance.

A tiara of stars crowned the firmament, its infinite pinpoints of brilliance reflecting the manmade luminescence of the city. It was a gorgeous night to be on the water. Ashby cut the engine and drifted about six hundred yards off James Island. He lay back against a seat cushion and savored the astral Broadway above him and the ripples kissing the boat's hull.

Digging through the backpack, he pulled out the whiskey and took a long hard pull. Hell, he deserved it. And it had been almost two weeks since he'd had a drink of any kind—a trip down to Market Street for a couple of beers with the guys.

The hundred proof seared his throat and made his eyes water, but it lit a nice relaxing fire in his belly and made the evening all the more pleasant. He was damned tired and closed his eyes while taking another big swig. No time to eat before he drove out to Jacobs' Landing. Time to enjoy a liquid dinner.

Cheers to you, Beauregard.

Half of the quart was gone in an hour or so. Ashby's boat floated where the eddies and currents took it. By now the heavens and the sea had started to spin, and he was not only drunk but also disoriented. He checked his watch and saw that it was about 11 P.M.

Through his alcoholic haze, Ashby saw a campfire flickering on a beach about half a mile distant. He lifted his binoculars.

His eyes widened when three figures wearing what appeared to be Confederate uniforms emerged from the darkness and approached the flames.

The whiskey sidewinding through his brain heightened the urgency of what was unfolding before him. Could this be the *Hunley* crew? A current of cold fear shot down his spine.

Rather than risk using his outboard, Ashby decided to row toward them. Twice his paddle almost slipped through his sweaty hands as he neared the fire and its owners.

A hundred yards out and silently closing.

Ashby took a double swallow of bravery from the bottle. He felt dizzy and struggled to focus on the scene ahead. Was this a portrait of his doom?

The Rebels were whooping it up. They capered around the blaze, yelling and slapping at each other. Moments later they were joined by several young women, one of whom was wearing pink hoop skirts that she held hiked around her knees.

Another wore a bikini top.

Ashby stumbled out of the boat into the thigh-deep surf and held onto the bow for support. Two of the Confederates waded into the water and helped him pull the craft ashore.

"How ya doin', partner," one of the Rebels slurred. "Looks like you could use a brewsky. Hey, officer of the keg! Bring this man a beer!"

"KA rules!" bellowed another soldier. Ashby recognized the yellow piping around the sleeves and collar of his uniform as that of a Confederate cavalryman—wearing a wristwatch.

As the soldiers and Ashby reached the high-tide mark, the beach filled with other yipping Rebels filtering through the sand dunes. Half expecting to meet the devil himself, Ashby was bewildered, drained, and drunk.

"Who the hell are you people?"

A Confederate officer banged him hard on the back with the flat of his palm. "We people? We are KA's from Mount Orion College in Juliasburg, Tennessee. Just arrived in the

Palmetto State after a damn long drive. Who the hell are you?"

Wordlessly Ashby produced his wallet and showed his Coast Guard credentials.

"You doin' a little fishin' tonight, lieutenant? Looks like you already caught a buzz, if you don't mind me sayin' so. You ain't here to bust us now are you?"

Ashby shook his head.

"I'm Thom Gordon, past president of the Kappa Alpha fraternity at Mount Orion. Class of '90. We got an alumni thing going here with about fifty folks from all over creation—well, at least the South."

A B-52's song suddenly blasted from a small stereo set up on two coolers. Most of the KA's and their honeys immediately broke into dance, gyrating around the fire. Amid the Rebel yells and war whoops, Ashby collapsed into a beach chair. Someone handed him a plastic cup brimming with beer.

"It's Conviviam, lieutenant." Gordon broke into his thoughts. "January 19. General Robert E. Lee's birthday. KA's across the country always celebrate it like a bunch of fools."

"Maybe I'm wrong, but Lee didn't drink or smoke like you guys are doin,' did he?"

"You've won the kewpie doll. We party hard, but we're still preserving Southern honor and heritage. I think old Bobby Lee would have admired our spirit."

They watched the bacchanalia engulfing them. "Man I can't believe this weather," Gordon said, finally. "When I left Chattanooga this morning, we had snow flurries. It's gotta be seventy degrees out here. I mean, look at these girls in their bathing suits."

Ashby was watching them in between pulls from his beer. In particular, he had his eye on an imposing redhead dancing amid a knot of other women just inside the firelight.

"I'm hearin' you, brother. Who's the girl in the slit skirt and silver top over there," Ashby said, motioning in her direction.

"You got good tastes, friend. I've been checkin' that out myself. She's a paralegal or law clerk or something from Savannah. A little sister, class of '87. Her name's Alison Curry, I think. I just met her tonight myself. Damned cute."

71

"Free Bird!" screeched a man wearing a Hawaiian-print shirt and a wide-brim straw hat. "Here you go, Thom." He sloshed beer in handing new cups to Gordon and Ashby.

"Let's cut to the chase, lieutenant. You weren't out on a joy ride when you ended up here. What's goin' on?"

"I'm looking for the *Hunley*," Ashby said, drawing from his new beer.

"The *Hunley*. You think you know where it sank? That's pretty cool stuff. I hear they're trying to find it and bring her up. Put it in a museum, I guess."

"You know about the *Hunley*?"

"Sure. The Confederate submarine that went down after it sank a Yank warship. To tell you an honest true fact, I'd forgotten all that happened in Charleston until you mentioned it. One of our guys did a term paper on it when I was a junior, I think. Yo, Badger!"

"This ain't no term paper, friend," Ashby slurred. "Everybody thinks I'm crazy to think the *Hunley* might still be out there sinking ships. But everything sure points to it." He was thinking aloud now more than talking to Gordon.

"That's a pretty wild hare idea," Gordon said, looking him hard in the face. "I mean, I kinda believe in UFO's and the Loch Ness Monster and ghosts in some form or fashion. Hell, but what you're talking about is a submarine that went to the bottom in the Civil War, more than 130 years ago, still being around today! Man, that is really, really wild. Either you've had way to much to drink, which I think is the case, or you need to see a shrink."

Ashby turned surly. "Buddy, I didn't ask for your opinion. I'm a trained Coast Guard investigator, and I don't give a royal rat's ass about what you think."

"Fine, friend. Hey you're the one who crashed our party. In fact, why don't we give you a little help."

Gordon stood, yelling and clapping to get everyone's attention. Most of them gathered in a semicircle around Ashby and him.

After quieting the throng, Gordon told them of Ashby's quest to find the *Hunley*. There was more to come after the laughter and hoots of derision slackened.

"Tell you what we're gonna do, lieutenant! Sutlive, you'll always be a damned pledge to me! Give this man your tunic and right now! Hey, Rice, yea you, you mother! Your head looks about the right size, throw me your kepi! The lieutenant here is trying to locate the *Hunley* and we gotta dress him accordingly."

The KA's clustered around Ashby, a dozen hands groping, grabbing, and pushing to put on the uniform jacket.

Dizzily he fell into the soft sand at least twice only to be lifted to his feet by the partiers.

Someone handed him another beer.

By now Ashby had resigned himself to go along with just about anything they wanted to do. His anger was awash in alcohol and, besides, he still had a chance to meet that cute girl if he played along with the KA's.

"This is gonna be a supreme test for one of our pledges," Gordon said to him. "We are gonna assign him to watch over you all night.

"Gentlemen! Lieutenant Ashby is now dressed appropriately, and pledge Mueller will be assigned to watch over him."

Gordon put both hands on Ashby's shoulders and explained his intent.

"What we're gonna do, lieutenant, is tether you out there about a hundred yards in this bateau and see if the *Hunley* comes callin'. One of our boys who lives up on the Stono River came down in this thing a few nights ago, so it must be pretty safe," Gordon said, eyeing the flat-bottomed, wooden boat.

"Mueller, you want to be a Kappa Alpha like nobody's business, right?"

A pudgy youth with close-cropped red hair and wearing a Confederate infantry uniform staggered toward them. "'Course, of course I do, Thom."

"Well, you're gonna spend the rest of this night on the other end of this rope from the lieutenant here. He's goin' fishin', so to speak, and you are gonna reel him in sometime around sunrise. We'll tell you when."

Two other KA's helped Ashby into the boat. A rolled sleeping bag, a Coleman lantern, and a fifth of vodka were put aboard with him. On Gordon's order they tossed the anchor aboard and pushed the boat off the sand, into the outgoing tide. A rope fastened to the bow uncoiled as the bateau rocked away. Mueller wrapped the other end of the line around one of his wrists before plopping down on the sand.

"Let him out about a hundred yards and keep an eye on him," Gordon said, patting the pledge on the shoulder. "He'll sleep it off, and we'll bring him in for some breakfast in the morning."

"I'll watch him, Thom. Just have somebody bring me a beer once in a while."

In the bateau Ashby's mind went into rewind from the last exhausting hours. The fire and the figures on the beach diminished as the boat drifted further and further off shore. The party commotion slowly drowned in the music of the ocean, and Ashby slumped against the sleeping bag. There were no thoughts of the *Hunley* now. His head was smothered in a vacuum of alcohol and sheer fatigue as he curled like a fetus.

Thoughts of the lovely redhead dancing through the flames filled his brain before he fell dead to the world.

"Hail to the picket boat!"

Ashby stirred, hitting his knee on the anchor. He cursed softly to himself, but did not awaken.

"Hey, picket, you'll be hung for sleepin' on duty. Get your ass up!"

Ashby started and slowly raised his head. A sharp pain angled through his neck from the contortion of his sleep. Groggily shaking the mental cobwebs, he tried to discern who was talking to him, their location, and the time of day. The latter was an impossibility. He had obviously drifted into a fog bank where visibility was limited to about thirty yards with the lantern, which was beginning to flicker.

Through the milky haze, he caught sight of something moving

off his port bow. It appeared to be a dark tree trunk floating toward him.

Twenty yards out and cleaving the water. This was no tree. By now Ashby could see that the thing was man-made, rows of rivets mailing its black metal. On its topside and near each end were what appeared to be hatches with portholes. The cover on one of these turrets was open.

Now the mystery vessel was parallel to his boat and about five feet away. Ashby was petrified almost beyond his senses. Sitting in the bateau, he was almost at eye level with the gaping hatch. A weak orange light escaped from the opening.

Momentarily a pale hand emerged from the turret, grasping the hatch ring. A head and the upper half of a body followed. Ashby was suddenly face to face with a man dressed in a Confederate officer's tunic, similar to the ones worn by the KA's.

This was no frat boy, however. The man appeared to be in his twenties, but his ashen features hinted at a life lived well beyond his years. A dark Vandyke accented his mouth and chin.

"I don't know who this poor buck is, but he's one purely luckless bastard," the officer said, nodding starboard.

In drop-jawed horror Ashby spied Mueller's body floating face down in the water. The pledge's wrist was still secured to the rope from the bateau's bow. He must have fallen asleep and been pulled out with the tide.

"We got no place to put him. Guess we'll have to cut him loose and leave him for the fishes."

The officer now turned his full attention to Ashby. "Who are you, boy, and what's your outfit? Didn't you hear me hail you?"

Ashby could feel his legs trembling, but he knew he had to appear calm. "Uh, I'm Sergeant Ashby of the 43rd South Carolina."

"The 43rd South Carolina. I don't believe I'm familiar with them, son. Where are you stationed?"

"Charleston, sir."

"Charleston's a big place, boy. You wanna tell me where the 43rd's bivouac is? And who's your commander?"

Ashby could not think quickly enough to answer. The silence roared in his ears like a speeding express train.

"I'm thinkin' there's something ain't exactly right about you, son. We got a Yankee fleet perched right out there just itchin' to find a way into Charleston, and you ain't exactly givin' me straight answers. If you are a bluebelly dressed in our uniform, you'll be shot. I can guarantee it."

"Sir, I'm not a spy, I don't know who you are, but—"

"It don't matter a tinker's cuss who we are," the officer snapped. "You and me are gonna have a little talk. Besides, those shoes ain't exactly Jeff Davis issue." The officer motioned toward Ashby's white Nikes, which almost seemed to glow in the dark.

"One of you boys in the stern get topside! I need you to guard this man and follow us to Pinckney!"

The back hatch cover swung open and another man crawled atop the vessel. Steadying himself on all fours, he crouched and sprung into the bateau. He fell heavily into the boat but, oddly, did not rock it.

Ashby studied his new companion in the lantern light. He had seen homeless people with shopping carts better groomed than this character. The sailor was slightly built with eyes and cheeks caved deeply into his skull. Shocks of hair splayed from beneath a dirty gray kepi. The boy had a trace of a mustache, little more than peach fuzz. His long-sleeved shirt, rolled up to the elbows, and gray trousers were threadbare and splotched with grime.

Ashby's mind played with a vision of the scarecrow in "The Wizard of Oz," but there was nothing nonsensical about his guardian. The sailor's hard-eyed impassiveness was backed up by what appeared to be a Colt Navy revolver leveled at Ashby's stomach. With a quick move, the seaman grabbed the lantern and whipped it over the side. He also pulled out a knife almost as long as his bony forearm and cut the rope holding Mueller. Ashby watched the body bobbing in the water, slowly drifting away from the boat.

"Now you pick up that paddle and you row," the man hissed.

As Ashby reached for the oar, the hatch covers on the other vessel clanked shut and he heard the squeaking of screws being tightened in the turrets.

The black craft moved off and Ashby rowed after her. The

seaman sat stoically facing him, his back to the bow. Who were these people? Had he actually made contact with the *Hunley* or was he mired in an alcohol-induced nightmare?

The officer and the man seated in front of him seemed real enough. And the maw of the guard's pistol seemed as large as a gaping cannon.

Ashby rowed hard, but the other craft steadily put yards between them. Gradually the mist seemed to lift and Ashby tried to get his bearings. It was still tar black and his watch had stopped at 12:01 A.M. Damned thing was supposed to be water and shock resistant.

Guessing at landmarks and seeing the Charleston skyline, he judged that they were past Fort Sumter and heading directly into the mouth of the city harbor. Ashby was comforted, somewhat, by the city's lights and the great framework of the Cooper River bridges looming in the distance. If these people were out of their century, at least he remained in his.

It appeared they were making directly for the Battery before the sailor ordered Ashby to take a more northerly course. By now they seemed almost close enough to Charleston to touch its waterfront buildings. Just a few hundred yards to the south, Ashby could see a cabin cruiser coming down the Ashley River, apparently headed for the open sea. He toyed with the idea of trying to signal the craft, but his sentinel's fixed gaze made him think otherwise.

Their course lay for Shute's Folly, a tiny island in the inner harbor. Its major characteristic was Castle Pinckney, a compact stone fortress that the Confederates had used to hold Union prisoners during the war. Nowadays it was all but abandoned and overgrown with underbrush and vines.

With the castle walls looming closer, Ashby jumped into the waves and pulled the bateau onto the beach.

The mystery craft lay about fifty yards away and in what appeared to be waist-deep water. A line from its bow stretched to an anchor on the strand. A guard stood at ease near the anchor, and about ten men were trudging from the direction of the vessel toward the fortress.

Ashby had not noticed that his bateau companion also had come ashore. Motioning with his gun, the Rebel silently ordered Ashby to join the group. Walking down the beach, he and his captor fell in with the column.

Ashby drank in the sight of this crew. Whether they were unsettled spirits with a killing bent or simply some hard-core group of Civil War reenactors, his mind was too numb to decide.

For sure, they were a sinewy lot and no two dressed alike. The officer from the hatch led the procession, wordlessly marching toward the castle. His uniform coat was bunched at his waist by a belt with a holstered revolver and a short sword in a scabbard.

By far he was the neatest-looking of the bunch. Several of the men who followed him were shirtless, their thin white bodies virtually aglow in the night. Some wore almost knee-high scuffed boots with their trousers tucked inside. Among the others, short gray jackets and kepis predominated. Most of the men looked to be in their late teens or early twenties. All had the coldly determined look of men who had fated themselves to live or die for a cause.

Carrying shovels, three of the crewmen stopped at a point near the wall. Silhouetted in the moonlight, they began digging. Moments later one of the shovels struck something with a metallic clang. Some of the men knelt beside the shallow hole and scooped the remaining sand out with their hands.

One of them reached into the chasm and, grasping a thumb-thick iron ring, flung open a thick-beamed door after several tugs.

The diggers stepped back and the commander stepped down into the hole. A match flared and the officer lit a torch. By the light Ashby could see that the torch jutted from a stone wall framing a spiral block stairwell twisting into the darkness below.

"Thas more for your benefit than our'n," one of the other sailors said, nudging Ashby. "We can see in the dark bettern' an ol' tomcat. Jest don't want you fallin' down them steps."

In single file the seaman followed the officer down the steps, halting periodically so that he could ignite other torches during the descent. Ashby was near the center of the column. The Rebel guarding him occasionally poked him in the back with the revolver barrel.

The passageway was so small that Ashby almost had to stoop to keep from hitting his head. He had no problem touching both side walls at the same time.

He guessed they had gone about sixty feet beneath the castle when the group stopped at the bottom of the stairs. Before them was a stout wooden door with rusted tin bands running its length. The leader pulled a key from a tunic pocket, worked the lock for a moment, and pulled the handle.

The door whined open slowly to reveal a hadean panorama.

Four large iron-barred cages filled with people lined the walls of this chamber. All of the captives rose with an agony of pleas and groans of the lost when they saw the landing party.

"Please let us go!"

"Help us!"

"Give us some food, you bastards!"

"Where's my husband?"

A stench of decaying flesh, human excrement, and sweat swept over Ashby, and he gagged momentarily. He felt the revolver's nose hard against his back.

"Stand right here, boy. Lieutenant's gotta decide what to do with you. And take off that jacket. You ain't gonna be needin' it."

"We'll find you a nice spot to settle in," one of the others said. "You're a lucky one. We don't take a lot of prisoners."

Ashby stood in front of one of the cages and glanced at its occupants. They appeared to be refugees from a costume party for the mad as they pressed against the bars, screaming and clawing at the newcomers.

Several of the men were dressed like Union sailors from the Civil War era. Some of these stood and shook their fists defiantly. At least two had their heads buried in their hands, sitting on the floor of the cages.

Another man was dressed in a black uniform of more recent origin. Around his neck he wore a Maltese cross medallion. His tunic was adorned with the eagle of the German military. He looked like a U-boat captain, Ashby thought.

A girl in a one-piece pink swimsuit removed her bathing cap and shook it in fury at the intruder nearest her.

"I've been in here since 1956! Where is my family? Are you ever going to let me go? Please have mercy! Sweet mercy!"

Two other women, one in a torn corset and flowing floor-length skirt, also tried to talk to the crewmen. They both spoke with pronounced New England accents.

"Sirs, we've not heard any news since our bark went down. I'm sure Mr. Rockwell Ellington of Newport is interested in our whereabouts."

"It would be in your best interests to free us."

Behind them on the floor crouched a teenage boy in a soiled white suit, a straw boater pulled low over his head. He was clutching a ukulele and appeared to be sobbing quietly to himself. A blonde in a purple-striped bikini knelt beside him, trying to comfort him with no obvious success.

"You watch, he'll fling that little guitar at the bars before we leave," one of the seamen said to another. "He does it every time."

Others in the cages appeared as though they had been plucked from a modern-day cruise ship. They wore tennis shoes, flip-flops, and sandals along with a variety of T-shirts emblazoned with slogans and scenes from places like Miami, Key West, the Nantucket Yachting Club, and Martha's Vineyard. Hell, these people could have been on a beach anywhere in the world yesterday afternoon.

Piled against the stone walls was a conglomeration of ships' rigging, pieces of masts, brass fittings, and nameplates from vessels. Strewn amid the rubble were cutlasses, old radio sets with tubes exposed, and more modern communications equipment.

In one corner of the chamber was a belt-high mound of moldering wallets, purses, gold and silver jewelry and flatware of every description, ornate china, and other treasures.

One wall was all but covered by U.S. flags of every size. Some of them were tattered or in pieces. Most were filthy and faded, and a few were splattered or stained with what appeared from a distance to be blood. Many of the banners boasted less than fifty stars.

A piece of paper folded into the size of a tooth filling fluttered through the air and hit Ashby in the forehead. He glanced down at it and then looked around to determine who had thrown it. An attractive woman with a gray blanket cloaked over her shoulders smiled and gave him a quick wave from one of the pens. Ashby noticed that she appeared sunburned.

"Go ahead and pick it up, boy," his guard said. "These folks ain't goin' no place less we say so."

Slowly Ashby knelt and picked up the paper, thrusting it into one of his jean pockets.

"You! You're going with us!" The officer pointed toward a tanned man in khaki shorts and an "Aruba—One Happy Island" tank top who was standing near the front of one of the cages.

"We need another body to power our boat. Lots of Yanks left to kill."

Two of the Confederates entered the cell and pulled the prisoner toward the door. He began kicking and screaming, and several of the other sailors rushed to help subdue him.

Ashby realized the chance of this unexpected diversion. Half expecting to strike air if these were indeed ghosts, he turned and swung blindly at the Rebel nearest him. The blow seemed to land on cloth and flesh, and the sailor teetered backwards off balance. Ashby dodged away from another seaman who lunged at him and darted up the stairs, the yells and screeches intensifying, seemingly following him upward. Strangely the wails appeared to be the only form of pursuit.

Near the top of the passage, the rush of cold salt air energized Ashby. He fell out of the pit and onto the beach, the sky as black as it was when he descended. There was no sign of his bateau or the other craft, and Ashby wasted little time in deciding what to do.

Splashing into the surf, he swam with all his might toward the lights of Charleston's Battery. His last energy quickly flagging, he dog-paddled and floated on his back, anything to stay above the waves, conscious, and inching toward the sea wall. To his right he saw a forest of white masts from a yacht club, but there was no one to call for help.

With a torturous slowness, the gleam of Charleston's street-lights burned brighter. The night was mild, but the water retained its January chill, which seeped into muscles, making his arms and legs feel almost like dead weight as he struggled.

After a virtual eternity, the ocean washed him sideways onto the slippery rocks at the base of the East Battery's seawall. Clutching at the algae-slimed boulders, Ashby staggered to his feet, almost blacking out and gasping for air. He didn't have long to catch his breath. The tide was raging in and he could easily be slammed into the concrete wall. He had to make a move.

Ashby waited for an incoming wave, timing it so that the water would help propel him to reach the wall's railing a few feet above him. If he guessed wrong, the sea would batter him like a piece of driftwood against the barrier. He jumped as the surge reached him. Rising with the water, his numb arms batted the iron poles of the railing above. Gripping it and pulling himself over the wall, he rolled onto the Battery's sidewalk.

Exhausted, he passed out where he lay, the rush of the tide and the devils that it held filling his fitful dreams.

6

1863–1864

MASKED IN CANVAS, the Confederacy's most secret weapon arrived in Charleston aboard two railroad flatcars on August 12, 1863. Bayonets fixed, edgy Rebel guards brushed back the curious as the train trundled in to the depot.

Charleston, the hotbed of secession fire in 1861, was in danger of being captured by Union forces that summer. The U.S. naval blockade had all but choked off all Confederate shipping to and from the port.

The sea noose was so tight that the prominent export firm of John Fraser & Company was offering a $100,000 reward for the destruction of the enemy's USS *New Ironsides* or USS *Wabash*, two of the most potent warships on the planet and stationed off Charleston. For anyone who could sink one of the less formidable but as troublesome Union monitors, the company agreed to pay $50,000.

Union troops were swarming over Morris Island just to the south of the harbor entrance and were menacing Battery Wagner, the Southerners' keystone earthwork in that sector. If the Federals could take Wagner, they could emplace guns in range to strike Fort Sumter and likely even Charleston itself.

Sumter, once the symbol of Yankee defiance at the war's outbreak, was now a Rebel fortress that had been all but battered into a mound of crumbled brick by the U.S. fleet.

Confederate General Pierre Gustave Toutant Beauregard, charged with Charleston's defense, needed any help he could get against the blue onslaught. "Please expedite transportation . . . from Mobile here," he wrote of his new weapon in August 7 orders to quartermasters and railroad agents before its arrival. "It is much needed."

Shaped like a trim Havana stogie, the little vessel was taken down to the Charleston waterfront. Any secrecy that the Confederates had implemented to this point was abandoned, and the city buzzed about the "porpoise" boat as many Charlestonians called it. Navy officers talked freely about the exciting new weapon that all hoped would be the death angel to smite the Yankee fleet.

A crew of ten or so men was being assembled, and soon the gallant porpoise would dive under the waves to bring Neptune's wrath to the damnable bluecoats.

The submersible was the newest version of an undersea boat first created some three years earlier by James McClintock and Baxter Watson of New Orleans. These machinists-inventors devised two machines to manufacture small-caliber ammunition for the Confederate States government shortly after hostilities erupted. The duo then turned their attention to development of a revolutionary tool of warfare on the order of gunpowder and cannon from previous ages.

A ship that sailed beneath the water and could strike at an enemy navy on the surface would be as lethal and innovative as the advent of the catapult, the arrow artillery of the English longbowmen at Crecy, or the Roman phalanx.

The United States had dabbled with the concept of the submarine since the nation's infancy. David Bushnell of Connecticut invented a contraption in 1775 that was the forerunner of these craft. Robert Fulton, czar of the steam engine, had furthered its development. The U.S. navy had launched its own submarine in late 1861. The naval brass basically ignored the *Alligator*, however. She sank in April 1863 while being towed off Cape

Hatteras, North Carolina. The handful of men in Mobile was the first to prescribe the vessel as an offensive tool of war.

Like Charleston, Savannah, and every other Southern port, the coils of the "Anaconda Plan" created by U.S. General Winfield Scott had gripped New Orleans by the throat. Scott's strategy called for Union land and sea forces to wrap around the Confederacy and suffocate the virus of secession.

The suffocation of New Orleans in autumn 1861 was caused by a U.S. naval squadron bottling up any access to or from the Gulf of Mexico. The Confederates simply did not have a navy strong enough to break the blockade. But they were working on it.

Based on their ideas and drawings, Watson and McClintock put their ironworkers to the task of assembling an underwater craft to attack the enemy. The ship was dubbed the *Pioneer* and mailed with 3/8-inch galvanized iron plates bolted to an iron frame. Approximately thirty-five feet long, it was built to hold a three-man crew. For propulsion, these men would hand crank a shaft to spin a propeller in the stern. The vessel dove or ascended by diving planes on each side of the hull.

A spar with a black powder-packed torpedo was the armament. Like ancient navies, the goal was to attack and ram the opponent like a mad unicorn. The lethal new difference was that the unicorn's horn was explosive.

McClintock and Watson were soon joined in the endeavor by Horace Lawson Hunley, the deputy collector of customs at New Orleans and also a prosperous planter and attorney. Three other investors also put their faith in the project. By February 1862 the team was testing the prototype vessel in the waters of Lake Pontchartrain. But the Federals were not going to wait to be assailed. They captured New Orleans on April 25, forcing the inventors to hastily scuttle the *Pioneer* in a vain attempt to keep her out of enemy hands. The submarine was recovered later by the Yankees.

Fleeing to Mobile, Alabama, with their blueprints and notebooks, Watson, Hunley, and McClintock began construction on an even larger submarine. The work was done at the Parks and Lyons machine shop, and the new craft was called the *American*

Diver, or the *Pioneer II*. The iron-hulled vessel was thirty-six feet long, and was powered manually like her predecessor. Rather than a spar, the *Pioneer II* was designed to attack with a torpedo attached to a rope and pulled behind her. The submarine would dive below an enemy ship and drag the torpedo against the vessel's side where it would detonate.

The first weeks of 1863 saw completion of the *Pioneer II*, and the Rebels wasted little time in getting her ready for combat. On a February day she was being towed out to meet the U.S. fleet blocking Mobile Harbor when the weather suddenly turned ugly. Swamped, the *Pioneer II* plummeted to the harbor floor, taking its creators' dreams, but fortunately no crewmen, with it.

Hunley was undaunted, however, leading a group of investors to put up money for a third vessel. Engineer William A. Alexander was put in charge of the construction, which also took place at the Parks and Lyons shop. Alexander was a young English immigrant who joined the Confederate service and was a lieutenant in the 21st Alabama Infantry. The regiment had been badly shot up at the battle of Shiloh in April 1862 and was sent to Mobile to recuperate. Because of his mechanical training, Alexander was assigned to the machine shop where the submarine soon took top priority.

For five months sweating workmen toiled away on the latest and most innovative of the subs. An old boiler cylinder, twenty-five feet long and four feet in diameter, was cut in half lengthwise. Two foot-wide iron strips were riveted between the halves to increase headroom for the crew.

Each end of the vessel was tapered and contained water ballast tanks with seacocks to the outside water for buoyancy control. The crew could submerge by opening the seacocks and flooding the tanks. A force pump to each tank allowed them to drain the water and surface.

Two lateral diving fins, or dive planes, were mounted forward and, controlled by an interior lever, allowed the captain to regulate his depth, which was indicated by a mercury gauge near the bow ballast tank. A forward shelf had space for a compass and a candle, the latter being the sole inside light when the craft was submerged. The boat was almost forty feet long. The captain, seated in the bow, steered by turning a wheel to guide a bow rudder.

The Parks and Lyons team experimented with electromagnetic and steam engines for the sub, but neither worked out. Like the previous two submersibles, this one also would rely on human muscle for propulsion. An eight-man crew would turn a crank-shaft attached to a three-bladed propeller. A circular iron collar protected the propeller from fouling on obstructions the most deadly of which was its torpedo. Like the *Pioneer II*, this boat also would tow a payload consisting of a copper cylinder filled with ninety pounds of gunpowder and attached to a two-hundred-foot line.

The crankshaft was forged into handgrips at different angles for the eight, all of whom would sit on a small ledge on the port side. With the men in place and cranking there was sparse room to move fore or aft. It was exhausting work in cramped, dark, damp quarters.

Her crew entered through narrow round hatches fore and aft, about sixteen feet apart. The hatches had watertight, rubber-gasketed covers that could be bolted shut on the inside. Each of these openings was atop a small conning tower. Each tower had a small glass window, or viewing port, for use and light if the vessel was running partially submerged or on the surface.

Each of the submarines relied on open hatches to replenish the oxygen supply, meaning the toiling sailors had only the air closed up with them to fill their lungs before they had to come up. But this midget dreadnought's creation took matters a step further. The inventors had built one of the first versions of a snorkel to ventilate the sub when she was submerged. The device was composed of an air box, located just aft of the forward hatch, from which elbow joints linked twin intake pipes, four feet tall. Stopcocks and a system of levers allowed the airflow to be regulated and the pipes to be lowered to the deck when the sub dove below four feet. The snorkel contraption needed more work, however, and the vessel would rely on its manholes for air. How long the crew could stay under was still a question.

During the construction, the submarine was christened the *H. L. Hunley* in honor of her primary backer.

In mid-July the latest Confederate "fish boat" was fit for action and she was eased down a wooden ramp into Mobile Bay. After a few days of trial runs in the harbor, McClintock, Hunley, and the others shook hands and declared their tiny leviathan combat ready.

Under the best conditions, meaning calm water, her top speed was about four miles per hour. If the sea was turbulent in the least, the vessel did well to avoid foundering, her lack of buoyancy a perpetual problem.

Some seven hundred miles across the Confederacy from Mobile, Charleston was in the cross hairs of a Union sea and land offensive. Warships of the U.S. South Atlantic Blockading Squadron of Admiral John Dahlgren were pounding the Confederate defenses with a blaze of heaven-rattling gunfire. Broadsides of eleven-inch shells from the *New Ironsides* were hammering Battery Wagner from a thousand yards off Morris Island. Union infantrymen were daily digging trenches closer to Wagner. Their shoveling often uncovered the moldering dead of previous assaults on the strong point.

The C.S. naval squadron at Charleston had few combat vessels and certainly nothing to tangle with Dahlgren's behemoths. But Charleston's land fortifications had many more fangs. Three bands of defenses girded the city, all except brick forts Sumter and Moultrie built of dirt and logs. Thousands of slaves brought in from Carolina plantations had constructed the bulk of these emplacements for the white soldiers in gray.

Their backbreaking war sculptures were based on the schematics of Beauregard and others who had studied military engineering at West Point and now used their education against their former country.

The outer harbor defenses ranged from besieged Morris Island northwest to Fort Sumter, standing astride the channel like the colossus of Southern rights. On the north side of the harbor was the comma-shaped Sullivan's Island with guns from the squat Fort Moultrie and the earthen Fort Beauregard posted seaward to give the Confederates a crossfire on anything bigger than a pelican heading into the main channel. The gigantic earthwork Battery Marshall was perched on the northeast end of Sullivan's, the sentinel of Breach Inlet. This swift-currented, deep, and narrow sluice of less than two hundred yards divided Sullivan's from Long Island, another quill-thin rise of barrier sand.

Besides the arsenal of big guns lining the Atlantic approaches, the Rebs also had sown a thick seeding of floating torpedoes in the harbor mouth, the entrances to the Cooper and Ashley rivers and the Folly Island channels. A great number of these mines were beer barrels, confiscated across the South, caulked, tar-pitched, and loaded with up to 120 pounds of powder. Armed with fuses and moored in the waterways, they were among the best weapons employed by the Richmond-based C.S. Torpedo Bureau. One industrious Rebel associated with this minor branch of the Confederate military invented the "coal torpedo," an explosive device of cast iron with a core containing some ten pounds of gunpowder. Made to resemble a piece of coal, these bombs were to be placed in enemy fuel dumps and later shoveled into the flaming boilers of Federal ships by unsuspecting firemen. The ensuing blast would destroy or badly damage the vessel. The Yankees blamed the coal torpedo for several mysterious explosions, including an eruption that demolished a general's headquarters boat on the James River in Virginia in November 1864.

A miasmic web of obstructions made of rope, logs, and chains stretched like a sea serpent across the main harbor from Cumming's Point to Sumter to Mount Pleasant on Sullivan's Island. This obstacle had a few openings to allow blockade-runners to slip through and access for the gunboats of the Confederate naval squadron, not that the latter was in any way ready to mount an offensive against the U.S. armada.

At Mobile the *Hunley* had put on an impressive display for C.S. Admiral Franklin Buchanan, who watched the sub destroy a barge in the bay during a mock attack. Buchanan was convinced the craft could help Beauregard in Charleston. "I am fully satisfied it can be used successfully in blowing up one or more of the enemy's ironclads in your harbor," he wrote to the Confederate authorities there. Beauregard took Buchanan's advice and, after a meeting with Watson and another *Hunley* investor, Gus Whitney, called for the submarine.

Charleston had been a curse on the previous Union navy commanders on blockade duty. Dahlgren's predecessor, Admiral Samuel F. Du Pont, had lost his job and his career trying to take the city. Du Pont led a down-the-throat, straight-into-the-harbor attack by eight of his monitors on April 7, 1863. The assault force was unable to forge past the outer harbor defenses, and the monitor USS *Keokuk* was riddled by shells. She sank the next day.

During the night Du Pont consulted his captains and decided not to renew the attack based on his damages and the stoutness of the enemy resistance. Du Pont immediately found himself under fire from a different sector—Secretary of the Navy Gideon Welles and a rabid Northern press.

Welles finally relieved Du Pont of duty in early June and replaced him with Commodore Andrew H. Foote. The fifty-seven-year-old rear admiral had seen action from the China coast to the river wars against the Rebs in Tennessee and on the Mississippi in his four decades of service.

Foote was en route to take over command from Du Pont when he died suddenly and unexpectedly. Thus, the lame-duck Du Pont remained on station until Welles's second choice, John Dahlgren, arrived in July.

Many blockade-runners dared to evade the Federal net, camouflaged in gray or black paint so as to steal past the Yankees and reach Charleston with their priceless cargoes of Enfields, bullets, swords, bolts of cloth, pickled beef, kegs of gunpowder, vintage champagne, and silk French fashions. The chess match was the same from Wilmington to Galveston as the Confederacy tried to carry on international commerce while "Old Abe's" tars waited by their lanyards for the next target practice. A few of the runners escaped the Unionists, but most did not. Others found destruction and death on the sandbars, in the shallows, and amid the tidal currents, their captains trying to navigate unfamiliar waters often in milk fog or the delirium of a sea squall.

Off Long Island alone the carcasses of the *Nellie, Samuel Adams, Stonewall Jackson, Tropic, Norseman,* and *Experiment* lay scattered and rotting, monuments to their masters' failures by August 1863.

A Confederate general at Savannah spoke as much for that city as Charleston when he issued a plea for area landowners to send slaves to strengthen Georgia coastal fortifications: "It is best to meet the enemy at the threshold and to hurl back the first wave of invasion. Once the breach is made, all the horrors of war must desolate your now peaceful and quiet homes. Let no man deceive himself. If Savannah falls, the fault will be yours, and your neglect will have brought the sword to your hearthstones."

Another Georgian whose light artillery unit was transferred from Savannah to James Island outside Charleston that month was awestruck at the buildup of Yankee might on the waves and on nearby Morris Island.

"You can almost imagine that you are looking upon Staten Island," wrote the colonel. "There is such an aggregation of shipping of every sort of description, and such a collection of tents, etc., that the island presents the appearance of a continuous village."

Thus it was into this carnival of despair, tattered flags and hopes, and the latest military technology of the age that McClintock, Whitney, and a small group of engineers and workmen arrived with the "porpoise." It had been a circuitous two-day journey; the South's railroads were in poor shape before the war, and the struggle had done nothing but worsen them.

Hunley and the others had stayed behind in Mobile, but the former made it ice clear how he wanted the submarine to be handled. Her debutante ball was to be a real blast.

"I'm anxious first and above all for a dead silence on our part that the enemy may be lost in uncertainty and mystery which is more dreadful than any understood evil even of the greatest magnitude," Hunley wrote to McClintock on August 15. If the submarine could make a successful assault, Hunley believed the enemy "while in a panic . . . might be possibly driven entirely from Morris Island, his works destroyed and guns spiked, even if it be not possible to take and permanently hold the island and prevent it from being retaken."

The master planner crowned his message with a burst of idyllic patriotism: "Remind your crew of Manassas & Shiloh and the consequences of faltering in the hour of success and make one grand effort."

"It certainly is a wonderful thing and we hope for its success," a Charleston belle wrote in her August 21 diary entry after a conversation with a handsome captain about the undersea boat.

Beauregard needed any and every advantage to stave off the Yankee sharks trolling the bar.

It was this elegant little general with the stature of a pier-front stevedore and the mindset of a Versailles aristocrat who had peered across Charleston Harbor's predawn sky awaiting the first blow on Friday, April 12, 1861. At 4:30 A.M. and on his order it came, a mortar round scarring the black heavens. The shell burst signaled cannoneers manning about fifty other big guns aimed at Fort Sumter to open fire.

On a grander scale the shot blew apart a nation. He was forty-two.

A voracious student of Napoleonic strategy, the Louisianan was well versed in military engineering, graduating second in the West Point class of 1838. He served on Winfield Scott's staff in the Mexican War and sharpened his skills improving navigable channels at the mouth of the Mississippi in the brief peacetime afterward.

For five days in January 1861 Beauregard was superintendent of the U.S. Military Academy, a huge career feather for any U.S. army officer. But his pro-South leanings at a time when the typhoid of secession already had claimed South Carolina quickly resulted in his expulsion. The new Southern government quickly offered him a brigadier general's commission.

The Cajun Caesar at Sumter and First Bull Run three months later rode his combat laurels to become second in command of the C.S. Army of Tennessee, which was, next to the Army of Northern Virginia, the largest armed force fielded by the Dixie republic. But the tarot cards of war turned against him. Beauregard was unable to earn an April 1862 victory at Shiloh after his superior, General Albert S. Johnston, bled to death from a leg wound. And he had evacuated the important railroad center at Corinth, Mississippi, when threatened by a larger Union force. These setbacks and friction between Beauregard and C.S. President Jefferson Davis ended with his being replaced by General Braxton Bragg in August 1862.

Yet posted to a much lesser role in command of the coastal defenses of South Carolina and Georgia, Beauregard regained some of his martial glitter.

An excited crowd gathered as word of the contraption's arrival filtered through the city streets. Laborers using blocks and tackles and mules eased the vessel off the train and loaded it on a wagon for the trip to its harbor slip. Cheering soldiers and civilians watched it pass, this possible savior from the blockade.

The Mobile contingent immediately set about becoming familiar with the waters around Charleston, being careful not to venture too close to the enemy navy, at least not until they were combat ready. There was not a great deal of time for practice. Enemy shells whistled through the sky night and day, and Charleston's defenses were taking a beating. Fort Sumter had been reduced to little more than a heap of dust and shattered brick by the Federal gunners, but still managed to hold out. Yet every day the gunfire rumbled louder, Union troops drawing ever closer to the city itself. McClintock, Whitney, and the others knew that Beauregard expected them to act quickly and that all of Charleston expected great things of the submarine. Several times in the last days of August they tried to make attacks, but were thwarted, weather conditions and the fact that they literally were inventing submarine warfare by trial and error accounting for the lack of success.

Hunley had arrived in Charleston by this time, but there was a far greater development on the night of August 21. Shells from a big Union gun slammed into the middle of Charleston. The Yankee "Swamp Angel" was bombarding the city from Morris Island. With Charleston now under direct assault and civilians becoming casualties, the Confederate brass became ever more impatient with the *Hunley*'s inability to fight.

Beauregard had had enough by August 24. He had the boat seized and placed under military authority. From now on the *Hunley* would operate as a Confederate navy vessel. Hunley stayed in Charleston, but most of the others of the Mobile team headed home.

Command of the *Hunley* was given to C.S. Navy Lieutenant John A. Payne, formerly of the ironclad CSS *Chicora* in the Rebel squadron at Charleston. Eight volunteers from the *Chicora* joined Payne to man the submarine.

Disaster struck swiftly, hard, and twice. On August 29 the odd little boat was performing for a score of soldiers and civilians who lined beaches and verandas to watch the activities. The men were invigorated by the prospect of making an upcoming attack.

After diving and surfacing about the harbor for more than an hour, the submarine made its way to Fort Johnson on James Island. There her crew tied a rope to the wharf near the docked C.S. transport steamer *Etiwan*.

Payne climbed into the forward hatch, savoring the fresh air. Inside the submersible, the other sailors were catching their breaths and resting their weary arms. The warm salt wind whirling through the "manheads" was priceless elixir for their starving lungs. Despite their fatigue, they were upbeat, operating as a unit and maneuvering the boat with the chance to soon sink a Union warship.

The *Etiwan* steamed away from the wharf, giving the *Hunley* a tow by a rope that was looped around the forward hatch combing. When they were away, Payne reached out to cast off the line, but became tangled in the rope. Trying to free himself, Payne's foot hit the lever controlling the diving fins, causing the vessel to dive unexpectedly.

Brine flooded down the still open hatchways, drenching the men and sinking the *Hunley* like the iron casket she was about to become. Payne struggled away and two others, one of them Charles Sprague, swam out of the aft hole. But six seamen were trapped within while the vessel plummeted more than forty feet to the bottom.

One of them, C.S. Navy Lieutenant Charles Hasker, fought

his way over the crankshaft and was halfway out the fore hole when the hatch cover crunched down on his back, pinning him to the falling boat. Squirming for freedom, he inched upward until the heavy lid held only his left leg.

The sub thudded into the seabed, and the crushing pressure of the ocean relaxed enough for Hasker to free himself and stroke toward the sun. Nearly drowned and exhausted, he was rescued by a longboat from the *Chicora*. In the water around Hasker the souls of five doomed Rebels bubbled from the abyss.

Beauregard, his army and navy commanders, and Charleston's civilians all were shocked by the tragedy, but the general didn't hesitate to order her raised and readied to make another effort. After ten days on the bottom, the *Hunley* was refloated and the sailors' corpses were removed from her embrace.

A frustrated Hunley asked Beauregard to allow him to bring an experienced crew from Mobile and make another attempt to attack Dahlgren's fleet. Beauregard agreed to his proposal.

Hunley was hell bent on proving the worth of his adventure. His patriotism was beyond question, but his sanity, or lack of it, in dreaming up the fish boat was street-corner fodder. Now thirty-nine, his law practice, plantation prosperity, and customs post had established him as a wealthy and savvy businessman who well recognized the importance of keeping the sea-lanes of commerce open between the South and her European allies.

Hunley was reorganizing and bringing his colleagues from Mobile when another bristling star stalked the Orion of Dahlgren's floating constellation, the *New Ironsides*.

The *David* was an experimental Confederate torpedo ram designed to run just above the surface. Several variations of these steam-driven craft were constructed ranging from forty to sixty feet long and made of wood or iron. The first was built at Charleston. The original *David* was about fifty feet long, cigar-shaped, and had a cockpit to carry a crew of up to four or five. It had a forward boiler connected to an aft engine by a crankshaft and vented by a short stack up front and was armed with a bow-spar torpedo. When at battle stations, the craft was so well submerged that only a portion of her stack, the upper one-fourth of her hull and her torpedo stanchion, showed above water.

The *David*'s Philistine was the 230-foot *New Ironsides*, certainly the Goliath of Dahlgren's squadron. On the night of October 5, the *David*, under Lieutenant W. T. Glassell, steamed out to fling a stone at her in the form of a sixty-pound torpedo. The night was hazy, and the *David*'s four-man crew was able to close within fifty yards of the warship, anchored off Morris Island, before a Yank sentinel hailed them. Glassell replied with a shotgun blast that mortally wounded the officer of the deck, and the *David* plowed into the side of the enemy ironclad.

The torpedo exploded and the immense concussion heaved a mountain of water over the *David*, drowning her engine and temporarily jamming her machinery. Dodging musket and revolver fire from the *New Ironsides* seamen, Glassell yelled to abandon ship. All except the pilot, who couldn't swim, dove overboard. Glassell and another crewman were captured, but the *David*'s engineer, James Tombs, climbed back aboard, worked with the pilot to rekindle the boiler fire, and brought the *David* home.

At first thought to be unscathed, on closer examination the *New Ironsides* showed significant damage. The attack heartened the Confederates and somewhat rattled Dahlgren's confidence, resulting in heightened precautions against any surprises the Johnnies might again try against his fleet.

Hunley's crew arrived from Mobile about the time of the *David*'s assault. These volunteers included young Lieutenant George E. Dixon, who replaced Payne as the skipper. Thomas Parks, son of the co-owner of the machine shop where the *Hunley* was built, also came to Charleston along with five or six others. Joining these men was Charles Sprague, a munitions expert and the only survivor of the first sinking to again step forward.

Over the next week Hunley and Dixon drilled their submariners in the waters around Charleston, taking care not to venture too far away from the protection of Rebel shore batteries and gunboats.

The Rebels had been forced to evacuate Battery Wagner in early

September after a merciless forty-two-hour naval bombardment basically transformed it into a sandy burial mound for maimed corpses of both sides. The loss of Wagner left Morris Island in total Union control. Yet even in the weeks before Wagner's fall, Charleston civilians were enduring the target practice of Yank artillerymen from the islands and marshes south of the city, beginning with the "Swamp Angel." Hurling shells almost six miles distant, these enemy guns killed and wounded residents as they slept in their homes or walked anywhere on the downtown streets.

The blue gunners on Morris and James islands sighted in on the graceful steeples of St. Michael's and St. Philip's churches. The barrages were sporadic and were indiscriminate in their carnage.

A black barber was decapitated by a shell fragment while working in his shop. The bodies of a newlywed couple were found entwined after a round crashed into their bedroom. Cemeteries were plowed up by the incoming ordnance. City Hall was hit repeatedly. Another shell ripped into a church and tore a Bible on the pulpit, leaving it open to a page containing the passage "An enemy hath done this."

Like everyone else in Charleston, the submariners suffered this existence, the mayhem and the cannonading intensifying each day, making their mission all the more critical. Amid this climate, Hunley and Dixon readied their men.

In George Dixon the Confederates possibly had found the man best suited to captain the submarine. A thin Kentuckian who was a mechanical engineer before the war, Dixon had enlisted in the 21st Alabama when the regiment was established at Mobile in October 1861, serving with Alexander. Promoted to lieutenant in Company A within a few months, Dixon and his unit joined the Rebel army massing at Corinth, Mississippi, for a hammer blow at the Union forces situated near Shiloh, a crude wood meetinghouse that lent its name to the coming holocaust.

On April 6-7, 1862, the armies collided, strewing almost twenty-three thousand dead and wounded in the Tennessee fields and woods.

Dixon was one of the approximately eleven thousand Rebels

to fall, severely wounded in the thigh by a Yankee bullet. The slug might have been fatal if it had not glanced off a $20 gold piece Dixon was carrying. The coin had been given to him as a token of affection by his fiancée, Queenie Bennett, when he was boarding a train to the front. Dixon had met Queenie while he was a steamboat engineer on the Mississippi River during peacetime. For the rest of his days Dixon carried the mangled coin with him as a good luck charm.

During his recuperation in Mobile, Dixon became involved with the submarine project. His leadership qualities, courage, and dedication, as well as his technical abilities caused Hunley, Alexander, and the other backers to place their trust in him.

The crew spent hours making simulated attacks on the *Indian Chief*, a Confederate receiving ship anchored in the Cooper River. Dixon's men were trying to perfect the "tow and dive" method, in which they would plunge under an enemy craft and drag the trailing torpedo against its hull. While damaged, the *New Ironsides* remained on station and was the primary target of the Southerners.

Ten days after the *David* episode, the crew was ready for another day of practice descents around the *Indian Chief*. Dixon was away for the day so Hunley decided to take the helm with Thomas Parks as his second officer. Both were as familiar with the machine's workings as any men alive.

Thursday, October 15, was cheerless and gray with rain and haze over Charleston. The *Hunley* left its wharf at 9:25 A.M., her crew cranking into the Cooper River to make a practice attack on the *Indian Chief*. Sailors on the starboard side of the ship and soldiers and civilians ashore watched the submarine plunge beneath the water, as she had done many times before.

Catastrophe roiled up from the fathoms. For whatever reason the *Hunley* did not reappear, beads of bubbles marking her point of final rest. In minutes eight more men, including Hunley and Parks, were added to the sub's death tally.

Divers found her on the bottom several days later, stern high at a thirty-five-degree angle and with her bow deeply burrowed in the mud. The Confederates raised the submarine from its grave some nine fathoms down, and she was brought to a dock in the Ashley River.

Beauregard had seen battlefield horrors from the Mexican War to Bull Run and Shiloh, but seems to have been especially affected when he saw the grisly haul from the *Hunley*'s womb: "When the boat was discovered, raised and opened, the spectacle was indescribably ghastly; the unfortunate men were contorted into all kinds of horrible attitudes; some clutching candles, evidently endeavoring to force open the man-holes; others lying in the bottom tightly grappled together, and the blackened faces of all presented the expression of their despair and agony."

Alexander also wrote of what they found when the hatches were pried open: "The holding-down bolts of each [hatch] cover had been removed. When the hatch covers were lifted, considerable air and gas escaped. Captain Hunley's body was forward, with his head in the forward hatchway, his right hand on top of his head (he had been trying, it would seem, to raise the hatch cover). In his left hand was a candle that had never been lighted, the sea cock on. . . . [His] ballast tank was wide open, the cock-wrench not on the plug, but lying on the bottom of the boat. Mr. Parks' body was found with his head in the after hatchway, his right hand above his head. He also had been trying to raise his hatch cover, but the pressure was too great. The sea cock to his tank was properly closed, and the tank nearly empty. The other bodies were floating in the water. Hunley and Parks were undoubtedly asphyxiated, the others drowned. The bolts that held the iron keel ballast had been partly turned, but not sufficient to release it."

Alexander also reconstructed what happened when Hunley began the fatal dive. The captain had "partly turned the fins to go down, but thought, no doubt, that he needed more ballast and opened his sea cock. Immediately the boat was in total darkness. He then undertook to light the candle. While trying to do this the tank [open at the top] quietly flooded . . . and soon overflowed, and the first intimation they would have of anything being wrong was the water rising fast, but noiselessly, about their feet in the bottom of the boat. . . . The water soon forced the air to the top of the boat and into the hatchways, where . . . Hunley and Parks were found. Parks had pumped his ballast tank dry, and no doubt Captain Hunley had exhausted himself on his pump, but had forgotten that he had not closed his sea cock."

Others speculated that Hunley was too familiar with the vessel to make such a deadly error and that he likely was trying to close the sea cock in the darkness when he dropped and lost his wrench in the rising water.

Thirteen bold souls had now gone to their gurgling deaths by this time, and Beauregard suspended further operations as winter engulfed Charleston.

Hunley and his men were buried with military honors in Charleston's Magnolia Cemetery. The Charleston *Mercury* ran his obituary the next day: "With everything before him to make life attractive, he came to Charleston, and voluntarily joined in a patriotic enterprise which promised success, but which was attended with great peril. Though feeling, as appears from the last letter which he wrote to his friends, a presentiment that he would perish in the adventure, he gave his whole heart, undeterred by the foreboding, to the undertaking, declaring that he would gladly sacrifice his life in the cause. That presentiment has been mournfully fulfilled. Yet who shall call that fate a sad one, which associates the name of its victim with those of his country's most unselfish martyrs?"

Rumors abounded that the vessel had drowned nine other sailors during a botched dive in Mobile Bay. Sure it was a weapon of war, but men on the wrong side were being killed.

And sailors in the Rebel fleet cursed and grumbled that the "murdering machine" had struck again.

7

1994

"HEY, FRIEND, we gotta move on."

Ashby jerked awake. It seemed he had only been asleep for a few minutes.

A Charleston police corporal was kneeling over him, shaking him firmly by the shoulder.

"If you don't have a place to stay, I can give you a ride to one of the homeless shelters. If you got a place to stay and just had a real bad night, like I'm thinking is the case, you still gotta clear outta here."

Ashby tried to stand as a foursome of elderly strollers stopped to watch the cop roust the bum. Swallowing hard for some dew-drop of moisture, Ashby came to his feet and suddenly felt the jackhammer at work in his head. He ached from cowlick to toes from all he had been through. A puddle outline marked the spot where he lay.

"That's a boy," the cop said. "Now where are we going from here?"

"I'll give him a ride, officer."

They both turned to see a pretty redhead with a rotund brown

Chihuahua straining at its leash. Ashby barely recognized her as the woman he had admired at the KA party.

"Officer, I'm Alison Curry in town from Savannah for a reunion. I met this gentleman last night and kind of feel responsible for him."

"Okay, ma'am, he's all yours. Looks like he could use some dry clothes and coffee. Hey, bud, stay off the sidewalk, huh?"

"Sure enough."

The cop strode back to his patrol car, and Ashby reached down to pet the Chihuahua.

"What's your name, bad boy?"

"That's Chico. He's about seventy in dog years and loves to eat, as if you can't tell."

In the excitement of meeting a new friend, Chico began wetting the sidewalk. "I do the same thing when I have guests over," Ashby said.

"Who doesn't?" Alison laughed.

Ashby introduced himself as the pedestrians who had been watching the show toddled down the Battery.

"Thom told me a little bit about you. I can't believe they put you out in that old boat. What happened? The last I saw of you, you were floating out there and that pledge was about to nod off."

"Some party animals you got there. What time did you leave them?"

"About two. I'm staying with some friends on the Isle of Palms. Everybody was pretty tanked up by then. Lot of them had been drinking all day."

Amid the small talk, the horrors of the night were gradually coming back to Ashby. He dared not share them with Alison. Looking out over the harbor, his eyes fell on Castle Pinckney. He glanced at his watch before remembering it was not working. It read 7:05.

"No way!" Ashby said, grabbing Alison's arm to check her watch, confirming that the time was correct.

"Are you all right?"

"Yeah, yeah, I'm okay. It's just been a pretty hairy night for me. Thanks for saving me from the cop."

"Not a problem. But what happened to you?"

"I'm not sure where your pledge is," Ashby lied, his mind replaying the sight of Mueller face down in the Atlantic. "The boat drifted off and I ended up here."

"I don't think you're telling me everything, but that's cool, as long as everybody's okay."

Ashby was quiet.

She studied him for a moment and sensed that it was hopeless to pursue the matter.

"So, Chico, should we bite him for being evasive or should we offer him a ride?" Hearing his name, the dog began to dance, his nails clicking on the cement.

"Chico, a ride would be great. I'm sorry, Alison, I just can't tell you a lot right now. There is a lot of stuff going on and I've got to figure it out. When everything is said and done, I'll buy you the best dinner in Charleston *or* Savannah."

"We'll see. So do you want a ride back to your boat or home or where?"

Ashby was focused on the Castle Pinckney prisoners. They had to be saved and he needed help to do it.

"If you don't mind, take me to the Coast Guard station. It's about a mile from here. I'll pick up the boat later."

They walked to Alison's Toyota Camry, and she gave him the address of a home on James Island that was the headquarters for the KA reunion. They drove out Lockwood Drive to Tradd Street, and she let him out in front of the Coast Guard base.

"Some of the guys pulled your boat up on the beach where it would be safe. If you want, come out this afternoon. We'll all be there. Sand, suds, and surf, and the cookout starts at four."

Ashby's thoughts had been racing for a plan to free the captives, but he could not ignore the beautiful woman before him.

Alison sat in the driver's seat, a crimson tide of hair flooding down on the shoulders of her gray sweatshirt. Even at this early hour, her jade eyes and easy manner reaped an Irish charm.

"Hey, I've got a question for you. If you partied so late, how come you and that dog are out so early this morning?"

"Chico and I are early risers. We always go for an early

morning walk, and the Battery is the place to be in Charleston. Any more questions?"

"Not now. I'll see you later, I think."

With a smile and a wave she was off. The car sped out of sight and Ashby trudged toward the Rice Mill. A cool breeze coasting off the Ashley River sent a chill through his body. Maybe it had all been a nightmare, so ghastly in its realism that he was beginning to believe it was true.

Even though his mind envisioned the *Hunley*, or at least a Confederate vessel of some type, there was the reality of the situation. The *Hunley*'s crew had gone to the bottom more than 130 years earlier. Despite what Ella Solomon and Hal Frye said, despite the strange occurrence with the button and "There's one for Beauregard," there was no solid basis to believe that a Confederate submarine still roamed the waters of Charleston harbor.

Hell, he had probably dreamed the whole thing last night, fell overboard after his encounter with the KA's, and swam to the Battery. That dumb-ass pledge was probably sleeping it off somewhere, playing a joke on his buddies. Even as he tried to rationalize it in this way, it all sounded highly improbable.

Ashby decided to go to his room and write down everything he could remember. He would then try to get some much-needed sleep. His jeans were dried out enough now so that he thrust his hands deep into the front pockets for warmth. His left-hand knuckles mashed what felt like a fortune cookie proverb. Probably inspector 4's tag from the factory.

Slumping on a bench in front of the admin building, he pulled out what appeared to be a minutely folded piece of paper. Oddly it seemed to be slowly yellowing, almost aging, as he unfolded it. Sudden exposure to the sun, maybe.

Carefully unpeeling it, he found what looked to be a section torn from an old envelope. There was pencil writing on it, some of which had been smeared and was illegible.

Although streaked with water, the most important line was readable. It was enough to petrify Ashby when he mumbled the words to himself.

"S.O.S. *H. G. Wells*. M. Wagner."

Rod Starnes was pounding on his door before Ashby had barely emerged from a hot shower.

"What the hell have you been doing, Eric," he blurted when Ashby answered. "We've got a report of a missing kid from Tennessee and witnesses that say you were the last one seen with him."

"Who's telling you this?"

"I don't know exactly, some people on James Island for a fraternity reunion. They're telling us you crashed their party talking some fool shit about looking for a Civil War submarine and that they put you adrift after you got too rowdy. The report says a nineteen-year-old named Mueller was assigned to watch you. He's a pledge or some crap. Whatever, they claim you and him and the boat disappeared sometime early this morning."

Ashby had listened calmly to this point. After reading the note he had gone to his room, trying to think rationally about a grotesquely irrational situation. He knew he would need Starnes's help, but the fact that the KA's were obviously blaming him for their missing pledge set him off.

"Hey, Rod, while you and I are sitting here talking about a bunch of dumb frat boys, we should be rescuing a dungeon-full of prisoners at Castle Pinckney."

"What the heck are you talking about, Eric?"

Ashby hesitated briefly, knowing how outlandish his story would sound to anyone who wasn't insane. No matter. Those wretches in their awful cages had to be freed. Just as important, their captors had to be stopped.

Ashby wearily fell onto his bed, playing with his bathrobe belt and avoiding Starnes's stare.

"I'm talking about the *Hunley*," he finally said, his voice barely above a whisper.

"The what?"

"The *Hunley*, the Confederate submarine that operated out of Charleston."

"I know about the *Hunley*, Eric. So what are you telling me?"

Harshly eyeing Ashby, Starnes dropped into a chair. He was

willing to hear this charade before choosing from a vast list of disciplinary actions he could level against Ashby.

The pent-up frustration, fatigue, self-doubt, and questions as to his own coherence flooded into a torrent of words as Ashby blurted out his story.

"Rod, all I know is that these guys have been fighting the war for more than a century. They've never stopped fighting! We're not dealing with Middle Eastern terrorists or some militia group or even some smart kids who've read too much about white supremacy.

"Somehow, some way, these are Confederate seamen who still kill just about any Yankee they come across. Doesn't matter whether you are a civilian or military. Anything with an American flag, they blow out of the water and it's been going on for decades."

"So you're saying that an old shipwreck is out there playing hell on the high seas? Are we talking zombies here, Eric?"

"You've got to believe this, Rod. This crew captured me sometime during the night. I've seen the *Hunley* and I was scared witless! Don't ask me if they're ghosts or what, but they play a damned deadly game.

"They've got a prison pen in a hellhole below Castle Pinckney, and there must be fifty or sixty people down there. I managed to get away from them and swim to the Battery. Oh, and that missing pledge—he was fish food when I last saw him. He must have passed out and floated out with the tide."

Starnes was quiet, slowly massaging his temples as Ashby rambled.

"Rod, we've got to rescue those people now! Can you sound general quarters, and we'll send everything we got out to Shute's Folly?"

Starnes pondered the situation, realizing that he had to order Ashby to undergo psychiatric testing. Any formal charges would have to come later.

"I tell you what we'll do, Eric," he said calmly. "We'll compromise. You head down to the infirmary right now and submit to a supervised drug screening."

"Whiz in a cup, is that what you're saying?"

"Yeah, just to cover my ass, momentarily, if all of this leads to something. Once you get back, we'll take a ride out to pick up your launch. I understand from the KA's that it's still out on James Island. Then you and me will cruise over to Shute's Folly on a reconnaissance before we turn out the whole base. How does that sound?"

"I know you think I'm wacko, Rod. But when you've been through what I've been through tonight, plus the death of that security guard on the *Yorktown* and the button thing that happened to me, it all adds up. I'll take your drug test and then we'll go."

Ashby dressed hurriedly and headed out. After giving his urine sample, he returned to his room where Starnes remained.

"There's one other thing that I forgot to mention. Probably the most important piece of the puzzle. When the Confederates took me down underneath Pinckney, I saw a woman prisoner who tossed me this."

Ashby handed him the scrap of paper. "I didn't get a good look at her, but as it says she must be Majorie Wagner from the *H. G. Wells*. She's alive, Rod!"

For the first time, Starnes's brow furrowed. Ashby had to be on a fantasy trip, yet the writing appeared to be that of a female who could be desperate for help.

"Tell you what, Eric, let me take this message and see if we can confirm if it was written by Ms. Wagner. Any problem with that?"

"No, but when are we going to get my boat?" Ashby appeared dead on his feet.

"You're more valuable to me with a little rest. Get a couple of hours of shut-eye before we hit the road. And at some point I want you to put in writing your case that the *Hunley* is still out there."

As eager as he was to embark for Castle Pinckney, Ashby's body was to the point where he could barely function. Sleep was imperative. Wordlessly he eased onto his bed, too tired even to think any more of the tormented souls and their haunting calls for help.

"Wake me," he murmured as Starnes softly closed the door.

Starnes headed directly for the communications center. He photocopied the tiny note, had it enlarged, and faxed it to a police investigator in Perth Amboy who had been their primary contact in the *Wells* case. In a brief cover memo Starnes wrote that a handwriting expert should be able to determine if Majorie Wagner wrote the message. He also offered to overnight the original note if necessary.

As the fax machine rasped, Starnes pondered all that Ashby had told him. Either Ashby was crazy or he had a problem that nothing in Coast Guard training or life, for that matter, had remotely begun to prepare him for.

"Outta the sack! Come on, let's hit it!"

It seemed to Ashby that every time he had been awakened lately something unpleasant was in the offing. His eyes flared open and the rest of his body jerked into instant tenseness.

The aroma of scrambled eggs and coffee aroused his nostrils, and he blearily watched Starnes place a breakfast tray on his nightstand.

"How long have I been asleep?"

"Oh, since about 10 A.M. yesterday. Happy Sunday morning."

"Damn, Rod, we need to be on the road!" Ashby bolted out of bed.

"Why the heck do you think I'm here? I called your KA buds and told them we would be out this morning. I also filed a preliminary report basically confirming that their pledge was missing at sea. Didn't give a lot of details, but there's about a three-paragraph story in the morning paper."

Ashby wolfed his breakfast as Starnes continued. "Naturally, the fraternity folks are pretty upset. I had Mike Green go out there yesterday afternoon and conduct some interviews, find out all he could about Mueller. We talked to his parents somewhere in south Florida last night and made a cursory search off the harbor side of James Island, but didn't find him."

Starnes paused, watching Ashby scarf up the last piece of jam-smeared toast. "You still sticking to your story, Eric?"

"Listen. I just want to know if my boat's still okay. What's the weather and tide table look like to get from James Island to Shute's Folly? Don't we have a metal detector? Might come in handy to locate the dungeon entrance."

"Yeah, yeah."

Less than half an hour later, they were headed across the Ashley River Bridge toward James Island with Starnes at the wheel of the orange and white Coast Guard Ford Explorer. Ashby had stowed the Fisher metal detector and two shovels on the back floorboard. Unknown to Starnes, he had also tucked a 9-millimeter Glock down the back of his jeans. It was hidden by his windbreaker.

They rode in silence, Ashby intent on his mission and Starnes wondering why he was being so patient with an obvious nut case. The sunny winter air greeted psychiatrist and case study with equal energy.

"You don't believe anything I've told you, do you?" Ashby finally said.

"Look, Eric, I mean, put yourself in my place. The story you're feeding me is like some wild drug trip or one of those bad science fiction movies. What am I supposed to believe?"

"I know everything I've said is pretty off the wall, and I sure as hell didn't ask to be put in the middle of it. Jesus, all I was doing was investigating a missing boat!"

"Speaking of missing, here's the preliminary report me and Green put together on Mueller. You might be interested."

Ashby opened a file folder Starnes retrieved from the dashboard. The report gave a description of Mueller and a brief narrative of the circumstances leading to his disappearance. Ashby noted that it contained nothing of what he had told Starnes about seeing Mueller floating in the ocean. The document listed six witnesses, none of whom Ashby recognized other than Thom Gordon. He vaguely recalled Gordon as the jerk who had instigated the whole incident.

"Rod, this only says that Mueller apparently fell asleep on the beach and was washed out to sea by the tide. It doesn't mention anything about me."

"That's why it's called a preliminary report, lieutenant. Green hooked up with an officer from the sheriff's department who is looking into the case. It's their jurisdiction, but Mike persuaded him to let us take the lead. They've had a rash of burglaries to solve and the deputy was pretty accommodating."

Ashby realized that Starnes and Green had both gone to some risk to protect him. Nobody had lied, but the truth of what happened at the party had only been half-told.

"Mike said the guy who owned the bateau you lost pretty much clammed up. Apparently he was supposed to be on a business trip to Columbia, but had come down to shack up with a KA little sister instead. The wife and kids are home watching "Jeopardy" and he don't want to jeopardize that."

"I really appreciate you and Mike covering for me. I don't know why you guys did it, but you probably saved my ass, at least for the time being."

"You're right on all counts there, partner. I'd be lying if I told you there wasn't some of that 'look out for your own' mentality in all this. Me and Mike have talked about it, and frankly we're not sure your butt is worth saving. Just remember, we're not going to the asylum with you."

Starnes stopped in front of an opulent beachfront home near the James Island Yacht Club. Several vehicles, some with out-of-state plates, were parked in the crescent driveway and along the edge of the lawn.

"This is the address," Starnes said, looking at the report. "Anton Francona, a contractor out of Memphis. This must just be his beach house."

"Helluva long way to come to the beach," Ashby answered as they climbed out of the Explorer. No one responded to Starnes's knock at the front door and, hearing voices in the backyard, they walked around the side of the house.

Fifteen to twenty people were gathered around a table containing platters of cubed fruit and cheeses and a huge silver punch bowl that Ashby thought looked larger than one of the *Hunley*'s hatches. Obviously they were interrupting brunch.

"Look at all the preppies," Starnes muttered as they were approached by a mahogany-tanned man in pressed khakis and a monogrammed maroon sweater.

"Morning, gentlemen, I'm Anton Francona," he said, glancing at the Coast Guard emblems on their jackets. Starnes handled the introductions as they shook hands. "May I offer y'all a mimosa?"

"No thank you, sir. We just want to get the lieutenant's boat, which we will take on a quick trip into the harbor, and we'll be out of your way. If it's okay, may I leave our vehicle parked out front for a couple of hours? We'll take the launch to a landing where the lieutenant left his pickup and trailer and then be back here without disturbing you."

"Not a problem. Any word about Pete Mueller? We're all pretty shocked by the whole thing."

Ashby saw Alison amid a trio of young women and gave her a quick wave. She responded with a playful and quick flicking of her middle finger when her friends weren't looking.

"No, sir, nothing new. Our search didn't turn up any trace of him. We spoke to his parents last night."

"Damned unfortunate." Francona shook his head. "Most of our guests are leaving shortly, but this sure cast a pall over the weekend."

There were a few seconds of respectful silence before Francona turned to Ashby.

"So lieutenant, you had quite an experience. You apparently partied just as hardy as a lot of the others here."

"I'm not offering any excuses for what happened."

"I'm not asking for any. I was back and forth from the house to the beach the other night and only saw you briefly. Most of us certainly don't condone what was done to you and Pete. I think those that helped Thom put you out in that boat are living to regret it. Certainly we want to be as helpful and discrete as possible. All of this is just as embarrassing to us as it is to you."

"That's a real comfort, Mr. Francona." Ashby was in no

mood for small talk. "I think we need to be on our way. And speaking of Thom, I don't see him."

"Old Thom's probably not feeling real well this morning. A bunch of us went out last night and I don't know when he made it back. He's staying with us and is probably still in the sack."

"Not exactly," Ashby said. Gordon emerged on the back deck looking like death warmed over. He made for the buffet table, finger-combing his hair and tucking a tattered rugby jersey into his gym shorts.

Spearing bites of cantaloupe and pineapple with a toothpick, he draped himself around a woman in a black warm-up suit. Gordon's eyes lazily scanned the crowd, brightening when they zeroed in on Ashby.

"Hey, Coast Guard! Wanna go for a boat ride?"

Ashby felt his face reddening.

"Jerk. He's responsible for Mueller's death as well as making a fool out of me."

"Maybe it is best that y'all leave," Francona said. "We don't need any more trouble. A couple of the guys will help you get the launch into the water."

They walked down to the beach, and Starnes put a duffel bag containing the shovels and the metal detector in the boat. Ashby had just put a spare can of gasoline in the stern when out of the corner of his eye he saw Gordon approaching from the house.

"Say, Ashby, goin' fishing for the *Hunley* again? Mueller must not have been the right bait. Maybe your friend here . . ."

Wordlessly Ashby wheeled and caught Gordon with a round-house left to the nose. His face spattered with blood, Gordon yelped in pain and tumbled backward into a pile of empty oyster shells.

"You're not getting away with this," Gordon sputtered, wiping his face with his arm and not attempting to get up.

"I just did," Ashby answered, turning back to the boat.

"Thom, you had to keep pushing," said Francona, helping Gordon to his feet. "Good seeing you, gentlemen," he called after them. Steadying Gordon by the arm, they headed back toward the house.

"Why the hell did you have to hit him?" Starnes whispered. "Damn good shot though."

Three of the other KA's helped the Guardsmen carry the boat to the tide line. One of them gave Ashby a hard slap on the back as he handed him the anchor.

"Thom deserved what he got. Pete wouldn't be dead if he hadn't pulled that stupid stunt. I'm glad he was already graduated when I joined the chapter."

"Yeah, he's a winner all right. Hey, friend, tell Alison Curry that I'm sorry I didn't get a chance to talk to her."

"Sure will, buddy."

With Ashby sitting in the bow and directing Starnes, they took aim at Castle Pinckney about a mile away across the harbor. After the rush of punching Gordon, the sight of the ancient fortress was a cold reminder to Ashby of why they were here.

A Coast Guard helicopter made several swoops around them and they waved to the crewmen. Starnes talked to the pilot by radio. Still no trace of Mueller.

Pretending to scratch his back, Ashby felt the outline of the pistol through his jacket. He had an extra clip in his front pocket. No telling what they might run into when they descended into the dungeon.

Ashby only prayed that a 9-millimeter hollow-point would be powerful enough to stop it. 🍂

Starnes killed the motor as they neared the little island. As close as Ashby could tell, this was almost the same route he had taken in the bateau. Even in total daylight his mind watched the Confederate sailors trooping up the sand. The launch glided into the shallows and Starnes was first into the surf, pulling her toward shore.

Grabbing a shovel from the bag, Ashby scrambled over the side and ran toward the castle wall.

"The hole was just about here!"

In a frenzy he attacked the sand, burrowing like a lunatic gravedigger.

Starnes watched half hoping that Ashby would come upon

something—anything. Ashby dug deeper and deeper. Nothing. He plunged into the sand at three other spots along the wall.

"I, I don't understand. That entrance was right along in here. We came ashore right down there and walked almost in a bee-line." Starnes did not reply and slowly sat down on the beach.

"Give me the metal detector. The door had a big iron ring on it. This thing will go crazy when it picks up that ring."

Ashby made several sweeps parallel to the wall, but the Fisher was mute.

"Maybe I've got my bearings a little fouled up. Let's check on the other side of the castle."

Ashby moved the detector back and forth, meticulously circling the entire fortress. The machine blared out several times, but the finds were only a long-rusted can, tin foil from a cigarette package, and a corroded nail.

The tide was beginning to recede, and the winter sun was dropping toward the Charleston cityscape. Starnes had been patient to this point, but they had to get moving if they didn't want to be caught by darkness or possibly some unseen mudbar.

"There's nothing here, Eric. Let's go."

"Just another couple of minutes, Rod. There's a sand mound up here that I want to dig into." Sand flew in all directions as Ashby burrowed into the little hill. Panting, he rose on his knees so that he could use the metal detector to sweep the area. The lack of noise from the machine meant defeat for Ashby.

"Come on, Eric. We need to get back." Starnes patted him gently on the shoulder.

"There should have been something here, Rod! There should have been something here!"

❧

Ashby was sullen as Starnes guided the launch up the Ashley to Jacobs' Landing. The water was choppy, but he was almost numb to the salty spray stinging his eyes and face.

The incubus of being shanghaied by Confederate sailors who should have been in their graves for more than a century was a horror burned into his brain. By the time they hauled the launch ashore at the landing and returned to Francona's home to pick up the Explorer it was almost nightfall. The party was obviously over since the house was dark and the visitors' cars were gone.

Starnes exited Ashby's pickup, but returned momentarily. "Here, this is addressed to you," he said, handing Ashby an envelope. "It was under one of my windshield wipers." As he had been for most of the return trip, Ashby was silent, placing the envelope on the seat beside him without looking at it. Leaning in the open truck window, Starnes tried to read Ashby's demeanor, but the dashboard light's illumination gave him no answers.

"Aren't you even going to read it, Eric?"

"Not right now," Ashby answered despondently.

Ashby followed Starnes back to Charleston, his mind leaping from the reality of the highway to the madness of his existence.

When they arrived at the base, Starnes asked that Ashby accompany him to his office. Ashby sank onto a wooden chair, its hardness as uninviting as what he knew was coming from Starnes.

"Eric. I'm going to level with you. No bullshit," Starnes said, leaning against his desk. "I'm gonna put you on administrative leave. Two weeks starting right now."

Ashby stared at his shoe tops. His face was an unchanging mask of depression.

"There's no argument that your behavior, off-duty judgment, and actions have been questionable at the very least," Starnes continued. "Now I've got a dead frat boy, maybe I should say presumed dead, who you apparently have a connection with. Eric, you taking all this in?"

"Yeah, Rod. I'm receiving you." Ashby slowly looked up, squarely eyeing Starnes.

"Thanks for putting up with me. I probably could use some downtime. Need to sort out some things."

"So what are you gonna do, boy?"

"Dunno. Right now, I'm just gonna hit the rack. I'll check you later, Rod."

"Just get yourself straightened out, okay?" Starnes laughed softly. "Heck, call up that Savannah babe you met at that party and go get laid."

They shook hands and Ashby slowly walked out of the office. He returned to his room and lay down on his bed. In the hushed darkness he thought about his options. Should he go home? No, this would be tough to explain to his parents. He could always look up an old school chum and go for a visit. Lingering in the back of his mind was, for him, a forbidden thought—Did he need mental counseling? He wasn't ready for a shrink just yet.

Realizing that he had not read what was in the envelope, he switched on a bedside lamp and opened it, reading the brief note aloud: "Call me if you get down to Savannah. Alison Curry."

Seconds later he was punching in Alison's telephone number.

Ashby was up before the sun's first rays danced across the Atlantic's horizon on Monday. Although he had awakened Alison, she seemed glad to hear from him and invited him for a visit. He packed his bags in the Mazda and embarked on the two-hour trip to Savannah. The route led him south out of Charleston, across the Ashley, and eventually into the countryside. It was a nice drive and helped take his mind off the whirlwind of everything that had happened to him.

Forget about it all and get to know Alison, he thought to himself as the car darted down the two-lane through a sea of brown marsh grass and over the narrow Combahee River. Less than an hour later he rounded a bend and the Savannah skyline appeared in the distance. It was dominated to the east by the gold dome of City Hall and an occasional "high rise" building of twelve or so stories. To the west was the magnificent and ominous presence of the Eugene Talmadge Bridge, towering over all so that mammoth container ships from around the world could pass under it on the Savannah River to reach berths upstream. Savannah and Charleston were considered "sister cities" because of their antebellum beauty and centuries of history, even though Charleston had been settled first.

James Oglethorpe, an English soldier and adventurer, had sailed up the Savannah and established a camp on the river bluffs in

1733 with a small band of followers. Knowing that the English needed an outpost to guard against Spanish raiders from Florida, Oglethorpe fortified the place. He also drew up plans for Savannah's growth as a settlement. The city squares he constructed remain, as does his distinction for planning the first city in the colonies.

Ashby slowly steered around the squares on Bull Street. For all the world it looked like God had picked up Charleston and dropped her in Georgia, the cities were so similar, Ashby thought. He had only been in Savannah one other time—during a road trip his lacrosse team had made to play a Christmas tournament in Jacksonville. On the way home the school van had broken down on Interstate 95, and the players had stayed overnight in a motel on Bay Street just above the Savannah River.

Some of the boys had used fake ID cards to get into bars on River Street, a strip of watering holes and shops along the waterfront. Ashby recalled that a few of the first-stringers had pooled their money to buy a hooker for Danny Wojeski, a pizza-faced freshman forward who was constantly being ragged about still being a virgin. Facing a dare of manhood from which he couldn't back down, Wojeski had taken the fifty-fivish whore back to the room he was sharing with Ashby for the night. Not in on the joke, Ashby had returned to the motel with another teammate and unexpectedly walked in on Wojeski. He remembered seeing his buddy lying atop the woman, groping at her body as his white ass bobbed up and down. Even more vivid was the memory of the prostitute, twisting a Salem in her fingers and grinning wickedly at him while Wojeski banged away at her.

Charleston was now two hours to the north by land behind Ashby. The *Hunley*, however, had traveled with him, silently roaring through his consciousness, surfacing and submerging in every thought.

The tour bus came full bore out of a blind side street. Ashby's instant reality was of the vehicle moving across his windshield, the tour driver barking his spiel into a microphone and oblivious to the yield sign he had just run. As he floored the brake pedal, Ashby could see a number of passengers on the open-air bus staring at him in open-mouthed terror. The Miata screeched over the asphalt, skidding toward a broadside crash. Ashby steeled for impact, but the car careened to a halt about three feet from the bus. Shaken and angry, Ashby climbed out of his seat and headed for the tour guide, who was trying to calm his passengers as he clambered out of the vehicle.

"Everything is okay, folks! Savannah has got some bad drivers! Yes ma'am, I'm sure we can get you a cold towel at the next stop."

Ashby snared the guide by the shoulders and spun him around so that they were nose to nose. The man had the size to be a Packers tight end. But he also had the puffiness of too many drive-through trips and the persona of a Memphis drag queen.

"Can't you read a road sign, jerk-off!"

Ashby was a cheap firecracker ready to go off at any time and on anyone at this point. Plank-board rigid, he stood eyeball to eyeball with the guide, his mind ready to send his body into any estuary of action.

"I should have gone down and rammed the hell out of you Yankees!"

Ashby felt himself mouth every syllable, but he was astonished by the words.

"Hey, buddy, what the heck are you talking about?" The guide backed up a few steps, sensing this guy was not to be taken lightly. "I might have missed that yield sign, but there ain't no need to get personal about it. Hell, I'm from Des Moines."

"Uh, it's no problem, man," Ashby stammered, calming down. "You shook me up pretty bad when you pulled out in front of me. Just watch it, okay?"

"Not to worry, brother. I got a load of Presbyterians from Mississippi that I need to get back to their hotel. You sure you're all right?"

Ashby didn't reply as he slowly walked back to his car. Where had that nonsense about the Yankees come from? It was as if he had been listening to someone else speak, except the words had come from his lips and he had no control over them.

So now he was hearing voices, or speaking in tongues, or was possessed by the phantoms he was battling. His mind was in a labyrinth of questions as he continued down Bull a few blocks and stopped at Forsyth Park. A group of kids was playing football and the sidewalks that bordered the park were busy with people walking their dogs or simply out for a stroll on the unseasonably warm afternoon. Through the trees Ashby could see the park's exquisite fountain, gleaming like lustrous ivory in the sunshine and ringed by an imperial guard of marble tritons spouting streams of water.

The tranquility and serenity of his surroundings could not have been more unreachable for Ashby. He was all but oblivious to everything other than the chrome-plated Colt .45 lying on the passenger seat. For a full half-hour after he pulled it from the glove compartment he focused on it, studying its lines, the curve of the trigger, and the diamond pattern of its grip.

Despite his inner turmoil, he was at peace with his decision. No banshees capered in his head for the moment, and he wanted to preserve the feeling. He wondered if a bullet coursing through his brain would still the demons. Gotta at least leave a note so somebody knows what happened. Something simple and to the point.

Ashby shook his head as he found himself thinking about the content and grammar of his suicide note. Mrs. Jarvis, his sophomore English teacher, would have been proud of him for the thought he was giving to this macabre homework.

No note, he decided. The shame of his suicide would be too intense for his parents. Let the cops rule it an unsolved murder if they couldn't figure out what he had done.

The rapping of knuckles on his window startled him. He turned and saw a black kid of about twelve years old straddling a bicycle and standing next to the car. Ashby lowered the window.

"What can I do for you?"

"Just wondering if you wanted to buy . . ."

The boy reached into the inside pocket of his jacket, fumbling for something. Ashby kept his eyes on him and groped for the pistol.

"I got one left. You wanna buy a candy bar that I gotta sell for my school? Two bucks for a good cause."

"Yeah, yeah, so what's the good cause?" Ashby had suddenly returned to earth, at least temporarily. He was embarrassed for reacting to the boy the way he had.

"You got me. Do you want it or not?"

"Gimme the chocolate." Ashby fished the money from his wallet.

"I appreciate that, man," the kid said, handing over the candy. "Say, whatcha' going to do with that piece?"

"To tell you the truth, I've been knocking over school kids selling chocolate bars and taking their good cause-money. Hey, son, this candy is as hard as an anchor!"

"Mister, I just sells it. I don't make it. Catch you later."

The boy pedaled away leaving Ashby again alone with his thoughts. Still, the minor intrusion had jolted him back to the reality of why he had come to Savannah—Alison. He desperately needed to confide in someone out of his Charleston inner circle, those who were increasingly predisposed to label him a psycho. Ashby shoved the gun back into the glove compartment and drove out into the traffic on Drayton Street. About a minute later he turned onto the red-brick-paved Jones Street, where Alison lived. He knew that she had taken the afternoon off from her job to clean up her house for the last-minute visit. He found the address and then drove around the historic district for a few hours. After all he wasn't expected until early evening.

Twilight was settling over the city when he returned to Jones Street. Like many of Savannah's downtown streets the avenue was lined on each side by colonial-style townhouses shaded by great contorted oaks. Driving slowly, he stopped in front of a thundercloud-gray, two-story home sandwiched between a pair of larger, more affluent row houses. Ashby ascended the stone stairs to the little front stoop and hammered the doorknocker.

In seconds the door swung open and Alison was giving him a bear hug. She had her hair pulled back in a ponytail and only a trace of makeup. Her faded Levis fit like they were tailored, and her black and green flannel shirt was crisp, smelling like it had just come out of the dryer. She looked great and appeared very happy to see him.

Neither of them knew what to expect from this visit. It was a much-needed getaway, perhaps one of sanity saving proportions for him. Certainly he had been struck by Alison's beauty and the way she looked at him, even though their first encounters had been bizarre in the extreme. She was good looking, intelligent, *and* mature, something Ashby had not found with many of the girls who hung out with the Coast Guard gang. He held the same view of himself and his buddies.

To Alison, Ashby was the last and unattainable answer to a crossword puzzle. She was attracted to him, even in the pitiable state in which she first encountered him lying on the Battery. He was full of crazy stories, but there was an earnestness that drew her to him.

Alison had told only her best friend and co-worker, Elizabeth Tattnall, about Ashby's visit. They both were law clerks at one of Savannah's largest legal firms. She and Liz were inseparable and had no secrets—until now. Alison had dated infrequently over the past few years, preferring instead to go out with groups of friends. Guys always hit on Liz and her when they went bar-hopping or to the beach at Tybee Island. From behind their sunshades they admired the boyish energy and muscular bodies of young servicemen who were always playing football or diving into the surf along the Tybee shore.

Liz had always been the more outgoing and flirty when any of these studs strutted up to their lounge chairs. Alison and their other girlfriends always called her "Lusty Liz," a nickname Liz treasured.

On one beach Saturday, Liz had connected with a handsome Ranger sergeant posted at Hunter Army Airfield in Savannah. They were an item for a couple of months before the Ranger revealed that he was supporting a kid he had fathered with a stripper in Panama. Liz cut him loose, but her eyes were always wandering.

Alison had given her sparse details about Ashby and his expected visit. With so much information missing about this mystery man, Liz mined her for more tidbits, but she remained tight-lipped—for good reason.

Ashby was on a magic carpet ride like no other man she had encountered. The unknown baggage and the skewed clockwork behind his eyes alternately scared and lured her. It was as if she was nose to nose with a diamondback rattler, death separating them by the thinness of a terrarium glass.

She also found herself wondering how he would be in bed. While Liz had done the dirty with several men in the last year or so, Alison had basically not been on the meat market. She had last been involved in a "meaningful" relationship with a criminal defense attorney from Atlanta, but they never agreed on the ethics of anything. Six months into this, she and Tom clashed in a stormy argument when he decided to defend a paroled and thrice-convicted child molester arrested on another offense.

A cop had stopped the man for weaving on a Smyrna back road. After finding a half-empty bottle of vodka under the seat, the deputy had searched the rest of the vehicle and discovered the corpse of a freshly killed eight-year-old boy, wrapped in aluminum foil and an old rug in the trunk.

"Think how this could jump-start my career if I can get this guy off, or at least a probated sentence!" Tom fantasized aloud to Alison. Her reply had been to spring from bed, pack her overnight bag, and get the hell out of his Buckhead apartment.

Alison had slept with Tom, but the sex had always been uninspired and over quickly. On the night she left he had tried to screw her, but she had turned into an ice goddess. Five months later she was glad to see her new friend from Charleston.

Ashby was not in Savannah for a quick lay. He was seeking an antidote for his mind poison. Perhaps Alison would be the madonna who would cuddle him to her bosom and exorcise the poltergeists.

❦

Because Ashby arrived so late and a cold hard rain had set in over the city, they decided to order a pizza rather than going out. The house was divided into four apartments with Alison's one-bedroom flat on the first floor facing the street. After the initial how-was-your-trip chitchat and other polite conversation, Ashby clutched a borrowed pink umbrella and headed out to his car to bring in his luggage. When he returned Alison had a small blaze flaring in the living room fireplace.

"How'd you get the fire going so quick?" he asked, brushing rainwater from his eyes and face. "And where's your fat Chihuahua?"

"Put your stuff away and I'll tell you the fire secret," she answered. "Mr. Chico is spending the night with a little girl down the street who feeds and walks him for me when I'm away. I let her keep him overnight sometimes, she loves him so much. Kind of a Mexican hairless slumber party, you know?"

Ashby stowed his bags in a hall closet and returned to the living room, where the fire was now crackling a cozy invitation. Alison had set out a bottle of cabernet and some cheese and bread sticks on a side table. The shadowy flames licking the walls and the opaque glow of a street lamp through the frosted windowpanes were the only light.

Wordlessly Ashby plopped down on the sofa beside her, and she nestled further into her corner to accommodate him. There was a safe distance of about a foot between them as they sat watching the fire dance.

"So what's the secret?" Ashby finally asked, his voice breaking over the snapping of the logs.

"Secret to what?" Alison was curled with an embroidered pillow clutched to her midriff.

"The fire. You started it really fast, remember?"

"Oh yeah. You gotta know, Ashby, I got so many secrets that you have to tell me which one you want answered." Alison prided herself on her precise grammar, but talking like a truck-stop waitress, as Liz put it, was one of her small pleasures. "I am a total woman of mystery and a purveyor of all that is feminine about my species. And I can tap dance like Ginger Rogers on crack."

She grinned and winked jokingly at Ashby, who was staring at her.

"Are you on something?" His question was half jest, half curiosity. Alison's playful nature, however, turned to granite.

"Not me, Ashby. But I bet a lot of your friends in Charleston are asking the same question about you."

Their eyes deadlocked for a few seconds before he looked away.

"I'm sure they are," he said softly, gazing into the blaze. Triumphant in her stare-down, Alison's harshness melted. She gently patted his forearm.

"I'm sorry, Eric. That was a cruel thing to say. You've been through so much and made a special trip down here just to see me, and I treat you like that—inexcusable. Where's that famous Southern hospitality?"

The awkwardness was interrupted by the knock of the pizza delivery girl. Minutes later Alison and Ashby sat at the apartment's small kitchen table and munched on their dinner.

Being together had grown uncomfortable for both of them, and Ashby made a move to repair the damage.

"I guess I owe you an apology, Alison." He paused, wiping his mouth self-consciously with a paper napkin as she watched him, waiting for more.

"I mean, I come down here and just . . . well, I just haven't been myself lately and I don't mean to drag you down or scare you. There is so much going on, and I don't have the answers to this crazy stuff. Do you want me to leave?"

Alison had listened to him while calmly eating pieces of pepperoni she plucked from a slice in the pizza box.

"So you're planning on bailing out on me tonight? Everybody thinks you got bats in the old bell tower and it's easiest to run away, is that it?"

"You have no idea . . ."

"Don't try to tell me what I know or believe, or don't have a clue about, Eric. And don't for a second deceive yourself that I am afraid of you." She was lying now.

Alison rose from her chair and retrieved a potato peeler from a drawer. "You see this buster? I can gut, slice, or dice you in a thousand ways with this little mutha. Self-defense class and survival training with an elite platoon of half-starved Green Berets on a deserted, enemy- and lice-infested island in the Fijis."

Ashby smiled at her, shaking his head. "God you are so full of shit."

"Maybe so, but at least I'm not some insane jerk-off."

For a second they looked at each other, feeling out the adversary. Both then imploded in laughter.

By the time they had cleared the table, washed the dishes, and had a second glass of wine by the fireplace, it was almost midnight. Alison liked Ashby's dry wit that occasionally shone through his serious demeanor. He liked her unpredictability and craziness, at times wondering if either of them owned their sanity.

"I'm going to bed, asylum boy, and you're not invited."

Early on, Alison had wanted to make it quite clear that she was off-limits, at least on the first night. Play the rest by ear and libido.

"The sofa is yours—and I'll cook you the best damned omelet you ever put in your mouth in the morning."

"Guess I'll see you then. Good night."

She hugged him and disappeared into her bedroom, closing the door behind her.

Ashby had expected as much. He stripped to his shorts and T-shirt and slid under the covers on the couch. A green pinecone burst in the fire, sending a torrent of sparks wiggling up the chimney flue.

Enthralled by the embers, he reflected on the night's events. Heck, with all that he'd been through, he wasn't sure if he would have been able to perform if Alison had come on to him. And truthfully, he was glad that she hadn't.

At least on the first night.

8

A RARE WINTER STORM blustered over Savannah during the night, and even rarer snowflakes swirled through the blackness. Lying on the couch under a pair of Alison's quilts, Ashby heard the wind whipping tree branches against the side of the house.

Watching the shadows of the trees waving across the walls in the orange gleam of the streetlight, he slowly drifted to sleep. In minutes he was deep in slumber. His tormented mind, however, was far from rest. The nightmare, whether real or imagined, churned in his subconciousness and could not have been more believable. He began to writhe on the sofa while the zombie prom broke loose in the ballroom of his cranium. It was as if Alison's departure, like a mother putting a scared four-year-old to bed with assurances that the bogeyman did not exist, had unleashed the demons.

The primeval hiss of the charred wood filled the room like the devil's last breath.

Unseen hands clutched at him, pulling his body down. Below him a coffin brimming with thumb-sized maggots awaited him. There were thousands of them squirming in their juicy existence, twisting over the sides of the casket, curling around its shiny handles—waiting for their feast.

Ashby tried to break free from the hands, but his descent was unchecked, the maggots becoming bigger and livelier by the second.

The worms! The worms! They'll make their nest eggs in your skull, Yank.

Ashby awoke screaming, throwing the covers away from him. The scraping trees were ceaseless, and his fevered gaze deadlocked on the frosted window. Four strands of dew ran down the glass as if one of his brain fiends had pawed the pane. The rasping of the branches seemed to heighten in volume. He sat up on the couch, his heart thundering. The room was suddenly washed in light as Alison came to him.

"Eric, come on, buddy, what's wrong? Come on."

Trembling and speechless, Ashby allowed her to nuzzle him into her lap, tenderly rocking him. The feel of her flannel bathrobe and the softness of her body beneath it slowly comforted him as he clutched at her waist.

Lying in her arms, Ashby calmed down even more when he noticed that the storm appeared to have blown over. He had no concept of time, but the trees had stopped their hellish clawing and he again closed his eyes.

Several hours elapsed before he stirred, a kettledrum of a headache booming over his eyes. His head was propped on Alison's upper thigh while she lay with her legs curled beneath her on the sofa. His movement roused her, and she glanced down at him in a sleepy glaze.

Early rays of sunlight were piercing the window as if in relief of the street lamp that had survived the night and gone home.

"Damn, Ashby," she said, rubbing her eyes. "You had one ride on the Hellbound Train last night."

"Hellbound Train?"

"Yeah. It was an old song my dad used to listen to on his eight track when he was out in his workshop looking at nudie magazines and pretending to build model airplanes. It was by some group called Savoy Brown. Sometimes he'd play it loud on the living room stereo and my mom would yell at him. Seems like every time they fought about him rattling the windows with the hi-fi, they'd end up heading upstairs to screw."

"So how were you so bright and so grown up to know that? You couldn't have been that old."

Alison was relieved to see that Ashby appeared rational, but she remained cautious as she steered the conversation.

"It was a dead giveaway when dad turned off Savoy Brown and put on Herb Alpert and the Tijuana Brass. All that horn music made my mom, well, horny."

"Yeah, that was pretty sexy stuff for my parents too. I think my mother had a crush on the drummer, especially when he wore that big sombrero." Ashby pillowed his head on Alison's leg as they talked.

"Nothing like a big sombrero to get a woman hot and bothered. But my parents were both cold tamales for the most part."

"So how do you figure that they were doing the dirty?"

"Who?"

"Your folks. You said they got all steamed up when they argued."

"Oh, I made all of that up, Ashby. My folks were Mormons. They didn't screw unless it was to make babies, and there wasn't any more room for more kids in the fallout shelter. Actually, my best friend Donna and I would listen to hear the mattress springs creaking."

Without warning Alison clambered off the couch, and Ashby had to grab a back cushion to avoid tumbling against the coffee table.

Gathering her robe around her, she headed toward the kitchen. "So are you ready for my horned toad and salsa killer El Paso omelet?"

❦

Ashby broke into a sweat as the spicy eggs and jalapeños tangoed along his tongue.

"It's not too hot for you, is it?" Alison sat across the table from him, dissecting his every move and trying not to appear too obvious.

"Are you talking about the omelet or last night?"

He knew he owed Alison an explanation, several in fact. How she had been able to stomach his wild excursions without taking him out with the other garbage was beyond his comprehension.

"So you had a nightmare. Who doesn't?"

"Alison, you know it's more than that."

"What I know is that I have a psychologist friend who I think would be great for you to talk to."

"I'm not ready to talk to a shrink just yet. Alison, there is something to all of this, and even though it doesn't make sense to anybody else it is something that I have to do."

"In all truth, Ashby, I don't think you're crazy at all although some of your stunts have been pretty bizarre. Hell, you think I'd let some Jack the Ripper spend the night on my couch?"

Ashby's fork played at the remnants of the omelet as he stared down at the plate.

"Guess you're right about that."

Clumsy silence filled the room for almost a minute before Alison broke in.

"And hey, you are such a brilliant conversationalist."

Ashby looked up and met her eyes.

"So what *do* you think of me, Alison?"

She reached across the table and grasped his hands in hers, inadvertently knocking the fork and some egg to the floor. Instantly a dart of black-and-white fur was at his feet. Slightly startled, Ashby saw a streamlined young cat gobbling up the omelet bits.

"That's Mona. She's been hiding since you got here. I found her hanging around a dumpster as a kitten and enticed her with sliced cheese. She's very skittish around strangers, but she's a sweetie."

The cat's debut diverted both of them and their hands broke apart. Alison was first to the next punch.

"So what do I think of you, Ashby?"

"Maybe I don't want to know the answer." He reached to pet Mona, but she scurried away, leaving a gnawed bell pepper in her wake.

Alison again took both of his hands, squeezing them tightly.

"Eric, you are a good-looking guy with a lot of great qualities. If I hadn't been attracted to you, you wouldn't be sitting in my townhouse and eating my omelet."

Blushing, Ashby glanced away from her, but Alison noticed his shy grin.

"You know what I meant you dirty-minded cretin. And don't try to touch my pussycat again. Mona and I are very particular girls."

❦

The Georgia morning broke cold and gray, but east winds soon flushed the snow flurries and clouds away from Savannah, across the salt marshes and out over the Atlantic.

By the time Alison and Ashby had showered and dressed to go out on a tour of the town, the day had warmed so that tennis players on the Forsyth Park courts could wear shorts.

With Alison at the wheel they set out to see Savannah's historic district. She drove slowly around the squares, each one an oasis of azalea bushes, impressive monuments, and princely oaks crowned by boas of Spanish moss.

"Spring is the most beautiful time to be in Savannah." Alison had assumed her best tour-guide voice. "The azaleas and dogwood are incredible, but it's trouble when we get a warm snap in February. The weather fools the flowers and they bloom early. When the freeze returns it can really zap them. Heck, sometimes by St. Patrick's Day a lot of the azaleas are long gone."

"So what do you do on St. Patrick's Day down here? I know it's one of the biggest and wildest parties around, right?"

"You got it, Ashby, and I've done it all."

They passed the opulent Cathedral of St. John on Abercorn Street.

"That's where all the real Irish gather to honor the religious aspects of St. Pat's. But even a lot of them are drinking whiskey shots by 6 A.M. that morning. They put on their green jackets, eat a plate full of green grits, and wash it down with red eye before the big parade."

"So Charleston doesn't celebrate like Savannah?"

Approaching Colonial Cemetery, Alison looked sharply at Ashby, her reaction telling him that he had asked a very dumb question, at least in her mind. She pulled into a parking space next to the ancient graveyard.

"Ashby, have you been reading that tourist brochure bull about Savannah and Charleston being sister cities? It just ain't so, my friend."

Ashby settled back into his seat, content on letting her launch into whatever tirade or opinion she chose. He obviously had tweaked a nerve and he wanted to see how she reacted.

"Charleston is Miss Scarlett in her hoop skirt, fanning herself on the veranda. Savannah is a big-titted bartender bending over to give you a cleavage view while she serves up a round of shooters for the house."

"Well, that's a pretty clear-cut picture, Alison."

"Well, Ashby, sometimes you sound like a clear-cut, card-carrying member of the major league dork club. Geeze, do you ever loosen up?"

"Not lately."

Another skirmish of tension and Alison's knuckles whitened on the steering wheel. Ashby had been absorbing the view of the cemetery during most of the encounter. Several small groups of tourists wound their way among the myriad gravestones and clay brick mausoleums. Above all was the eternal gray shroud of the moss wreathing the trees like funeral bunting.

"So who are all the old dead white guys buried in there?" Ashby tried to change the subject, but Alison would have none of it, her patience nearing a breaking point after the night's circus of the crazed.

"You wanna join them? Look, Ashby, I find you washed up on the Battery like some vagrant, panhandling whale, I invite you down here to see me, and you freak out on my couch. You have such a shit-load of bats hanging in your belfry."

Ashby flung open the car door, ready to walk.

"So are you trying to make a point here, Alison?" He had had enough banter about his problems.

She shook her head and grimaced. "Oh come on, Ashby. You

know you're a psycho mass murderer waiting to happen as much as I do. Maybe you should get a job with the postal service. Now shut the door and let's find some lunch, okay?"

The slow clip-clopping of a horse-drawn carriage drew their attention. A massive gray-and-white speckled mare pulling a carriage filled with about fifteen tourists trudged alongside the car.

"On our right is Colonial Cemetery, one of Savannah's earliest burial grounds," a prim tour guide in a navy blazer related from the driver's bench. "Among those who rest here are Button Gwinnett, a signer of the Declaration of Independence, a number of prominent war heroes, and many citizens who died in the city's yellow fever epidemics. The early colonists . . ."

Alison wondered why the guide had stopped her narration, noticing at the same time that Ashby had vaunted out of the car and climbed atop its roof, his footsteps booming like July thunder. She thrust her head out the window with the carriage astride them a few feet away. The guide and the tourists were staring at the wild man atop her car in open-mouthed amazement, derision, or a combination of both. The horse snorted.

"Behold, ye heathens, I am the guardian of this underworld, uh, place, and anyone who passes through these portals is subject to a baggage check or a full body search if you pay extra."

Never in his life would Ashby ever have expected to be on top of an auto and feeding lines of undistilled nonsense to a face-to-face captive audience of tourists. But times had changed radically and violently, and life suddenly had very little meaning to him. What was the point of it all when he was so tortured? And why should he play civilized when there were no societal norms in the sinister world he had found?

"Sit down, jerk! What the hell are you smoking?" A portly man with cotton-white hair and a flaming yellow shirt yelled at Ashby from the carriage. Others of the tourists seated around him were laughing or clapping in support.

"Climb off that cloud, you drugged-out freak!"

Ashby went for him. He bounced down onto the car trunk and then bounded to the pavement, keeping the jeerer in sight. A woman screamed on the carriage. The instant his feet hit ground he lunged for the tourist. But a fist around his right ankle tripped him, sending him face first toward the street.

Ashby braced his fall with his palms, the burn of the asphalt and the impact sending streaks of pain up his arms. His left knee came down hard, ripping open his jeans and kneecap. As he bit the gravel, Ashby glimpsed Alison letting go of his leg. He also saw the rear of the carriage as the horse headed down Abercorn.

"The Marines would've used you for crab bait on Tarawa!" shouted the white-headed man from among the tourists.

Ashby rolled in the street, clutching his knee.

"Alison, what the hell . . ."

"Answer your own question, Ashby. You go berserk on some tourist! What were you gonna do to the old guy, snap his neck?" He hadn't even told her about the incident with the tour bus driver the previous day. If she'd known about that, she likely would have accused him of having a death wish for tourists.

She pulled a T-shirt from the back seat and flung it at him. "Here, clean yourself up, I'm hungry."

Ashby limped to the curb and sat down, gently dabbing at his wounded knee with the shirt.

Alison settled back into the car and scolded him, shouting to be heard.

"Such a spectacle and you a representative of the United States Coast Guard. I would've expected better. Hey, can you move it a little bit? I've got low blood sugar like my Aunt Amanda on my mom's side. You know what that means, Ashby? Probably not. It means I gotta eat and now!"

From his curbside perch Ashby seethed, holding the shirt to his bloodied leg.

"Sit right there, Ashby," Alison continued impatiently. "It'll be March before long and the St. Patrick's parade comes right by here on Abercorn. Since you got here so early you'll have the best damned seat in the house."

❦

Within thirty minutes Ashby was hobbling after Alison on the ballastones of River Street. His knee had stopped bleeding, but pained him as he limped to keep up with her.

"Did you purposely park so far away from this restaurant so that you could enjoy my suffering?"

"Don't whine to me, Ashby," she called over her shoulder. "I didn't go mad-dog rabid over a tourist. Just try to keep up."

A frigid wind gusting upstream from the ocean made Ashby hunch deeper into his jacket. Ahead of him Alison had disappeared amid knots of milling pedestrians. One side of the street was a strip of taverns, seafood eateries, and souvenir shops. The other was the Savannah River, a gentle, muddy waterway about a quarter-mile across at this point, snaking some seventeen miles east to the Atlantic. The river was the boundary between Georgia and South Carolina and for more than two centuries had been the global artery of Savannah's shipping industry.

Ashby had learned the basics of the region's geography through his Coast Guard briefing about his Charleston assignment. Savannah's sidewalks were another matter. Stepping aside to evade a guitar-playing panhandler lolling in his path, he suddenly felt something splash on his shoulder.

Cursing the dive-bomber seagull under his breath, Ashby looked up to see Alison standing on a canopied balcony above him holding an outstretched cup of beer. With her were two guys both peering down at him from the second floor of the pub.

"Want another sip, Ashby?" Alison called to the hoots and laughter of her compadres. Frustrated, but more curious then angry, at least until he could determine what game Alison and her friends were playing with him, Ashby headed into the bar.

The interior of "The Golden Hind" was loud and crowded, but offered welcome warmth. Like most of the River Street businesses, the tavern was located in one of a line of old brick warehouses used to store cotton and other wares in the days when masted ships plied the Savannah. A steel spiral staircase led to the lounge's upper deck, and Ashby took the steps two at a time despite his banged-up leg.

Alison met him at the top, grinning at him.

"Enjoy your drink, Ashby?"

Behind her a preppy young couple sat at one of the six tables. Through open French doors Ashby could see Alison's friends watching him while leaning with their backs to the balcony railing.

"Buy you a beer, Ashby? No hard feelings, right? Come on out and meet my eunuchs."

Ashby had yet to answer her. He was too busy sizing up what appeared to be his competition and how Alison fit into the equation.

"Mavis, bring my friend here a Heineken, please ma'am," Alison called to a passing waitress.

Ashby followed Alison out to the balcony and was introduced to the others. Tim Thornton and Rex Warren worked for a shipping line in Savannah. They both were clean-cut guys, Thornton being the taller and more muscular. Warren, however, had a cleft chin and lady-killer blue eyes, and Ashby pegged him as the Casanova.

"I met these characters back in late August, I think. I was down here with some of the girls from my office, and they were having crab races at Commodore's. That's this great oyster bar just down the street, and I always put my money on this little fiddler called Herman's Hermit. Anyway, this one particular Saturday night, Rex here was the official crab-racing association commissioner."

"The bar staff names a new commissioner every week, so it's not all that great of an honor," Thornton chimed in.

"Well there was controversy in the Triple Crown Crustacean Preakness, and all of us who bet on Herman complained to Rex that the race was fixed. I mean this other crab was down the track like he was on some kind of steroids. We still lost our bets, but Rex and Tim bought me and the girls a bunch of strawberry daiquiris."

"Yeah, I used all that big payoff money I got to fix the race," Warren laughed, "and then I decreed that the losers would be deviled and served with a twist of lemon."

"Damn that Herman was tasty!" Alison blurted. The three of them shared the laughter while Ashby tried to smile politely.

"That's quite a story," he offered. "Never been much of a crab fan. They're bottom feeders, eat the stuff everything else in the ocean won't touch. I remember a case we worked out of Wilmington, where this twin-engine Cessna went down in a marsh. The pilot was this big-wig New York architect, and he went right through the windshield on impact with the mud and water."

The laughter had stopped by now, Alison and the boys frozen in stillness as they listened.

"We had a big air-and-sea search for this guy for three days before we found the body, or what passed for it."

"Eric, I'm not sure . . .," Alison started, but Ashby cut her off.

"Well, Rex, the crabs had had their way with him, no doubt. There wasn't enough left of his face for his mother to kiss. Guess they'd rather be snacking on a bloated fat architect than racing."

Thornton took a long pull from his Budweiser in the awkward silence that followed before Alison gathered her wits.

"Eric, you sure know how to kill a conversation—and my appetite."

"Sorry, Ally, just trying to make small talk. You guys didn't mind I hope."

"Not at all, Eric," Warren replied, thrusting his hands deep in the back pockets of his chinos. "So not to change an unpleasant subject, but I understand you are a big Civil War buff."

"You could say that." Ashby wondered how much of his story Alison had shared with these two.

"I guess you know all about General Sherman giving Savannah to President Abraham Lincoln as a Christmas gift."

"Yeah, I read something about that. Let's eat."

Around an inside table overlooking the river, the foursome shared steaming plates of Lowcountry Boil, a conglomeration of boiled shrimp, potatoes, ears of corn, and sliced links of kielbasa. Seasoned and cooked together, the sumptuous concoction was dumped on newspapers spread before them.

After the meal Alison and Ashby parted from the boys and headed down River Street. A mammoth container ship, some ten stories high, made its way ponderously down the Savannah. Ashby studied its immensity and felt the throb of its engines beneath him, the power reverberating through the water. The vessel, of Norwegian registry, towered over the five- and six-story riverfront buildings. A tan-and-white tug hovered at the bow, dwarfed by the size of the colossus.

"Ally?"

"What?"

"Look at that baby." The passing ship absorbed Ashby.

"I know, Ashby, they come in and out of here all the time. Savannah is an international port."

Alison paused and watched him staring in fascination.

"The boys liked you. You feeling lucky?"

"Lucky about what?" Ashby answered without looking away from the vessel.

"Lucky in love, cupid," Alison cooed. "I could see you checking out Rex's package. Never figured you to be on the hunt for the elusive trouser snake."

"What the hell are you talking about?" Ashby had now turned his full attention to her.

"Oh come on, Ashby, you can't tell a couple of bathhouse Romeos when you see them?"

"Are you telling me that your buddies are fags?"

"Queerer than the Gay Nineties. And fags is a term they might take exception to."

"I thought you had the hots for that Rex guy."

"Where'd you get that idea, cupid?"

"I don't know, he's not bad looking and he is your friend."

"So you admit that Rex is handsome. Who had the hots for who?"

"Hey, I'm no fag, that's for sure. Your boys hump each other or do they fly solo?"

"Well, that's a pretty raunchy way to describe a relationship between two consenting adults who hide the sausage in the privacy of their own homes, don't you think?"

"Alison, I don't give a rip about anything that has to do with either of them." Ashby wheeled away from her and walked down to the river's edge, stopping at an iron guardrail. The tide was going out at his feet, and the Savannah's current looked as if the water was being suctioned out by the ocean's pull.

Across the stream was the ruin of an old kaolin plant, the

blue-and-white paint fading and peeling off the one-story building. Rotting wooden docks from a forgotten age sagged on the
opposite bank and beyond them were snatches of brown salt
marshes broken by pockets of pine and cypress trees.

The orange stern of the Norwegian freighter grew smaller in
the distance as Alison joined him.

"You called me Ally back there. I hate that name," she said,
watching the ship's wake dissipate in the river.

"You called me cupid. Lose it."

"Now that the fourth-grade stuff is out of the way, you wanna
go back to my place and make out?"

Ashby didn't change expression, staring at the water.

"Or maybe you want to call Rex or Tim." Alison stifled a laugh.

"Do I have something to prove to you?" Ashby was serious,
turning to face her. She studied his features at this close range.

"Nothing," she replied softly, raising a hand to quickly, gently
caress his cheek in an almost motherly manner. "Let's go home,
okay?"

She clasped his arm and tried to lead him, but he slipped from
her grasp. Wordlessly Alison came nose to nose with him, and
she saw his eyes begin to water.

"It's just that I'm in no mood to be screwed with right now,
Alison. Jokes are jokes and that's great, but I got too much happening to deal with bullshit people or their crap."

"Yeah, yeah. Tell it to your mom, Ashby." Alison tried to
keep the moment light. She had a slight beer buzz, but didn't
want to provoke him into a confrontation. Despite her friends'
warnings, she felt that she had seen enough of him to feel secure
in virtually any situation. If she was playing carefree and careless,
it was the first time she had ever done so in any relationship.
Alison felt dangerous; Ashby was worth it.

She tiptoed to kiss him, enjoying the softness of his lips and
the feel of her arms around his slim waist.

At first he was rigid in her embrace, but he almost instantly
relaxed, his mouth opening to accept her tongue. For a few
seconds they tasted each other, Ashby wrapping around her to
pull her close.

Alison then eased away from him.

"Come on home, Eric."

Despite his problems he didn't need a second invitation.

Rod Starnes's message on Alison's answering machine was insistent: Call as soon as possible. Starnes had not used any of the codes denoting a Coast Guard emergency, but Ashby knew the urgent tone. Ashby routinely wore a pager, but a man on administrative leave tended to leave such tools behind.

A minute later he had Starnes on the phone.

"Eric, you remember Hal Frye, that old detective you talked to? Well he's dead. Somebody killed him and a young woman in his trailer. The Mount Pleasant cops obviously know that you were with him recently, and they are damned antsy to question you. They may be calling in the state or even the FBI to help with the case. Assign it some sort of serial killer status because they also had that guy cut up on the *Yorktown*."

Ashby was stunned.

"Who was the woman? Do they think all three crimes are related?"

"I dunno. Could be the girl is a local stripper. You know her too?"

"How were they murdered?"

"Can't talk about that right now, Eric, sorry. You know the girl?"

"I just might. I'll be on the road in less than an hour, Rod."

"Take your time, buddy. The lead investigator is your friend Detective Lord and he's pretty busy right now as you could guess. Probably won't be able to interview you until sometime tomorrow."

"I'm headed back anyway. Later."

Ashby clicked off the receiver and looked up to see Alison standing in the den doorway.

"So you gotta leave me, sailor?"

"I'm afraid so. Alison, I'm so sorry about everything, but I have to get back to Charleston tonight." He sighed. "Damn, it's kind of like how it must feel to be in the eye of a hurricane."

"What do you mean?"

"Never mind. Thanks for a great time. I'll be back—if you want me back."

"Sure, big fella." She came to him, and they embraced as he stood up from the couch. For Ashby there was no time now for anything but to find out what was happening in Charleston. Alison would have to wait, and she realized that fact as much as he did. In less than ten minutes he had stuffed all his gear into his bags and was ready to go.

"See you around, Ashby." Alison was teary as they shared a final kiss at her front door. He was almost overwhelmed by emotion while pulling away from her and heading down the stairs to the street. How could anyone have stood by him through this wildness? Yet she had done it.

Speeding out of the downtown area, Ashby's car ascended the Talmadge Bridge with Savannah sprawled below him. It was only about 5:30 P.M., but night already had settled and the city sparkled with pearls of light. Below him was the river, aglow in faint silver. From the bridge pinnacle Ashby could also see vast stretches of marsh grass carpeting the northern horizon. South Carolina.

Well off to the northeast, possibly somewhere over the sea islands between the ocean and the city, he glimpsed what appeared to be a lightning strike. Strangely, there were no clouds and Ashby rationalized that the flash could have been a beacon or some other light from an inbound freighter. Sadly he wondered if he would see Alison and Savannah ever again.

Two hours later Ashby parked near his residence hall and was pulling his luggage from the car trunk when he saw Starnes and Cliff Okai walking briskly toward him.

"Eric! Glad to have you back!" Okai said, pumping Ashby's hand.

"Sorry to cut off your downtime." Starnes was more formal.

"So what is the deal, Rod? I'm on administrative leave. Heck, I didn't remember that until I was halfway back to Charleston."

Okai and Starnes looked at each other.

"I think I can safely say you are restored to duty," Okai said, grinning.

"So what gives? Somebody say I killed Frye and the woman?"

"Ease up there, hoss. We got even more shit to handle."

"Rod, what is going on?

"We got an overdue cabin cruiser registered to some honcho out of Bangor. It was headed up the Intracoastal from Pompano, I guess cruising back to Maine, when some ham radio operator near Beaufort picked up a broken-up distress call. The radio guy called us. Said somebody on the boat sounded excited and yelled something about intruders coming on board. The transmission went dead and that's all that was heard."

"Rod's boys here have found out that the boat is a thirty-five-foot Magnum Sport called *Gretchen's Wanderlust*," Okai added. "Registered to the owner of a wilderness outfitting company in Bangor. Let's see . . ." Okai flipped through a notebook, looking for the ID.

"*Gretchen's Wanderlust*," Ashby mulled over the name. "It sounds like a German porno flick."

"The guy's name is Goldenberg." Starnes continued the briefing without cracking a smile. "He and his wife left Pompano a couple of days ago, and then we get this call a few hours earlier. Our guys from Wilmington to Tybee to St. Simons and Miami have been trying to raise them since the reported distress call.

"Tybee station actually had the last official communication with them at 5:38 P.M. Goldenberg reported his position then as about forty miles north of Port Royal and heading into the Charleston vicinity where they planned to dock for the night, probably at one of the Edisto Island marinas. We got the call from this ham operator about twenty minutes later. I talked to him personally," Starnes said.

"We sent up a chopper, but they haven't reported seeing anything" Okai said. "New kid named Roman is flying the mission.

He's headed back now. I thought I'd go up for a look as soon as he gets back to the perch."

"You kosher with everything so far Ashby?" Starnes asked.

"Sure, captain, but just one question. Why are you telling me all this?"

"Heck, Eric, haven't you been on missing-boat detail lately? Like going back to the Civil War?"

"Come on, Rod," Okai said, laughing halfheartedly and punching Starnes on the shoulder.

Ashby had by now cocooned himself in a callous shell, impervious almost to any remarks from the other Guardsmen, including his friends like Starnes and Okai. He bit back at Starnes.

"Captain, I came back to Charleston because of a homicide investigation being conducted by the local authorities. So bite my ass if you want me for anything else while I'm on administrative leave."

Starnes didn't hesitate in storming within kissing distance of Ashby's face.

"Don't give me any back talk, lieutenant! Just do as I say. The proper channels, namely me, have cleared up this administrative leave cow crap and I want you to assist in this case. Questions, Lieutenant Ashby?"

The spittle from Starnes's nose-to-nose tirade had sprayed Ashby's face, but he didn't flinch. Eyes straight ahead he endured the brief lacing with no show of emotion.

"No questions, captain."

"Then get the fuck out of my sight, Ashby. Here's a copy of my incident report. The police can wait until morning, everybody will still be dead. Cliff, get this mother out of here and you get airborne."

Okai grabbed him by the arm and hustled him toward his Jeep. Ashby would go to the Coast Guard Air Station for a briefing on the aerial search. Ashby looked back to see Starnes standing in the parking lot, glaring after him. He couldn't resist the temptation to shout a farewell.

"Hey, captain, I don't know why your mama would ever call you Rod. You will always be a needle dick!"

"Yeah, yeah, Ashby, just find the boat," Starnes yelled back.

"He's always backed you up, you know that," Okai said as they settled into the Jeep.

"I know, Cliff, I just had to get in a shot."

9

AT THE HELICOPTER BASE Ashby and Okai met with Roman and his crew before Okai filed his flight plan and lifted off into the sable sky. The shrill whir of the Dolphin HH-1's twin engines engulfed the night as the chopper ascended. It was about 11 P.M.

With assurances from the Air Station crew chief that he would be notified of any overnight developments, Ashby headed back to his quarters. A young Guardsman drove him through Charleston's quiet streets back to the base.

Overdue boaters were a dime a dozen to the Coast Guard. Everybody from the Florida Keys to the Great Lakes to Puget Sound and Malibu was a weekend admiral. They headed out in anything that would float—from lowly dinghies to majestic three-masters to the sleek and sexy speedsters—dragging their families and friends along for the ride.

Trouble was that most of them didn't know a damn thing about navigation, tide tables, or direction finding. They couldn't find their longitude if it was hanging by a spar line from the North Star.

The Coast Guard spent infinite hours rescuing dumb-asses.

Always had. Whether hung up on a sandbar, stranded by a dead battery, or just plain too ignorant to figure out how to run a boat's engines, they had to be rescued. Ashby had been on a number of these missions in Baltimore and Wilmington. Many times the "skipper" was completely drunk and baked to lobster redness from his time on the water. Many times they were arrogant, blaming everything but their own stupidity for their plight.

Ashby could remember an incident near Wrightsville Beach, where a call had come in about a boater who had issued a distress signal. When the Coast Guard craft arrived on scene, the crewmen were confronted by a three-hundred-pound man in the tiniest of Speedos, enough gold around his neck to fill a galleon's hold, whose only dilemma had been a shortage of sunscreen.

Saving the marooned or looking for the drowned proved to be a steady diet for any station. Routine stuff, especially in summer when the sea virtually bubbled with armadas of the brainless.

But nothing was routine these days, and the missing Goldenbergs could easily be another episode in the asylum story where Ashby existed.

He unloaded his luggage from the Miata, where he had left it when Starnes and Okai found him, and headed into the residence hall. In his room there were three messages on his answering machine. He fell heavily on his bed to listen to them.

Alison hoped he'd had a safe trip and wanted him to know she was thinking about him. Call her when he got a chance.

Detective Lord knew he was on leave, but needed to talk to him about "an ongoing felony investigation" as quickly as possible.

The last message, left about three hours earlier, was from "Snapper" Gould. Call when you get a chance. Found something you might be interested in about the *Hunley*. Ashby dialed Gould, but got a busy signal. Repeatedly he tried with the same result.

The phantoms were waltzing wildly when he fell asleep.

Okai's sweeps found no trace of the *Wanderlust*, and three UTB's, one each from the Charleston, Georgetown, and Tybee stations, embarked at dawn to renew the search.

Ashby awoke about 6 A.M. and lay in bed trying to piece together his latest nightmare. Strangely his mind and body were becoming accustomed to these intrusions, and they weren't exacting the toll they had in the beginning. He rolled on his side and saw that his telephone receiver was off its caddy. Must've left it off the hook when he dozed, he thought.

Starnes was at his door a few minutes later.

"Mount Pleasant cops want to see you right now. You might want to read this before we head out there." Starnes shoved a copy of the Charleston *Herald*'s sunrise edition into his belly. Standing in the door in his bathrobe, Ashby unfolded the paper and stared in disbelief at the front page.

"Double Murder Probed by Police," blared the headline. "Ex-Officer Killed in Mount Pleasant Slayings," read the subhead. Inserted in the story's columns were thumb-sized facial photos of Hal Frye, about twenty years younger than Ashby remembered him, and a pretty blonde identified in the caption only as Lagrange. Ashby immediately knew he had seen her before.

"A retired Mount Pleasant police detective and a Sullivan's Island exotic dancer were found slain early yesterday in the officer's mobile home," the account began. "Mount Pleasant police are searching for clues, but had not revealed any information about possible suspects as of late last night. The victims, Hal W. Frye, 69, a longtime officer with the department, and Gwendolyn Lagrange, 28, a dancer at the Gold Bug Bar, were found about 7 A.M. yesterday in Frye's residence at 120 Rest Eaz-Zee Trailer Park off U.S. Highway 17 in Mount Pleasant. Autopsies were scheduled for today at the Medical University of South Carolina to try to determine the causes of death, MPPD Chief Louis Kraus said. He would not speculate on how the pair was killed. An unidentified neighbor made the grisly discovery when she went to Frye's trailer to . . ."

Ashby couldn't read any more. He handed the paper back to Starnes. "Give me twenty minutes to get ready."

By 8:30 A.M. Starnes was trying to inch into the jammed parking lot of the Mount Pleasant police department. The primary

roadblock was a pack of four television news vans, their reporters, and video technicians who were set up outside the building.
From a motorcycle cop in an orange vest Ashby and Starnes
learned that the police chief had scheduled a 10 A.M. news conference, but that all of the media crews had been on the scene
overnight. The officer directed them to a back lot reserved for
official vehicles.

"Guess they don't know anything yet about *Gretchen's Wanderlust*," Ashby said under his breath while watching the TV
personnel.

"Yeah, I guess something like this overshadows a missing yacht.
You'll have to decide when and if we issue a public statement
about the Goldenbergs, unless they show up safe and sound."

Ashby and Starnes edged into the building, getting clearance
from an officer at the front door.

"How ya doin' Ashby?" a cameraman yelled. Ashby gave him
a wave.

"Lieutenant, hold up!" a young woman called. "Is the Coast
Guard involved in this case? What can you tell me?"

As fast as her high heels would allow, the reporter picked her
way toward them over the gravel with the dexterity of a fire walker.

"You'll have to talk to the police, Angela," Ashby answered.
"We're just here in a support role. I'm sorry but I'm late. Catch
me later if you need to."

The Guardsmen were in street clothes to draw less attention
from the media circus, but Ashby was a familiar face to some of
the Charleston journalists with whom he had worked on stories.

"Sergeant Lord said to expect you," the door cop said. "We got
this entrance guarded to keep them damned nosy reporters from
camping out inside." Ashby noticed that the officer was wearing
a black band across his badge in honor of a fallen comrade—
Frye.

The secretary, Margaret, met them in the small reception area.
She was a well-proportioned lady in her early forties, Ashby
guessed. Smartly dressed in a charcoal skirt and black blouse and
well coifed, she noticed the unspoken compliments that both of
the visitors lavished on her with their brief stares.

"Hi," Ashby greeted her with a touch on the arm. "Rod, this nice lady saved me from a case of police brutality the last time I was in here. I'm sorry, but I don't think we've ever been introduced. I'm Lieutenant Eric Ashby and this is Captain Rod Starnes."

"I'm just charmed," Margaret riposted. It had been a long twenty-four hours since the bodies were found. Everybody in the fifty-employee department was working at least double shifts to help solve the case. She had snatched a few hours sleep on an interrogation waiting room couch before being roused at 3 A.M. to take down a statement from a trailer park Peeping Tom. The pervert had been known to cruise the Rest Eaz-Zee, but none of the investigators believed he had the guts to slice and dice Frye or the stripper. Margaret was in no mood for flirting right now.

"I think you know the way," she said, leading Ashby down the corridor toward Jeremy Lord's office. "Your buddy can just have a seat."

The narrow hall was busy with uniformed and plainclothes cops talking in groups or hurrying in or out of side doors to offices. Ashby caught snippets of a hundred conversations about blood spatter patterns, fingerprint dusting, Gwen's fine-looking corpse, and sperm on the bed sheets. A stout black meter maid hunched by herself on a small chair in a corner, sobbing quietly. There was talk of Hal Frye's good nature and devotion—and, why was he shacked up with that whore babe from the Gold Bug?

"Shit, the county vice squad probably nailed Gwen for prostitution about five times within the last year," he heard a bull-necked officer with a crew cut and gold insignia on his collar tell another man who was dressed in a dark suit. Both of them nodded a greeting to Ashby as he brushed by them, and he felt their eyes burrowing through him.

"Who were those guys?" Ashby asked Margaret quietly when they were out of earshot.

"That was Chief Kraus and Agent something or other. He's with SLED. You know, the State Law Enforcement Division."

"I know, Margaret, thanks. When did the SLED boys get here from Columbia?"

"Sometime mid-afternoon yesterday. They brought in blood-hounds, but all the dogs found was a dead possum under some-body's trailer."

Margaret laughed as they approached Lord's office.

"So did you ever find that button? You were white as a sheet that day you left here."

Ashby shuffled his feet and felt his face redden.

"Nope, never found it. And I can't explain what happened to it."

"Oh, it'll turn up, honey," Margaret answered. She whipped into Lord's doorway and saw the detective settled back in his chair, his head slowly bobbing in the process of nodding off.

"Sorry to disturb you, Jer, but, you remember our friend here, right?"

Lord bolted awake as if he had been shocked by jumper cables.

"Fine, Margaret."

Lord finger-combed his hair, coughed, and grabbed for his pack of Camels, not yet acknowledging Ashby's presence.

"Good luck," Margaret offered, heading back down the hall.

Ashby plopped down into the same old wooden chair he had occupied weeks earlier with the photo of Hal Frye looking down on him. The office had not changed in any detail, and he found himself tingling with a sense of foreboding. The button was long gone, but his return there was as if he had gone back to the scene of a barbarous murder.

"We checked with this, uh, Alison Curry in Savannah last night to verify your whereabouts," Lord mumbled, still looking at the unwieldy stacks of paperwork growing on his desktop.

Lord looked like he had been awake for a year; and Ashby, despite his anxiety, noticed that the cop had aged noticeably since he last saw him. Because he had knocked the phone off its hook, Alison had been unable to contact him about Lord's call to her, he reasoned.

"Obviously we can't consider you a prime suspect, but you did know both of the victims so it is routine that we bring you in for an interview, you understand."

Lord spoke in an almost trance-like monotone. The strain of

what could be a serial killer's first brush strokes was getting to him. The Hoyle murder case on the *Yorktown* was lodged against a stone wall, and now he had a double killing that on first appearance could well be related to Hoyle's death.

Lord's subdued demeanor seemed to coldcock Ashby out of his funk. He had expected a tooth-and-nail confrontation, but his opponent already seemed beaten.

"So," Ashby hesitated, "what are your questions?"

"You just stay close to home so that I can find you if I need to talk to you again," Lord barked suddenly. "And remember your buddies this way!"

Lord reached into one of his paper piles and pulled out a handful of photos that he flipped onto the desk in front of Ashby.

Spread before Ashby was a panorama of gore—dozens of crime scene photos. The grotesque images of the victims were sprawled amid the carnage of Frye's home. Like rag dolls dipped in ketchup, Hal and his dancer-friend were the top-bill stars of the eight-by-tens, both captured in deathlike color from many angles by the police photographer.

The bloody grin of a throat cut from ear to ear was Frye's most prominent feature. Wearing white boxers and a gray T-shirt all but saturated in crimson, his body was draped over a straight-back chair, the only upright piece of furniture in a kitchen that looked as if it had taken a Kansas tornado hit. Ashby saw that at least two cupboards were knocked off their mountings, and Frye's little two-burner stove had been ripped from the floor and set back down sideways. Everything on the shelves and from the open-doored refrigerator had been flung out, the food and debris scattered about the floor.

Ashby winced at some of the pictures before his eyes settled on several of Gwen Lagrange. His grimace almost turned to nausea and Lord chuckled at his reaction.

"Pretty grim stuff, ain't it, Coast Guard?"

The stripper was lying face up on the now-red carpet of Frye's living room area. Her pink bra was bunched around her throat, and Ashby recognized the finely done rose tattoo on her thigh.

Frye's recliner and sofa looked as if they had been dropped into the room from a thousand feet. Everything was accented in blood, whether in thick black goo adhering to the bodies or in red speckles garnishing the ceiling light fixtures.

What convulsed him most was the killer's coup de grace. Gwen had essentially been split from her navel to her neckline, a horrific highway running over her upper torso. The butchery had left her wide-eyed and opened-mouthed, as if entreating heaven for some answer to her doom. Ashby swallowed hard and tried to retain his composure.

"How were they killed?" he asked.

"No need to answer that one, sergeant."

Ashby pivoted to see the suit and Chief Kraus standing in the doorway. "Even if we knew the answer to the question, it wouldn't be appropriate to share it with someone not directly involved in the case," the suit continued. "Are we on the same wave length, chief?"

"Certainly, Madison. SLED has free rein around here, you know that."

Lord watched the exchange without moving a muscle or changing his doleful expression. The Camel in his fist burned toward his knuckles.

Kraus introduced himself and SLED Agent Craig Madison to Ashby.

"I was away on a second honeymoon in Tahiti when you, uh, lost that piece of evidence in the Hoyle case." Kraus was friendly but firm. And Ashby could sense that Madison was the puppeteer of the two.

"You don't have anything to shed light on how these folks were killed, much less how that button disappeared, is that right?"

"Chief, if I could turn rain into beer I'd do it in a second."

"Well, beer turns to piss real quick, Ashby," Madison said, moving into the office.

"Were you fucking Lagrange?"

"No. I saw her once at the Gold Bug and met her briefly at Frye's. That's all."

"So you never tucked a few bills into her garter or offered her money for sex?"

"Did you ever try to screw yourself?" Ashby was getting irritated.

"Easy, easy," Kraus intervened, stepping between them as a precaution. "No need to get any feathers ruffled here."

Over the chief's shoulder Ashby could see the agent smiling smugly at him.

"Detective Lord, if you have nothing further, I guess we can let the lieutenant go." Lord nodded and Ashby rose to leave.

"Just one more thing, Mr. Ashby. The name Peter Mueller mean anything to you?" Ashby stopped in his tracks and stared at the wall ahead of him while Kraus continued.

"Missing kid from Florida who disappeared off James Island a few days ago. A family out on a picnic found what was left of him yesterday afternoon. Washed up on a beach somewhere along the Stono River. Know anything about him?"

In the mirrored reflection of a framed wall plaque, Ashby could see Kraus and Madison looking at him like hunters peering at a rabbit just snared in their trap. He had to stay calm. And lie.

"I have heard of him, yes. We are working with the sheriff's department, and the last I knew he was still missing."

"Okay, son, we'll be talking to you."

"Sorry to hear he turned up dead."

Ashby again started out of the office but hesitated. "Chief, why are you asking me about a missing persons case being handled by another agency?"

"Well now, Ashby, there's been so many corpses found around Charleston just recently that we in law enforcement are looking at everything and everybody, you included." Madison's tone was confrontational.

"I hope you find Hal Frye's murderer," Ashby said to Kraus, ignoring the agent on his way out of Lord's cubbyhole.

"Me too, son."

Ashby all but collided with Margaret when he entered the hall.

"Uh, chief, it's almost time for the press conference. There is a lot of reporters out there."

"I'll be along in just a minute, darlin', thanks. Just got to get a briefing from Sergeant Lord here before I meet the press."

"Hey, chief, that pretty young thing from Channel 45 asked me to tell you thanks for the hot chocolate you sent out to her. She wants an interview with you as soon as possible."

"They all do, Margaret. Thank you. Say, why don't you go home and get some rest. You been here all night. Jennifer just came in, she can take over. Just shut that door on your way out, will you, sweetie?"

Ashby followed Margaret back down the hall, most of the cops having cleared out by now.

"So I got a parole, yippee!" she said to him as they walked.

"You gotta be whipped."

"Actually I'm more wired than whipped. These diet pills I've been taking are like some kind of speed, I guess."

"Well, can I buy you breakfast? I owe you, you know."

"Like I said, I'm on a diet, honey. No blueberry pancakes for these thunder hips right now," she said, slapping her sides.

"You promised me a drink, if I recall correctly."

"I did, but it's ten o'clock in the morning."

"And I've been here more than twenty-four hours. I'm getting off now and it's happy hour."

"It's hard to argue with that kind of logic, Margaret. I'm your man as long as the old salt out there in the waiting room gives me permission."

"He already has, sweet pea."

Before Ashby could answer they were in the reception area, where he saw Starnes impatiently thumbing through an ancient copy of *Good Housekeeping*.

"Give me a minute with the captain, okay?"

"Yep, I'll get my stuff and be right back."

Margaret headed off and Ashby returned to talk to Starnes.

"So how'd it go?"

"No problems. Hey, I got nothing to hide."

Ashby lowered his voice. "Rod, they know something about Mueller. They asked a couple of questions about him. Said he had been found."

"That's true, a sheriff's deputy I know just told me about it. Very decomposed body. Must have surfaced yesterday. With all the stuff going on with the Goldenbergs, he kinda got lost in the shuffle."

"Anything new in that case?"

"Not a trace of nothing. The search is ongoing and I need to get back. Margaret says she has to go over some paperwork with you, and there's no need for me to hang around. Take care of it, and I'll beep you if there are any developments."

Starnes was distracted by the hubbub of reporters and camera trucks all hunkered outside. Blinding lights, a swarm of snaking cables, and satellite dishes all were ready for Chief Kraus's debut.

"Hey, captain buddy, I sense that you have ulterior motives."

"Sure do, lieutenant. Melanie Potemkin from Channel 4 is out there, and she gave me the once-over when we came in."

"Rod, she's looking for a scoop and sees you walking into the police station. She probably thinks you're a murder suspect. Hell, you look like a child molester to me."

"Vote of confidence noted," Starnes said, cupping his hand over his mouth to check his breath.

"Get the hell away from me, will ya, Eric. Take care of business here and find your way back to base."

Starnes opened the front door, and was immediately swallowed in the white lights of the television crews. Ashby was about to follow Starnes out into the glare when he was yanked backward by Margaret.

"We'll go out another door. No need to deal with all of that," she said, pulling him aside.

"Captain, you are on your own," Ashby called to Starnes and gave him a salute. "I'll grab a taxi back into town."

Ashby opened the driver's side door of Margaret's black Pontiac. "Such a gentleman. You've got some Southern blood in you, I bet," she said, climbing in.

Margaret headed north on Highway 17 out of Mount Pleasant. An early morning fog had burned away and the air was salty and crisp—another balmy January day in Carolina. It had been almost a year now since Ashby traveled this road looking for any leads in the Wagner case. So much had happened to him in that time, but he still was no closer to solving that mystery than jumping over Jupiter. He was beginning to understand why Snapper Gould would forever remain so obsessed with the *Sea Lynx* disaster. And he himself would not and could not exorcise the faces of the Castle Pinckney captives from his mind.

"So where are we gonna find a bar open before 10 A.M. in this county? Isn't there some ordnance about no alcohol served after 1 A.M. or before noon? Heck, even the winos can't get a drink this time of morning."

"I know a place. A bunch of the night-shift guys go there when they get off duty at 7 A.M. Doubt if it will be crowded today since all of them have been working so hard on this murder case. I know the SLED guys were out last night talking to a lot of Hal's friends who hang out at the Gold Bug."

"Did you work with him before he retired?"

"Oh, I guess for about seven years. We always got along. Always had a nasty joke or two that I never wanted to hear."

They were about three miles out of Mount Pleasant by now, the malls and fast food strips replaced by pinewoods and modest rural homes.

"I just can't believe somebody would do something this awful to old Hal and that girl. And I can tell you this, Jer, Detective Lord, doesn't have a clue who did it or why, and I don't think those tight-assed suits from Columbia do either. You got a cigarette?"

"What about Chief Kraus? No, I don't smoke, sorry."

"Oh, he's only been with us for about three years. Came from some small department in middle-of-nowhere Iowa or somewhere and nobody seems to know anything much about his record there. Rumor is he might have shot another officer out there while dry firing his weapon."

"Dry firing?"

"You know, pulling the trigger when you think the gun isn't loaded. It's a big no-no, but some cops do it just like some dumb-ass who just bought his first revolver from the Western Auto. A lot of times the gun *is* loaded. Really really stupid."

"Chief wears his badge on his pecker anyway," Margaret

continued. "He's always sniffin' after those young TV reporters. They could give two shakes about him if there wasn't three un-solved homicides, but he don't have a clue about that either. Hell, he's even invited me over to his apartment for a drink, but I wasn't born yesterday, you know?"

"So you think we got us a Boston Strangler–type psycho in Mount Pleasant?" Margaret looked away from the highway, her eyes impaling him.

"Honey, I don't know what's happening around here, but I can assure *you* that if you aren't on the up and up and try some-thing funny with me, I am prepared."

Ashby laughed.

"I'm sorry, I'm sorry. Hey, I owe you, remember? That's the only reason I'm here." Margaret softened.

"I know, sugar. I've seen all kinds and you ain't one of those kinds. Oh, here we are, almost missed my turn."

She wheeled the Trans Am off the highway onto a dirt road flanked by two vast weeping willows whipping in the breeze like giant green hydras. Behind the curtain of willows Margaret stopped at a rundown, pale yellow wooden building with a screened-in porch running the length of its front. Flattened beer cans and bottle caps littered the gray sand parking lot.

"Keith's Crabhouse—Fireworks and Bait," read a worn ply-wood sign anchored on rusty supports over the porch. "Night-crawlers—Ice Cold Beer."

"You sure this is the place?" Ashby said. "Did you see the movie *Deliverance*?"

"Sure did, honey. Come on in, I'll protect you." Margaret sidled out of the driver's seat. "You shore do have a purty mouth."

"Most famous line in movie history."

"You might get an argument about that sweetie, but it's way up on the list."

The whiny screen door clattered shut behind them as they entered. On the porch was a row of wooden boxes with wire tops where the live bait was kept. A glee club of crickets sang for their liberation.

With Margaret in the lead they went through another doorway that opened into a big room with a diner-style bar and stools at one end. Four linoleum tables with old kitchenette chairs, none from the same group, it seemed, were spread out over the oily-brown wooden floor. Along one wall were shelves filled with canned goods, sacks of flour, and other groceries.

They seated themselves on low barstools, and a black woman wearing a grease-smeared white apron emerged from a back kitchen area.

"Y'all want some breakfast? Too early for booze I guess you know. My my, you are a sweet-looking man."

"Isn't your name Ethel? You don't remember me do you?"

Ethel stared blankly at Margaret. "I get a lot of customers. The menu's on the chalkboard right there by the door. We got fried catfish for the lunch special today."

Margaret pulled her wallet out of her purse and showed her police identification card. A wave of recognition rolled over Ethel's face.

"Oh yeah, you've been in here before with some of your cop buddies, yes ma'am, how you been doin?"

Ashby could tell that Ethel didn't know Margaret any more than the last alien who landed in the crabhouse parking lot. Margaret sensed it too, but went along with the game.

"Oh, we've been doing just fine, just working real hard on these murders that have been happening."

"I heard something about that on the news. Just a terrible, terrible thing."

"It truly is. Ethel, I need a light beer for me and whatever my friend here is having. It's on his tab."

"Bud in a bottle if you got it. Is there a pay phone around here?"

"Naw, baby, but you can use that phone right around the end of the counter there if you're making a local call."

"I need to check in with the base and see if anything is going on," he said to Margaret.

"I'll start without you. Skoal." She raised a Miller Lite long-neck and took a big swig.

Ashby's call was transferred to Mike Green, the petty officer who had been on duty when the *H. G. Wells* went down. Green told him there had been no new developments in the Goldenberg case, but that Okai's Dolphins and those from the Air Station in Savannah, along with a forty-one-footer from Station Tybee, still were actively combing the area. The local media was so immersed in the "slashing slayings," as one reporter described it, that a sea-and-air search for an overdue boater was being ignored. He told Green that he could be paged if needed and asked about Starnes.

"He's tied up in some meeting with Grizzly and some guys from the Corps of Engineers. Probably about harbor dredging or something equally as exciting," Green said. "Anything new on the murders?"

"I'm still meeting with a police official. Tell Rod to page me if he needs me. Otherwise, I'll be back to base as soon as I can."

"Hey, Eric, I know they brought you back off administrative leave because of this case. Me and some of the other guys know you're dealing with a pretty full plate and . . ." Green paused.

"Mike, just don't have me packed off to the funny farm just yet, okay?"

"That's pretty much what I wanted to say, Eric. Rod and me are pretty good judges of character—at least we think so. Just know that you are still one of us. Hell, you'd do the same for me, I know it."

"I appreciate that, Mike. That means a lot to me. I haven't been exactly Mr. Friendly lately, and that doesn't look like it's going to change until I get some puzzles solved. Just bear with me."

The conversation with Green was some reassurance to Ashby that the other Guardsmen had not turned on him or written him off as a basket case. But at the same time he knew that Starnes had not shared the particulars of his leave with the other officers. As real as it had been to him, if they knew about his Castle Pinckney episode the entire station would likely shun him. Disbelief, shock, shame, and pity would infect all like a rampant distemper, and it would likely lead to the end of his Coast Guard career.

"So, are you gonna leave a lady to drink all by herself?" Margaret called. Ashby looked down the bar to see her and Ethel watching him.

"He shore does have a fine butt, missy. You are a lucky lady," Ethel said.

"Oh, he's not mine. We're just out for a drink."

"Then maybe I still got a chance, you think so, sugar?"

"Ethel, you always got a chance with me. Now that I know where you are, I'll come back to see you."

"Sugar, I'd be all over you like white on rice. You think you could stand it?" Ethel laughed.

"If I can't stand it, I'd die with a smile on my kisser and a pecker like Mount Rushmore. And you'd be one happy lady."

"I can believe that. You want that beer cooled down?" Ashby had left his bottle on the bar when he went to make his call.

"Just get me a cold one, thanks Ethel."

"Mount Rushmore," Margaret giggled.

Ashby turned to her as she sat on the stool with her legs crossed. Four longnecks were in a platoon on the bar in front of her.

"What happened when the Pope went to Mount Olive?"

"Huh?"

"Popeye beat the shit outta him! That was one of Hal Frye's favorite jokes!"

"Y'all call me if you need anything. I got to put my breaded catfish in the fryer." Ethel headed to the kitchen, shaking her head. "Crazy woman talking about Popeye and the Pope."

Margaret was feeling no pain, a euphoria that she enjoyed. A decade of police work, even a desk job in a department as small as Mount Pleasant, could do that to anyone. Daily exposure to the worst of human nature eclipsed the sun of even the most upbeat.

"Ethel said she would hump you right here on the bar if I wasn't here to take care of you."

"Is that a fact? Were you gals planning to gang bang me?"

"That float your boat, Ashby?" Margaret leaned toward him, slightly unsteady on the stool. "Me and Ethel making a man sandwich out of you?"

"Hey, I'm open to new experiences. Why don't we bring along a Great Dane too."

"You wouldn't need Ethel or anything else if I got a hold of you." Caressing a bottle, she looked him up and down as if he was a Chippendale dancer. "How about another beer?"

"No thanks. Two's my limit before noon, and even though I'm in civvies I'm still on duty."

Margaret drained number six and added it to the collection.

"Look at all the dead soldiers," she slurred, gazing at the bottles. "Time to go." Ashby paid Ethel and, steadying Margaret by the arm, they headed outside.

"Y'all come back soon, especially you, mister fine-looking gentleman," Ethel called after them.

"We'll see you later. Thanks." They walked out to the car.

"You always drink like that?"

"Like what?"

"You killed a six pack, and we were only in there about an hour and a half. Maybe I better take those car keys."

"I'm perfectly fine to drive. And there's nothing wrong with me having a few drinks after a long night and to mourn the loss of a friend is there?"

"I guess not," he replied, watching her as she settled into the driver's seat.

"Besides, we're not done yet. I'm taking you to the spot."

"The spot?"

"You'll see."

Margaret gripped the steering wheel as if she were at the helm of the *Queen Mary*. Fishtailing out of the lot in a tire sandstorm, she drove around Keith's and sped through a pecan grove on a narrow dirt lane. Thin tree branches slashed across the windshield as the Trans Am hurtled through the underbrush. Ashby braced for the first big limb to come crashing in, decapitating him in Jayne Mansfield fashion.

The road and the trees ended on a high dirt bank overlooking a swampy pond. The dark water was stabbed by hundreds of cypress trees and almost totally carpeted by saucer-size lily pads. Down the bank about fifty yards to their left were the rotting ruins of an old sawmill, its tin roof caved in as if an ogre's fist had punched it. A small mountain of burnt orange sawdust some two-stories high rose beside the mill, and rusty pieces of machinery were strewn in the weeds.

Ashby got out of the car and stood on the bank taking in the view. Two brown wood ducks came whipping across the skyline, quacking in tandem. It was a beautiful setting to him although he realized that some city slicker might stand on the same spot and see only a nasty, smelly swamp. Certainly in the furnace of summer this place would be the empire of the cottonmouth with air forces of horseflies and mosquitoes patrolling the territory.

"Like what you see?"

"I bet there are a ton of snakes in here . . ."

Ashby stopped in mid-sentence as he turned toward Margaret, his eyes widening in surprise.

She had removed her blouse to expose a skimpy lavender lace bra overburdened with her pearl-white breasts.

"I asked you if you like what you see, Eric." Margaret was leaning against the grill of the Pontiac. He couldn't find the words to answer her, standing transfixed while she slowly walked toward him.

Within a few steps of him she reached behind her, undid the clasp and let the bra fall to the ground. Wordlessly she embraced him, and he could feel her full bosom against his own chest. At the same time he could feel his hardness brushing against her thighs. There was no stopping it now.

"Uhnnnn, do you want to screw me, Eric?"

His answer was to run his hands over her back, kissing and licking her neck before finding her lips. His fingers massaged and kneaded her flesh as she gasped. His tongue slipped from her mouth and coursed down her throat, over her serpentine necklace, and down to her breasts.

Margaret groped over his stomach and used her palm to massage the bulge in his jeans as Ashby buried his face in her chest.

Between gulps for air she murmured, "Over there," and pointed to the sawdust pile. Ashby came up for breath and led her to the mound. She lay down at its base, and he attacked her body with ravenous lust. There were no thoughts of Alison now. He was intent on the luscious woman writhing beneath him.

Ashby kicked off his shoes and squirmed out of his shirt and pants while tongue-dancing with Margaret. He unzipped her skirt and pulled it free, pausing for a moment to stack it neatly to the side.

Margaret lay on her back in the sawdust, now wearing nothing but black thong panties. Her arms were stretched above her head, and her breasts heaved with her heavy breathing. Sweaty sawdust lined her cleavage and glistened over her torso and legs.

"Come and get me, big boy," she purred.

Ashby was feeling the sting of Margaret's fingernail claws on his back as they headed back to Mount Pleasant. Both of them were brushing and picking sawdust out of their hair and clothing.

"You're a real jaguar," he said, reaching over to stroke her neck as she drove.

"Soooo are you, lover. That's what I call interaction between departments."

They basked in carnal contentment as Margaret headed into Charleston and dropped him at the base. Around the corner from the main gate she had stopped the car for the good-bye kiss—long, deep, and passionate.

At the gate Ashby adjusted his clothing and got out of the car.

"Thanks, Margaret. You are an incredible lady. Can I call you?"

"I'll be disappointed if you don't, Eric." She grasped his hands.

A last peck on his cheek and she was gone, the Trans Am's thunder fading on Tradd Street.

10

1864

THE BODIES OF Horace Hunley and his honored crew were just beginning to enrich the soil of Magnolia Cemetery when George Dixon made his request. Despite the submarine's death count and repeated failures, despite Beauregard's ban on its operations, Dixon wanted another chance with the craft.

The general did not spend a lot of time contemplating this decision. Charleston was under attack by a superior enemy, civilians were being killed in the periodic bombardments, and Beauregard needed any and all weapons. He consented to Dixon's entreaty on the condition that the sub operate only on the surface like the *David*.

Dixon recruited yet another crew; and William Alexander, his comrade from the 21st Alabama, signed on as his second officer. Two of the men came from the Parks and Lyons shop in Mobile. Dixon obtained five other sailors from the *Indian Chief*. Despite the sub's record and notoriety, there apparently was no lack of patriotic volunteers.

"The honor of being the first to engage the enemy in this novel way overshadowed all else," Alexander would recall.

By now the *Hunley* was in dry dock at Mount Pleasant, where black laborers had scrubbed her down using brushes, soap, and lime. For a time, Dixon and Alexander drilled the new squad out of the water, acquainting them with the craft's functions and apparatus. Mechanics also repaired, fine-tuned, and lubricated her equipment to bring her back to fighting trim. Like the two companies of lost souls before them, this crew began war maneuvers in the harbor, diving and ascending in mock attacks.

Early in December 1863 Dixon decided he and his men were ready to take the offensive, and Beauregard again readily agreed.

Under Special Orders, Number 271, Dixon was instructed on December 14 to "take command and direction of the submarine torpedo-boat *H. L. Hunley*, and proceed . . . to the mouth of the harbor or as far as capacity of the vessel will allow, and will sink and destroy any vessel of the enemy with which he can come in conflict."

Beauregard's mandate also stated that "all army officers are commanded and all navy officers requested to give all possible assistance to Lieutenant Dixon."

Rough weather prevented any immediate strikes against the U.S. fleet, so Dixon had to be content with trial runs in and around the harbor. To save the energy of the men, the *David* towed the *Hunley* to its area of maneuvers. It was during these exercises that the sub's torpedo, pulled behind it, almost blew up both vessels. Changes had to be made, the first being that the *David*'s days of towing the submarine were ended.

The Confederates also decided to mount the *Hunley* with a spar torpedo like the *David*. The first was a twenty-two-foot pine lance with the warhead attached to the end. The spar shortly afterward was replaced by an iron version armed with a ninety-pound canister of gunpowder. Like others of its kind, this torpedo was designed so that the vessel could ram it into an enemy ship and ignite it by reversing course, thus causing a tripline to detonate the explosive. The torpedo spar was designed so that it could deliver its blow beneath the waterline.

Admiral Dahlgren had tightened security for his squadron after the *David*'s attack on the *New Ironsides*. The ships were equipped with defensive chain booms and high-beam calcium lights, which could illuminate large areas. Anchor chains were ready for slipping, and high steam was maintained so that the vessels could quickly move out of an intruder's path.

Dixon's submariners were quartered at Mount Pleasant while the *Hunley* was moored about seven miles away at Breach Inlet near Battery Marshall. Each morning the crewmen had to walk this distance by way of the beach, sometimes exposed to fire from Dahlgren's gunners.

The daily routine involved the hike to Breach Inlet and then some two hours of diving drills in Conch Creek, which Alexander referred to as the "back bay" behind Sullivan's Island. Late each day Dixon and Alexander would lie on the beach and, using a compass, coordinate the bearings of the closest Federal vessel as she took her post for the evening.

The Confederates realized their best bet to destroy an enemy ship lay in attacking one of the more vulnerable wooden-hull vessels stationed outside the harbor bar. It would be a longer mission to and from the objective, but they were more likely to puncture one of these ships with the torpedo than Dahlgren's iron-plated monitors.

There was no shortage of available targets, but getting close enough to ram home the charge was quite another matter. Once the prey was marked, the submarine's boom and stinger were bolted on. The crew settled into their places and, when darkness descended, cranked out to find the glory grail that had claimed the lives of so many comrades.

A conspiracy of wind, tides, sea, and limited human endurance scuttled every planned attack. This winter also was particularly harsh for this region of the Deep South. After each failure the *Hunley* returned to its dock and the torpedo was removed for safekeeping, under guard, at Battery Marshall.

Muscles screaming and knuckles bleeding from the cranking, the crewmen trudged back to their camp to have breakfast and rest. This grueling routine was performed about four times a week in November and December 1863 and January 1864. The *Hunley* would ride out with ebb tide and head back when the current was flooding ashore. A cloudy night or evening when the moon was dark was also essential to keep from being spotted by the enemy.

On several occasions Dixon surfaced for air so close to Union picket boats that through the open hatches the Rebels could hear the Yankees talking or singing.

One aspect of their conditioning was to determine how long they could stay submerged without surfacing for air. Alexander described a test dive of stamina in the back bay. "It was . . . agreed upon that if anyone in the boat felt that he must come to the surface for air, and he gave the word 'up,' we would at once bring the boat to the surface."

Late one afternoon both Dixon and Alexander looked at their watches, noted the time, and dove. A number of soldiers crowded the banks to watch the exciting experiment. Would the deadly Porpoise again claim another bunch of fools?

Everyone on land held his breath as the minutes mounted. Everyone sweating and cranking several fathoms down was breathless.

The candle died in twenty-five minutes, but the crew continued to work the shaft in the blackness.

Alexander continued: "Each man had determined that he would not be the first to say 'up!' Not a word was said, except the occasional 'How is it,' between Dixon and myself, until it was as the voice of one man, the word 'up' came from all nine. We started the pumps. Dixon's worked all right, but I soon realized that my pump was not . . ." Alexander quickly guessed the nature of the problem. Even while others in the tight little chamber were beginning to panic, he uncapped the pump by feel alone, the interior being like the inside of a burial vault. He yanked out some seaweed that had clogged the valve, reset the mechanism, and desperately began to pump.

The sub already was down by the stern, Alexander's post. Gravity, fear, and borderline chaos reigned among the men.

"Thick darkness prevailed. All the hands had already endured what they thought was the utmost limit. Some of the crew almost lost control of themselves. It was a terrible few minutes . . ."

Alexander furiously worked the pump, and the boat ever so

slowly ascended from the deep. Lungs and senses long pushed past human limits, the men coughed, heaved, slumped like half-open jackknives, and vomited, taking in any microbe of oxygen that a comrade expelled through a fart, sweat, loose clothing, earlier blow-hard talk, or even shoes. Any and everything within the hull held a piece of trapped breath, and they all dueled for it.

Eternity brought them to the surface and the hatches were flung open.

"Fresh air! What an experience!"

From shore a lone awestruck Rebel private watched the wheezing crewmen crawl from the sub's manheads. The sun was gone to China and darkness prevailed. The other spectators had sulked away long ago, figuring that the accursed Porpoise was doomed again. Indeed, a message had been dispatched to Beauregard telling him of the supposed disaster. Exhausted Dixon and Alexander checked their watches and were tiredly ecstatic. They were submerged for two hours and thirty-five minutes, including the twenty-five or so minutes it had taken the candle to die when they first embarked.

The dive not only showed the great strength of this crew but its ability to survive a crisis, something two previous squads had been unable to do.

On February 5 the *Hunley* camp suffered a setback when Alexander was reassigned to special duty in Mobile, where he was to help construct a new type of breach-loading cannon. Alexander was crushed by the news and Dixon was little better.

"This was a terrible blow both to Dixon and myself, after we had gone through so much together," Alexander would later write.

From his Mount Pleasant quarters that same day, Dixon wrote to his friend John Cothran, who was also his captain in the 21st Alabama. Cothran had been trying to lure Dixon back to the regiment, which was in action near Mobile. Dixon felt his destiny compelled him to stay at his current post.

"Beyond a doubt I am fastened to Charleston and its approaches until I am able to blow up some of their Yankee ships . . ." he wrote. "I have been here over three months, have worked very hard, in fact I am working all the time. My headquarters are on Sullivan's Island, and a more uncomfortable place could not be found in the Confederacy. You spoke of being on the front and holding the post of honor. Now, John, make one trip to the besieged city of Charleston and your post of honor and all danger that threatens Mobile will fade away . . . for if you wish to see war every day and night, this is the place to see it.

"Charleston and its defenders will occupy the most conspicuous place in the history of the war, and it shall be as much glory as I shall wish if I can inscribe myself as one of its defenders."

Dixon's inscription came on the night of February 17, 1864. That day he took aim at a U.S. steam sloop-of-war anchored in the harbor's north channel about three miles off Breach Inlet near Rattlesnake Shoal. He had been watching her movements for several days as she stood off the bar waiting to intercept any wayward blockade runners trying to reach Charleston.

The USS *Housatonic* had been commissioned less than two years before and saw her first combat when she was assigned to the South Atlantic Blockading Squadron. The 1,240-ton, 207-foot steamship bristled with 13 heavy guns and had a crew of about 160. Under the command of Captain Charles W. Pickering, she had taken part in several bombardments of the Charleston forts. She was a formidable opponent for anything the Rebels had afloat.

None of this was any matter to Dixon as he peered at her through his telescope, watching the bluebellies moving about on her deck. He intended to take the *Hunley* out and send her to the bottom when night fell.

Dixon took his men for a dry run in Conch Creek that afternoon and made final preparations for the attack. At last it seemed the wind and tides would give them a chance for immortality.

Dixon had done all he could to steel his boys for this opportunity. Weeks of training had hardened them into veteran submariners. James A. Wicks, Arnold Becker, F. J. Collins, C. F. Simpkins, and Joseph Ridgeway—all were volunteer navy men from the *Indian Chief*. Corporal C. F. Carlson, a South Carolina artilleryman, had come aboard with Alexander's departure. Two other are known only to history as White and Miller.

An ivory full moon hovered over mist-veiled Charleston that cold Wednesday night. A slight breeze blew from the northwest, but the sea was calm.

Determined sweaty doom churned a fathom beneath the peaceful waves.

After dark Dixon and his men had cranked away from the Battery Marshall dock, and the *Hunley* headed out Breach Inlet toward the open sea. The *Housatonic* was in their bull's-eye, but it would take them about two hours to reach her. The Rebels knew they would have to surface a few times to replenish their air. This would be extremely risky because the night was so bright, but they had no choices.

Dixon stayed on the surface until the sub broke through Breach Inlet's wicked currents. He took one last sighting on the warship before submerging the *Hunley*. His aim and his compass would now have to guide them to the foe.

About 8:45 P.M. Acting Master John Crosby and one of six lookouts aboard the *Housatonic* spotted a log-like object floating about a hundred yards off the starboard beam. At first thinking it might be a dolphin, Crosby squinted at the form and saw that it rippled the water, moving toward his ship at three or four knots. Could it be a Secesh vessel? He wasn't about to take any chances. Crosby immediately called the crew to quarters, but the phantom was now too close to the *Housatonic* for any gun to be brought to bear on it.

With his hatches just above water so that he could see through his porthole to make the final thrust, Dixon urged his men to crank like mad, the starboard side of the ship now towering over them.

Yelling Union sailors frantically fired muskets and revolvers at the dark mass. Silently it kept coming as the bullets pinged off it or zipped into the water. Captain Pickering, who had been in his cabin reviewing some charts, came topside expecting the alarm to be the sighting of a blockade-runner. Grabbing his double-barrel shotgun, he also fired at the intruder. The sloop's cable was slipped and the engine reversed, drawing on twenty-five pounds of steam, but it was too late.

The *Hunley*'s ram harpooned the *Housatonic* like a fat tuna, bashing a hole in her side below the waterline. Righting themselves after the impact, Dixon's mariners reversed cranking to pull out of the wound so that the torpedo could be detonated by its tripline. Less than three minutes after Crosby's sighting, the *Housatonic* was lifted almost out of the sea by the tremendous underwater explosion.

The titanic blast tore off the ship's stern, sending up a column of water and spraying the eviscerated vessel with a deadly sleet of wood splinters, glass, and iron shards. Timbers cracked like dry pine saplings, and the ocean gushed into her innards.

Within minutes the *Housatonic* buckled to port and quickly settled by the stern on the ocean floor only five fathoms down. The water was so shallow that many of her seamen saved themselves by climbing into the rigging of her three masts, still above water, while others hastily escaped in two lifeboats. Five Yanks met their deaths in the attack.

Because the torpedo ignited below the surface, there was very little noise and no visible flames. Thus the rest of Dahlgren's fleet was unaware of the attack until one of the *Housatonic*'s lifeboats approached the warship USS *Canandaigua*. She was the first to reach the *Housatonic* about 9:35 P.M., pulling her shocked survivors aboard.

As the *Canandaigua* closed on the smoking hulk of the *Housatonic*, a seaman in the fore rigging of the rescue ship saw something odd—a blue light playing over the swells off the bow of the *Canandaigua* and on the starboard side of the *Housatonic*. The sailor made a mental note of it, but was too absorbed in the rescue effort to make much out of it at the time.

At Battery Marshall the Confederate commander Lieutenant Colonel O. M. Dantzler waited for some word from his sentries or lookouts about the *Hunley*. He was well aware of the sub's mission and knew that an orange eruption at sea would mean Dixon was successful in destroying or damaging a Yankee ship. Dantzler had arranged lantern signals with Dixon so Rebels ashore could use beacon lamps to direct the *Hunley* back to Breach Inlet. The night passed and Dantzler heard nothing.

Hazy conditions the next day prevented the Confederates from seeing that one of the enemy blockaders was missing. But Dantzler finally learned that the submarine had not yet returned to base, even though she apparently gave a signal to the fort the previous night.

On Saturday, February 20, the *Hunley* was still unaccounted for, but what the Rebels believed was her lethal handiwork was evident on the ocean. Three masts of a sunken vessel were seen sticking out of the water some three miles offshore while Union tugs and other ships hovered in the vicinity.

Dantzler fired off a message to headquarters. An enemy gunboat was down, probably the work of the missing submarine.

Confederate Charleston celebrated the victory—but what of the *Hunley*? For days the city waited for word of its naval heroes. Possibly they had been captured after sinking the Yank warship. Maybe she had been borne out to sea by the tides and was late making her way back to port. Rumor had it that due to strong winds and currents, Dixon was forced to find a haven at Georgetown, about forty miles up the coast.

Pickets and officers on patrol scanned the Atlantic's horizon for some sign of the submarine. There was nothing—no messages from the enemy fleet trumpeting the capture of the *Hunley*, no bodies washed ashore, and, ultimately, no triumphant return of Dixon and his tiny craft.

The February 29 Charleston *Daily Courier* paid tribute to the lost submariners: "The glorious success of our little torpedo boat under command of Lieutenant Dixon of Mobile has raised the hopes of our people, and the most sanguine expectations are now entertained of our being able to raise the siege in a way little dreamed of by the enemy." But the siege could not be broken even though Charleston held on for another year. Confederate forces evacuated in February 1865, and the city was occupied by Federal troops.

❦

The *Hunley* was the first submarine in the history of warfare to sink an enemy ship. Lost in the hour of her greatest glory, she and her crew remained at their posts in the ocean depths, forever the sentinels of Charleston.

II

Larry GOLDENBERG was dead before he hit the water. The neat circular bullet hole in his forehead was evidence of that. Even more revealing was the fact that the killer had done nothing to camouflage the crime.

Someone had pumped a round into his brain and fed him to the fish. The fate of his wife, Bella, and their boat, *Gretchen's Wanderlust*, was still a mystery when a Coast Guard UTB hauled Goldenberg's mud-crusted body out of a salt marsh south of Folly Island five days after they vanished. An islander checking his crab traps discovered the corpse.

Goldenberg had been one of the biggest wholesale outfitters of hunting and wilderness travel gear in the country. To the sea dwellers he was merely supper.

Despite the decomposition, suicide didn't look to be the cause of death. The victim's face was contorted in a death grimace as if he were still fighting not only for his life but for his soul.

The autopsy told even more. A pathologist found the bullet and sent it to the SLED crime lab in Columbia. Luckily there had not been an exit wound. Forensics identified the ball-bearing-shaped round as a 36-caliber lead projectile. Their tests and examinations by a university archaeologist showed that the bullet likely came from a Colt Navy revolver of the type carried by soldiers and sailors in the Civil War.

Ashby watched a sheriff's investigator discuss the slaying on the 6 P.M. local news. The Coast Guard was assisting in the case, but Charleston County was handling the brunt of the probe. The cop didn't elaborate publicly on the murder weapon other than to say it apparently was a "large-caliber handgun."

The sheriff's investigators believed the gun was a reproduction of the Colt. Several companies in the United States and in Europe, primarily Spain and Italy, manufactured working muskets and revolvers modeled after the nineteenth-century originals. Tens of thousands of them were owned by Civil War reenactors who spent their weekends dressed as Rebels or Yankees, recreating camp life and battles.

Ashby didn't buy this. To him Goldenberg's blood dripped from the hands of the ghouls who prowled Charleston's waters. And if she was not dead too, his wife likely had joined the pitiful ranks of the damned in the Castle Pinckney dungeon. It was the faces of these unfortunates and his powerlessness to help them that haunted him most. He planned to make at least one more trip to the tiny island and try to find some way into the subterranean chamber where they were held.

The ball cut out of Goldenberg's cerebellum was the latest of the deadly puzzle pieces being dangled before Ashby like a table scrap waved in front of a ravenous Rottweiler.

In the two weeks after his return from Savannah, Ashby talked to Alison and Margaret. Both wanted to see him, but for different reasons. Alison cared about his mental well-being. She wanted to come to Charleston to see him. Margaret's needs were more primal. She wanted to be screwed fast long and hard.

He put both of them off. There were more pressing matters than his sanity or even getting laid. And the fact that he didn't care about the latter made him doubt the former.

Because Snapper Gould's telephone message had not sounded urgent, Ashby had not tried him again after his efforts the night he got back from Savannah.

With the Goldenberg case going nowhere except into the "active but unsolved" file with the others in the last week of January, he finally returned the call. Gould was not exactly pleasant on the phone.

"I called you weeks ago and you're just now getting back to me? You frigging think I hit the speed dial to make small talk, Ashby?"

"Snapper, I'm sorry, I . . ."

"Or maybe you think I'm just some broken-down old fart-sniffer who is out here pissing into the wind cause he don't know no better, is that it? Boy, when I call you I mean business, you reading me?"

"Yeah, Snapper."

"Anyway, I got some information I ran across about the *Hunley* you might be interested in with that notion of yours about, well, you know." Gould's tirade had gusted out to sea, and the small craft advisory was lifted. "Why don't you come out to see us sometime soon and give it a look-see?"

Ashby agreed to drive out to Edisto on Saturday morning. Gould was glad to see him. Ashby told him about the Goldenberg investigation and the cause of death.

Gould whistled under his breath. "The Confederacy strikes again, eh?"

"Any insane person would think so. My straight jacket's tailor made you know." Ashby was joking, but he wasn't sure whether there might be a great measure of truth in the statement. Gould sensed his dejection.

"Ah come on, boy, it ain't all that bad. Hell, we're not about to hit the Normandy beaches in the morning or lead Pickett's Charge. And you're not Custer's bugler. Now *those* guys had it bad."

They went into Gould's study, a manly landfill of navigational charts, Coast Guard manuals, and books on maritime and military history forming a debris field around Snapper's battered mahogany desk.

"So what time did the bomb go off in here?" Ashby said, surveying the room.

"Think this is bad? You should see my workshop out back. The lovely Rita got buried in all that junk, and I didn't see her for two weeks!"

"So where is the lovely Rita today?"

"I knew you were coming here to sniff around her tail, so I sent her to the store to pick up a few things. She'll be back in a while."

Ashby's eyes settled on a jagged piece of dirty-white wood lying on Gould's desk. The mast section was about a yard long and a foot in diameter.

"That's my little souvenir from the *Sea Lynx*. Canadian pine. I keep it as a reminder of all those who died on her." He paused for a moment. "And of my failure to find out what happened to them."

"No self-pity now, Snapper. I'm dealing with enough of that myself these days. You know as well as I do that ships of all kinds and from every country in the world can be lost at sea without leaving the least bit of a clue. It's happened for centuries and it always will. The Coast Guard has thousands of unsolved disappearances."

"Sure they do, boy." Gould's tone was excessively sharp. "But I only got this one and it eats at me every day. Anyway, here's what I wanted to show you."

Gould plowed into a mountain range of papers, magazines, and bulging folders on the desk and pulled out a thick book, its yellowing pages hinting at its age.

"*Official Records of the Union and Confederate Navies in the War of the Rebellion*," Ashby read the title aloud.

"This is only one of about 130 volumes," Gould said. "About twenty years after the war the U.S. government started putting together this collection. It's got battle reports, daily correspondence, quartermaster records, telegraph dispatches—heck if a Yankee took a leak off the side of a gunboat, it's probably in the OR, the *Official Records*. Government Printing Office took over forty years to compile and publish all this stuff. The Marine who sold me the crappy rowboat has the whole collection, and I found this for you. He let me borrow it so don't mess it up or he'll use me for chum. Check the bookmark."

"Snapper, only you would use a crab claw for a bookmark."

"I know, I know, just read what's there. I put a pencil mark beside it."

Ashby found Gould's notation and read:

Headquarters Battery Marshall
Sullivan's Island, February 19, 1864

Lieutenant: I have the honor to report that the torpedo boat stationed at this post went out on the night of the 17th instant and has not yet returned. The signals agreed upon to be given in case the boat wished a light to be exposed at this post as a guide for its return were observed and answered . . .

The report was written from a Lieutenant Colonel O. M. Dantzler, the commander of Battery Marshall, to another officer. It was forwarded the same day to Beauregard's headquarters.

"So this Dantzler claims he, or some of his soldiers at least, were in contact with the *Hunley* after her attack on the *Housatonic*, am I reading this right?"

"You are. I have other documentation that Dixon, the sub's skipper, would show a blue lantern from the *Hunley* when he was ready to return from the mission. Dantzler was then to burn a white light near the mouth of Breach Inlet to guide the *Hunley* back to her nest. The Confederates in the forts around Charleston had lamps with blue- and red-tinted lenses so that they could communicate. Obviously the white light came from a lantern with clear glass. Called these things calcium lights."

"Snapper, most of the stuff I've seen says the sub rammed the ship and probably went down with her. I even read something about divers after the war finding her with skeletons inside."

"Yeah, I read that stuff too and it's garbage. A lot of folks thought the *Hunley* went down so close to the *Housatonic* that when the Yankees cleared the wreckage they scooped up the sub as well without even knowing it. Army engineers about eighty years ago blew up what was left of the Yank ship to clear the harbor entrance, and they didn't find the sub.

"Hell, even old P. T. Barnum the circus king offered a reward of $100,000 to anyone who could raise the *Hunley*. Wanted it for his show. Plenty of takers but no finders."

"So what about Dantzler? Did he record anything else about the *Hunley*?"

"Sorry, Ashby, but this was a soldier who didn't have a hell of a lot of time to write—or live—for that matter."

"What do you mean?"

"He was with a South Carolina regiment, the 20th, I believe, and was transferred to Virginia a few months after the *Hunley* disappeared. Got himself killed in June 1864 in the fighting around Petersburg."

❧

"What are they, Mommy?"

"I'm not sure, honey. Let's ask your father, okay?"

"Looks like a pair of them old time beer kegs to me. Think I can get a drink out of it?" the dad laughed.

From the guardrail on the flight deck of the *Yorktown*, a knot of tourists leaned over the water to see two barrel-like objects bobbing in the pea-green water near the aircraft carrier's bow. Behind them a Patriots Point guide began his introduction to a class of seventh graders and their teachers on a field trip.

"The USS *Yorktown* is the fourth United States navy ship to bear the name. Her sailors called her the 'Fighting Lady' because of her extensive combat service in World War II and the Vietnam War. Commissioned in 1943, she has been with us here in Charleston since 1975."

A charter fishing boat heading seaward out of the Cooper River passed about fifty yards from the *Yorktown*, the fishermen waving to the people watching them from the railing. But the charter's faint wake generated a low swell that shoved one of the barrels against the side of the carrier.

A cannon shot of noise cracked the calm morning, and an enormous gusher of water spat up the bow flank. Yells and screams of the schoolchildren and tourists rent the air as the explosion's sound waves inundated Charleston and thundered over the outlying islands. Everyone on the flattop literally hit the deck, many of the kids cupping their ears, and visitors within the carrier's interior were jarred off their feet. One man dropped to the tarmac in the exact spot where Charles Hoyle was murdered, faded crimson still blotching the surface.

Police, fire, and emergency medical squads were immediately sent to the ship and evacuated everyone as quickly as possible. Three people below decks had broken arms or legs and had to be taken to hospitals. Others appeared to be in shock. The barrel had ignited, and its sister was still in the river virtually brushing the carrier. Law enforcement cordoned off all roads leading to the *Yorktown*. On the water, patrol boats from the Charleston Naval Base descended on the scene, and Cliff Okai was aloft in his Dolphin, everyone tense and ready for anything. Okai was in contact with the Navy craft and a sheriff's captain who was coordinating the operation on the ground.

A black smudge scar slivered up the bow of the *Yorktown* from the detonation of the strange keg, witnesses were describing. The carrier did not look to be seriously damaged, but the prime dilemma was that the other barrel was rocking in the water about five yards from the point of the first blast.

Coast Guard Charleston had also scrambled two UTB's, and these were on scene in less than twenty minutes, assisting the Navy in sealing off all harbor traffic along the Cooper River channel. In minutes a Navy demolitions team in a gray launch cautiously approached the floating object. An explosives expert went over the side and soon could be seen examining the barrel. Another diver went in.

The frogmen worked on the device for about half an hour before one waved his arms above the slight swells, indicating all clear. A Navy tender then moved in, and crewmen used a small crane to carefully hoist the barrel aboard and lower it into a yellow bombproof cylinder.

Ashby watched the event with binoculars from the foredeck of one of the utility boats stationed about a quarter mile from the *Yorktown*. He had earlier been in radio contact with the captain of a German tanker heading into Charleston. Now the tanker was at a dead stop about two miles out of the harbor, waiting for word that the emergency was over. Even as he saw the barrel slip softly into the cylinder, Ashby had an ominous feeling that the emergency was just beginning.

The main shipping channel was reopened just after noon, and Starnes and Ashby headed to the Naval Base to get a closer look at the bomb.

A gate sentry gave them directions to the command center of the Explosive Ordnance Disposal Mobile Unit shore detachment that had handled the incident.

Ten minutes later they were introduced to Navy Lieutenant Vincent Patterson, the squad leader who had been the first man in the water. Patterson filled out his uniform with the build of a fullback. Second generation Navy, he had seen action in Panama and in Desert Storm.

"Gentlemen, let me show you what we got. It is indeed a piece of work."

Patterson ushered them into what appeared to be a classroom with about fifty folding metal chairs set up in rows facing a chalkboard and several maps posted on the walls. On a rectangular table at the front of the room was the explosive device, a wooden barrel with tin straps and conical metal attachments on each end.

"Don't worry. This thing was filled with about a hundred pounds of crude grade black powder, but we siphoned all that out. You could kick it or run over it with a car right now and nothing would happen. Nothing in it left to explode. It was her sister that gave everybody the big scare. Draining the powder out of this one was the only way we could diffuse her. Very very tricky operation."

"So what do you make of all this, lieutenant?" Starnes asked.

"Captain, what we got is a very primitive but, as you saw today, very effective form of floating sea mine. I just finished up with the guys from NCIS, I mean, the Naval Criminal Investigative Service. They had two agents out here and took a sample of the gunpowder and wood fragments we found from the other device. I guess they'll be sending them to Washington to have it analyzed. Hey, it's out of my hands after we neutralize these things. Someone dropped her and her twin into the harbor around the *Yorktown*. It's a classic reproduction, a real piece of fine work."

Patterson flipped open a book and leafed through the pages. Ashby could see the title in gold lettering, *Confederate Torpedoes and Mines in the Late War*.

"This is it." Patterson laid the book on the table, and Ashby and Starnes saw a line drawing almost exactly like the barrel bomb beside it.

"The baby we have here with us is a carbon copy of this Civil War era model," Patterson said, pointing to the rendition. "Now it is not uncommon for us to have to deal with ordnance from that period. Thousands of artillery rounds of many calibers were fired by both sides in the fighting around Charleston, some exploding, others landing and waiting to explode later, years and years later in many instances. These shells are on the ocean bottom or in some farmer's field or in some new housing development. Sooner or later somebody runs across them by accident or chance. Same way with any of the thousands of Civil War battlefields."

As Patterson talked Ashby remembered the story of a Maryland farmer plowing his cornfield near Sharpsburg, where the battle of Antietam had been fought a decade earlier. His plow hit something hard and the farmer dug up an old musket. Figuring he could use the iron of the gun barrel to reshoe his mules, he tried to melt it down and reshape it using his forge and anvil.

The heat triggered the gunpowder and musket ball still in the barrel. The man's wife found him spread-eagled on the floor of his barn, the bullet having split his face like an overripe melon.

"Lieutenant Patterson, you are talking about land artillery, obviously," Starnes interrupted his thoughts.

"This device was at sea. Are you saying that it is Civil War vintage? There is no way that wood and metal of this type could have survived the elements for over a century. You know that as well as I do."

"Captain, I also can't disregard the facts of what I am having to deal with and with an implement that could have blown me to atoms with one wrong move. No matter if it was constructed a century ago or Tuesday, this instrument was designed for maximum damage. Obviously it has to be a reproduction and it is a dandy.

"Occasionally a shrimp boat or some other fishing vessel with her nets dredging along the bottom will come up with an unexploded shell—Parrott, Blakely, Enfield—army or navy, Union or Confederate ordnance. We always inform the Coast Guard as I am sure you are aware."

Starnes nodded.

"These pieces are always potentially of a highly volatile nature. Some of the other projectiles are from the time of the world wars. All are unstable, carrying a payload of gunpowder that could blow up anything from a warship to a Chrysler. Gunpowder is just like a mother-in-law. The older they get, the crankier they are and more likely to go off on you."

"But why would anyone drop two of these things at the *Yorktown?*" Starnes asked. "Even if this was some terrorist deal, she's an out-of-service tourist attraction now. You guys certainly are more of a military target. And why would someone try to recreate an old sea mine like this when the technology and capacity for a lot more serious damage has evolved so much?"

"You're asking the wrong man, captain. I get paid to disarm these things and try to go home to dinner every night with all my parts intact. I do have this, though." Patterson pulled a few sheets of paper from a folder he was carrying.

"This is what we know about this bomb so far. I got some faxed information from our intelligence guys about half an hour ago. Seems this is a to-scale replica of a type of sea mine used by the Confederate armed forces in the war. The Southerners collected all these beer barrels, filled them with powder, caulked and sealed them with pitch, and put them out to blow up Yankee ships. A lot of them were moored to river or harbor bottoms with ropes and weights. Both sides called these things floating torpedoes."

Patterson pointed to what looked to be five iron nipples protruding from one side of the barrel on the table.

"These friction fuses ignited them. A boat moves over this mine, her hull depresses one of these fuses, and it's time for blast-off. Damned primitive but efficient, the best the Confederacy had. During the war the U.S. Navy found a lot of these things around Charleston. And now I got one myself." Patterson laughed.

"Let's see what else we got here. Uh, a Confederate general, Gabriel James Rains, designed this weapon and some others like it. West Point class of 1827. He always liked explosives and was the inventor of the antipersonnel land mine. That's damned interesting. We could have used him in Kuwait. Says here he developed land and sea mines in Charleston, Mobile, and Richmond. Headed the Rebel Torpedo Bureau late in the war."

Starnes and Ashby left the naval base, both quietly dealing with their thoughts. Ashby's mind twirled with Castle Pinckney, the frozen button, the slaughter of Hal Frye and the stripper. Foremost, he concentrated on the words of Ella Solomon about the devils from Revelations that killed Iceman Turner, and the vagrant who foretold the attack on the *Yorktown* after encountering the murdering phantoms, possibly the same ones who kidnapped him.

"Eric, you think that sea mine is the genuine article, don't you?" Starnes broke the quiet. "Planted by your buddies on the *Hunley*. They knocked off Goldenberg too, is that right?"

"You got a better explanation, captain? We got this homeless guy who tells us about the threat to the *Yorktown* well in advance. We got this dead guy from Maine with a Civil War bullet in the brain. The keg mine is Civil War. I was shanghaied by whatever these things are—ghosts, goblins with a drawl, or whatever. Or maybe we got a serial killer or group of hard-shell militants out there who use Civil War era weapons to commit their crimes. You buy that one, Rod?"

Starnes drove without a reply.

"Explain it all to me, Rod, if you got a better theory. All I know is that a lot of people, a lot of school kids included, could have died today if the *Yorktown* had been blown to hell. I couldn't deal with that on my conscience if I had some prior knowledge that could have stopped it, regardless how insane the information sounds to me or anyone else."

"You're right, Eric. To tell you the truth, a lot of the stuff you have been saying all along is starting to piece together for me, if that makes any sense. Maybe you are on to something about that serial slayer using weapons from the war, but there is no pattern to any of the crimes that we know of."

Ashby whispered his reply.

"The *Hunley.*"

The unexplained explosion that jarred the *Yorktown* drew a ten-second mention on the national news telecasts and was the lead story for all of Charleston's local stations and newspapers. The Navy did not publicly display the sister bomb or even mention that two devices were involved. News crews had gotten some video of the intact mine being hoisted from the harbor, but it had been cocooned in a blast-proof sleeve in the transfer to the vessel. There was really nothing to see in the fuzzy, long-distance tape.

The Navy's news release merely referred to the other weapon as an "unidentified floating object taken aboard merely as a precaution." Why panic the public with spring about to blossom in Charleston? At least not in the initial phase of the investigation. NCIS agents nationwide tried in vain to locate Bobby Windrow, the hobo who first got wind of the plan to blast the *Yorktown.*

Focused more on the blast itself and the survival stories of the children and others on the *Yorktown*, the city's media was led away from the other mine. In a few days it was dismissed totally, a Navy spokesman saying that the other object pulled from the water proved to be an oil tank probably dropped from a long-gone freighter.

Ashby by now believed he was battling foes from another epoch. Life expectancies, stress tests, or high blood sugar did not bind them to their ages.

Indeed, Charleston was an otherworldly mecca for the lost. So much history unfurled there that the past and present twined in a kudzu ecstasy.

The children dancing in a circle were unmindful of a Volvo and a metro bus that plowed through them in the middle of Meeting Street. An innocent who died in one of the yellow fever scourges lightly kissed her little brother on the forehead; he in turn embraced a black slave child killed by a copperhead's strike in a cotton field.

Tourists strolling White Point Gardens unknowingly brushed the buckled shoes of pirates dangling from the gallows there, sending the bodies into a slow, hideous pirouette.

In Marion Square, Continental regulars grabbed snatches of sleep in their trenches, awaiting another British attack from north of the city while picnickers spread their blankets for a peaceful afternoon. On Hayne Street partiers bar-hopped among the watering holes, oblivious to the cries from the slave auction going on a few feet from them.

"What is my bid for this sturdy young buck? He is another of the fine lot just arrived from Captain Sterner's good ship the *Alexia*."

Shoppers ambled through art galleries and boutiques on Bay Street, not seeing the long column of ragamuffin Rebel infantry parting on the avenue to let pass a battery of Confederate artillery, the cannoneers yelling and lashing at the sweaty horses.

From the dungeon of the Old Exchange at the intersection of Broad and Bay, prisoners begged for water, while a senior citizens group from Nebraska followed a guide through the catacombs.

The late-night tolling of the St. Michael's bells was a clarion for those in the cemeteries to enjoy their own promenade. Among the tombstones they conversed and cavorted, talking of old times and relations while the children scuttled about, playing hide-and-seek in the crypts.

They spoke of the fires, hurricanes, and floods. They reminisced about the old country, states of affairs, presidents, czars, and kings. They discussed the many wars and opined about the military Caesars of their times.

One guy always went off on a rambling tangent about his cavalry captain in the Mexican War. Everyone tried to avoid him.

Another believed Warren G. Harding was on the up and up. This one always found a good argument.

"Hear about the *General Slocum?* Awful fire in New York Harbor, I think it was."

"Oh, my family didn't have power for about two weeks after Hugo."

"So the potatoes didn't sprout and the likes of everyone from Kinsale's Head to Dublin town was in a wee pile a dung."

Yanks and Rebs turned out as well. Thousands who fought and died among the palmettos and sand dunes of Charleston's islands and on the waters now gathered to talk of the old days when they walked and killed among the living.

The five bluejackets who died on the *Housatonic* were there, and they always wondered about the fates of the undersea Johnny Rebs who sent them to their deaths. No one in tattered gray had any answers for them.

The *Hunley* was still missing.

12

In THE FIRST WEEK of February Ashby decided to take a look at the site of Battery Marshall and Breach Inlet, where the submarine embarked on its last mission.

The *Yorktown*'s bow had been repainted to cover her latest battle scar, and tourists once again swarmed her decks. Despite the Navy's array of resources, the bombing probe could not have been more stagnant.

Equally as decomposing were the Hoyle case, the other Mount Pleasant murders, and the Coast Guard's dead/missing boater files. The investigations had been coldcocked at every turn.

Ashby had expected Grizzly Vandencomp and his flunky Kapowski to have been breathing down Starnes's throat until something was resolved, but the commander was on extended assignment in Washington, serving as an advisor to a congressional committee studying drug intervention strategies and tactics on the open seas. He'd taken Kapowski with him, and Starnes wondered aloud to his friends about the convenience of Grizzly's absence when Station Charleston was under such duress.

"He doesn't want to take a fall. Too close to retirement," Rod had said. No one disagreed with him.

Ashby drove through Mount Pleasant and veered onto South Carolina 703, the lone two-lane route leading across the creeks and salt marshes to Sullivan's Island. The girded Ben Sawyer Memorial Bridge arched the Intracoastal Waterway, and could be rotated sideways so that masted vessels or other larger craft could pass it. Anyone who drove 703 regularly was used to the delays.

Hurricane Hugo had spun the Ben Sawyer like a beanie propeller.

On the island Ashby made a left at the only stop light and turned onto Jasper Boulevard. The main drag bisected the island north to south. Sullivan's was a serene beach community of about two thousand people. Even in the summers it rarely stirred from its hammock of tranquility.

The houses and cottages along Jasper ran the gamut of 1950's era bungalows to sumptuous three-story seafront villas, often side by side. There was no business district other than a couple of convenience stores, a little seafood café, and two seedy-looking taverns, one of which was the Gold Bug. Ashby passed that bar and remembered meeting Hal Frye for the first time—and seeing Gwen Lagrange in all her fleshy wonder. So much had happened since then.

There was nothing to note where Battery Marshall once stood other than a street named Marshall Boulevard on the north end of Sullivan's. Private homes now occupied the ground, a developer's bulldozers long ago razing any remnants of the earthen fort to sell this prime real estate.

An ancient concrete bridge linked Sullivan's with the Isle of Palms, formerly called Long Island, spanning Breach Inlet. Near the spot where the *Hunley* likely was moored, a small paved parking lot offered a beautiful vista of the glistening Atlantic.

"Swimming Prohibited—Dangerous Currents and Undertow," warned a sign posted in the shallows. A sliver of white-sand beach adorned both sides of the inlet, each flanked by gray rock jetties of riprap the Army Corps of Engineers had positioned to prevent shore erosion.

Ashby looked out over the ocean, watching hundreds of white caps flashing at the same moment on the olive sea. It was a sunny day and warm for the most part, but sporadic wind gusts reminded him that winter still presided. Ashby thought of George Dixon taking compass locations and targeting Federal ships, probably very near where he was standing.

The Carolina weather of February likely had tantalized Dixon even though the winter of 1863–1864 was harsher than usual. There had to be an occasional balmy afternoon like this when Dixon honed in on one of Dahlgren's blockaders and readied the *Hunley* to attack. But the offshore swells would have been too great, threatening to swamp the sub, the tides didn't cooperate, and the wearied crew would have to crank back to base—until they got their final chance.

Ashby had read several accounts about the *Hunley* written by William Alexander some forty years after the war. He also turned up some of Beauregard's correspondence and memoirs giving other input about the submarine. He obtained much of this information the previous weekend during a trip to the state archives in Columbia. Snapper Gould had pointed him in the right direction, and he dug through rows of musty old books and stacks of hundreds of letters and documents to find what he wanted.

Alexander's reminiscences and the fact that he survived to write of his incredible experiences particularly fascinated Ashby. He also marveled at the bravery, dedication, toughness, and endurance of the submariners, especially Dixon's men, who had volunteered after two previous crews died in the same contraption. *Two* previous crews—he knew that Hunley, Parks, and the six others drowned in the second fatal dive were buried at Magnolia Cemetery along the Cooper River. Ashby had visited Hunley's grave and the "*Hunley* Circle," where his comrades lay.

He went to the cemetery to try to find any hint of a clue to the mysteries. It had been a bleak day with rain threatening at any time. A grounds-keeper had directed him to the Hunley site. Hunley, Parks, and the others—Brockbank, Patterson, McHugh, Beard, Marshall, and Sprague—rested together in a well-kept plot surrounded by a marble border. Azalea bushes, a dogwood, and a large palmetto tree adorned the gravesites, along with a granite monument briefly detailing the October 1863 disaster. Ashby had left the cemetery with nothing more to go on.

But what of the first five, who had gone down due to Lieutenant Payne's blunder? Their bodies had been recovered, but he had found no record of where these men were interred. They were not at Magnolia. Nothing in the manuscripts he had sifted through alluded to their resting places.

"I know where those lads are, Eric."

To Ashby's luck, Snapper Gould made one of his frequent visits to the Coast Guard station two days later. They sat on a bench outside the Rice Mill, and Ashby asked if he knew anything about the Payne crew.

"You want me to show you where they are? Let's take a ride." Gould's clunker of a pickup truck wheezed out Lockwood Drive, leaving drivers behind him in a stinking cloud of blue 30-weight oil smoke.

"Damn, Snapper, can't you afford anything better than this jalopy? Smells like seagull crap in here."

"Easy, boy. This old Nissan may not look like much to you, but when you're jouncing over Edisto Island and all those moon craters we call potholes, you'd rather be in here with me than in some rich fat jerk's limousine. Guarantee you that. We ain't heading to the Oscars, son."

They traveled in heavy traffic before Gould started again.

"If you're in to ghost ships, why couldn't these marauders of yours be from old Blackbeard's bunch?"

Gould relished sharing his knowledge of history with others whether they wanted the experience or not, and settled into the tale.

"I've heard of him, Snapper."

"Most notorious pirate of the buccaneer age. Just a devil afloat, an Englishman named Edward Teach. Had this long black beard, and when he went into battle he would braid

lighted candles in it. His enemies musta thought they were looking at old Lucifer himself."

Gould braked to avoid an Escort that dodged into his lane.
After a few choice words shouted to the driver, he returned to
his story.

"That son of a . . . As I was saying, Blackbeard sailed these
waters. Had a base up at Ocracoke Inlet in North Carolina."

"Snapper, why are you telling me this stuff?" Ashby interrupted.
"It's interesting, but what does it have to do with—anything?"

"Will you just let me finish?"

"Sure. Just stop tailgating, okay?"

"Old Blackbeard blockaded Charleston in 1718, I believe it
was. Flat sails up in his ship the *Queen Anne's Revenge* and just
says nobody gets in or out of the harbor. South Carolina was
still a British colony then, but there wasn't a Royal Navy warship
around to do anything about it. So Blackbeard takes a bunch of
civilian hostages from other ships and threatens to hang them if
Charleston don't give him medical supplies, especially any relief
for syphilis. Him and his crew had been screwing all these native
gals and whores from the Caribbean to the Carolinas and got
themselves a first-class epidemic of VD. Guess this wasn't no
Kathie Lee Gifford cruise! Ain't we got fun!"

Gould saw that Ashby was not laughing with him.

"Anyway, the huffy citizens of Charleston send out chests of
potions and remedies to Blackbeard, and he releases his prisoners, but not before relieving them of their money, jewelry, and
other valuables."

"So, Snapper, do you have some theory that Blackbeard or
the *Queen Anne's Revenge* or both sank the *Sea Lynx*?"

"Not at all, my friend. You're the intermediary with the spirit
world here. No 'Seances Are Us' for me. Probably a backed-up
line, someone tossing a cancer stick too near a fuel tank, or major engine malfunction killed the *Sea Lynx*. Manifest didn't list
any inflammatory cargo."

"So you think I'm crazy for hounding this theory about the
Hunley still being out there?"

Gould wheeled off Spring Street onto Hagood Avenue and

immediately stopped in the middle of the road. His tone was sharp and direct as he spoke.

"Ashby, I spent a lot of years with the Coast Guard here, and I saw a lot of things in that time. I don't pretend to know anything about the Atlantic other than we had a pretty good record of rescuing people when I had the helm. That ocean out there holds a big ol' trove of secrets. If we could just roll it back like a green layer of shag pile carpet for even just one day, we'd find shipwrecks and other stuff that would clear up questions for a lot of centuries probably.

"You haven't answered my question, Snapper."

"What I am trying to say is that you'd likely find your *Hunley* buried in mud a couple of miles out, maybe closer, who's to say? Her hull would be caked with coral and other sea life. Dig her out, pop open her hatches, and there would be some evidence of her crew, personal items, a revolver, belt buckles, maybe some bones, who knows?"

Gould paused for a moment, the truck's motor sputtering.

"There are no ghosts, Ashby. The *Hunley*'s out there, somewhere on the bottom. She's been there for 130 years or so and hasn't moved. Iceman Turner and the *Sea Lynx* are just coincidental. I guarantee it."

Ashby was silent. There was nothing he could do to convince anyone about what he had experienced unless they had lived through the same bad dream. He believed a lot of people who entered the nightmare never emerged.

"Didn't mean to bore you there, Eric. If I didn't think you were a good kid and worth my time, I wouldn't be here right now, you know that.

"You're not crazy, Eric. You just have to find a better grip on reality. Right now, however, I'm gonna show you where your sailors are buried."

Gould punched the gas and the truck shuddered ahead.

Hagood Avenue was the main street leading to The Citadel, South Carolina's tradition-steeped military college. Sky-blue paw prints painted on the pavement showed they were in the territory of the Citadel's Bulldogs, the nickname for its sports teams.

The faint red brick walls of Johnson Hagood Stadium quickly appeared on their right. The brown turf of the football field could be seen through a wire gate. The avenue and the arena were named for a Confederate general and Citadel graduate.

"Bulldogs had a back, Stump Mitchell, who was just a hell of a runner. Played for the Cardinals in the pros." Gould pulled into the stadium parking lot and stopped, the brakes squealing.

"Here we are, Ashby."

"Here we are what? I thought you were taking me to the cemetery where the five crewmen are buried."

"We're there, friend. They built this stadium right after World War II, 1947 I think. Only thing was they forgot that the Rebs had used this area as a burial ground for some of their sailors and marines in the war about eighty years earlier. "Your boys are probably right around the fifty-yard line. I know a couple of season ticket holders who would love to have their seats!" Gould laughed, slapping the steering wheel with his palms.

"Say, you wanna go to a Citadel game with me this year? The lovely Rita hates football. I think we're gonna make a run for the conference title. Gotta beat Georgia Southern though."

Ashby didn't question or doubt Gould's knowledge that the five men rested beneath the stadium. He trusted Snapper; hell, he was one of the few who didn't actually call him a lunatic to his face. So here he stood with his nose pressed against another stone wall, waiting for the bad guys to make the next move and helpless to prevent it.

The weekly investigations update that Starnes had implemented was always the same. No new leads. A special agent from the Naval Criminal Investigative Service had been coming to these conferences since the *Yorktown* bombing. He had no more to offer than the eight frustrated Coast Guardsmen around the table.

The meetings centered on unraveling the Wagner case, the Hoyle slaying, and the subsequent attack on the *Yorktown*, since they seemed to be related to the shooting of Larry Goldenberg and the fate of his wife and their vessel. Starnes had assigned teams to work each of these cases, but he and Ashby worked individually. Starnes also stayed in touch with the Mount Pleasant police about the trailer murders, but Jeremy Lord was at a standstill as well. Starnes also checked regularly on the Peter Mueller case. The news was no better there.

Ashby never brought up his *Hunley* theory in these conferences although Starnes and Mike Green certainly knew where he stood. Cliff Okai meanwhile had been transferred to an air station in Galveston. He had family in the region and wanted to be closer to them.

The media clamor about a possible serial killer quickly fizzled, and by early February the victims, the missing yachts, and sailboats were all but forgotten, at least in the public eye. Charleston and the rest of the world moved on although the *Yorktown* incident sporadically remained in the news for several weeks. The Navy carefully avoided using the word "attack" in all references to the carrier explosion even though it was being investigated as such.

One drizzly afternoon Ashby stopped by Rod Starnes's office to drop off some monthly reports. Starnes was just hanging up the phone.

"Since my public relations guy hasn't been much of any help, I've decided to take matters into my own hands." Starnes looked serious.

"What have I done now, Rod?" A kicked dog could not have looked any more forlorn than the Guardsman standing before Starnes.

"Ashby, it's what you haven't done. Your assignment early on was to fix me up with Melanie Potemkin, and you have failed miserably. Don't you agree?"

"Well, we've been kind of busy with dead people and sea mines and missing boats for me to give your love life a kick in the pants."

"Then you admit that you have bungled this assignment. Correct, lieutenant?"

"Captain, may I go now? I have work to do."

"Ease up, Ashby. Since you were getting me nowhere with

this babe, I took the initiative to send her a dozen red roses for Valentine's Day next week."

"So how do you know that she doesn't have a boyfriend who is going to come kick your butt when the florist shows up with flowers for his lady?"

"Oh, Ashby, you think that bothers me? Bring the loser on. He's got no idea who he's dealing with here. And besides, I called Leo, the camera guy who usually goes on stories with her. He says she is fair game."

"Go for it, hoss."

The afternoon was drippy and cold as Ashby left the Rice Mill and walked across the base compound, as always deep in thought about the cases. Fog over the Ashley curtained the cutters at their moorings, but some Guardsmen could be seen going about their tasks on the docks and in the repair bay.

So Rod had time to worry about ordering roses for Valentine's Day. Ashby at first was irritated that his captain wasn't as focused as he was on putting the puzzle together—and stopping the killers from adding more pieces. His ire dulled somewhat when he realized that the investigations were as chilled as Goldenberg's cadaver. Why shouldn't Rod spend some time trying to woo a sweetheart? Everything else was whirling blindly down a dead-end street.

Hunkered in his windbreaker, Ashby did not see a figure in a black raincoat and carrying an umbrella step from the shelter of a tree and approach him from behind. Hearing the splash of footsteps on the sidewalk he turned.

"Alison."

"So you thought you'd ditch me before you slept with me, Eric? Now that's a novel concept. The guys' book of slimy dating etiquette says you got it backwards. Screw 'em then lose 'em."

The water coursing down her cheeks was not from the rain. They stood facing each other, gusts of cold wind clutching at her open umbrella.

"Alison, I've been under an awful strain here. I'm sorry that I haven't called."

"Don't hand me excuses, Eric. I came to make sure you are okay, at least for the time being. I talked to Rod and told him I was coming. I told him not to tell you."

"He didn't, the bastard."

"Rod cares a great deal about you, Eric. I've been calling him to keep tabs on you since you haven't extended me the same courtesy. It's been kind of like checking my shares on the lunatic stock market—Ashby up or down a quarter of an insanity point."

"So you drove all the way from Savannah to insult me?"

"Don't flatter yourself. I'm here for a couple of days consulting with law librarians from two firms. My attorneys need some background on a client who is originally from Charleston County.

Ashby looked up and caught sight of Starnes watching them from his office window. Rod ducked away.

"So do you want to grab a cup of coffee or something?"

"I can't. I've got a meeting in half an hour somewhere on Beaufain Street."

"Are you staying in Charleston overnight? Maybe we could have dinner."

"Sorry, Eric, I've got a working dinner session with another law clerk. Could be several hours. By then I'll be pooped."

"I see. I just wish I had more time to make this up to you, Alison. You helped me through a rough time. I just wish things weren't so screwy."

"Me too. I read about the *Yorktown*. Pretty heavy stuff. Rod tells me y'all don't really have jack to work with in any of these cases."

"He's pretty much on the mark about that."

"Eric, I hope you find what you're looking for before it kills you. I know you won't call me so I'll check in with Rod every once in a while."

"Too many innocent people have died already, or worse, for me to stop now. You know me well enough to understand that, Alison." Ashby tried to appear stern, but he clearly cared for her and she saw through his chameleon act.

"Hope you aren't a poker player, Eric. You'd be living in a refrigerator carton under a bridge if you were."

The distant baritone of a freighter's foghorn moaned through the mistiness, a fitting dirge for what Ashby believed was the end of his relationship with Alison. She came to him and kissed him delicately on the cheek.

"Mona and Chico say hi. Be seeing you, Ashby."

With a forlorn smile Alison walked away. He watched her, knowing that the best thing to ever happen to him was sliding through his fingers. He tried to call to her, but there were no words. Alison would be a lucky catch for any man. Would she wait for him? Who knew?

What he did know was that something else was waiting for him, a dynamism that resisted its own demise to serve death and timeless anguish on others, perhaps thousands of others.

Tuesday was Valentine's Day and Ashby called his mother, the only sweetheart he had. He tried Alison, but got no answer and didn't leave a message. Margaret had stopped phoning him weeks ago after he never bothered to return her calls.

It had been almost a year since he had been home, taking a few days before his transfer from Wilmington to Charleston. He talked to his parents every other week and always put on the positive spin—everything was still going great, he loved Charleston and his assignment. Of course they had heard about the *Yorktown* and were concerned. But he had reassured his father that night that all was well. The Navy or the Feds would catch the crackpot responsible.

His parents were now planning an April trip to Charleston to see him and the treasures of a Deep South spring. He tried to sound excited when his mother told him, but his mind instantly began devising ways to shield them from the madness that inundated him.

Ashby hung up, lay back on his bed, and closed his eyes. As always his sleep time was a restless adventure.

Valentine's Day fell on a Sunday in 1864. From the folder of hand-scribbled notes and photocopied documents he had retained from the archives and from Snapper Gould's books,

Ashby knew of George Dixon's heartthrob, Queenie Bennett. Surely Dixon had taken time to pen some romantic missive to his lover in Alabama, unaware that he would be lost in combat at sea three days later.

The sudden realization that the anniversary was upon him jarred him awake like the first tremors of an earthquake.

At almost the same instant on the sea the reality was much deadlier for others.

13

"HAPPY VALENTINE'S DAY."

In the cockpit of the *Cynthia Lee*, Douglas Segui lowered his Ray Bans to get a better look at his girlfriend as her unfastened bikini top fell to the teak deck.

"Wanna play with the ladies?" she said jiggling her showgirl breasts in front of him.

"You know I do, babe, but right now I have to get us through this drawbridge up ahead. Get me a pop will you, Sandy?"

"You know where to find me," Sandy Madison said in a sing-song. "First girl sunbathing topless on the stern."

"Be with you shortly, baby."

Segui throttled up to nine knots and waved to the bridge tender high above in his tower. Segui could see cars and other vehicles lined up on both sides of the span as the bridge unlocked in the middle, each half grinding upward to allow the two-masted schooner to pass. Seeing the string of autos, Sandy pranced gingerly to the bow and stood there shimmying to the delight of several drivers who honked their horns in approval.

"Hey, if they have to wait for us, might as well give them a cheap thrill!" she shouted back to Segui.

The pair had set out from Sussex Shores, Delaware, a few days earlier heading down the Intracoastal Waterway toward Jacksonville for Segui's college class reunion. Segui had taken his first vacation in two years to attend the event and planned it so that he and Sandy could make a leisurely voyage south.

He had bought the *Cynthia Lee* three years earlier and had become an efficient sailor, taking the rakish seventy-footer on weekend sallies into the Atlantic and exploring the New Jersey capes. Still, his career as a biochemist for a research corporation's Dover plant was his first priority.

Both in their early fifties, he and Sandy, an ophthalmologist, were twice divorced. Friends had set them up for a dinner date two years ago, and they had practically been together ever since. This cruise to north Florida was the first extended trip they had made with the *Cynthia Lee*, but Segui was confident in his abilities.

With the bridge shrinking behind them, Segui looked at his direction finder, compass, and Decca radar. It had been a brilliant day, and even though they had escaped the Delaware cold it wasn't much warmer along the South Carolina coast. Sandy was intent, however, on starting her tanning early, or at least tantalizing him with her many curves. He checked his maps and determined they were near Bulls Bay between Charleston and the fishing hamlet of McClellanville.

The sun was fading behind the trees, turning the western sky into a canvas of tangerines with bolls of magenta clouds. The bay at this point, between Bull and Cape islands, was expansive enough that Segui decided to steer east a few hundred yards out of the main waterway and drop anchor for the night. He cut his diesels, which he had been using for most of the trip because of a lack of wind, and minutes later the reassuring splash of the anchor hurtling to the bottom ended the day's trek.

Daylight's end dropped the mercury and forced Sandy to put on a sweat suit, at least temporarily. They went below to warm up and have a quick bite of dinner before Segui saw Sandy hauling a sleeping bag topside.

"What are you doing? It's probably going to be pretty cold out there tonight."

"A good Camp Fire Girl is always prepared. Besides, I have to earn my merit badge."

"Merit badge in what?" Segui laughed. Sandy leaned to whisper in his ear and his face reddened.

"You are such a little boy sometimes. Join me on deck, my captain courageous."

The evening was calm, and when Sandy switched off a floodlight they were engulfed in the darkness, the moon hiding behind a bank of high clouds. As his eyes adjusted to the murkiness, Segui could see Sandy twisting into the sleeping bag like a butterfly trying to return to its cocoon. She had spread the bag near the stern, piling her sweat suit and underwear beside it. Segui quickly looked around the perimeter. They were alone, and it would not have been too far out of his imagination to believe they were the last humans on Earth had it not been for two or three twinkling lights marking the coast several hundred yards away.

"Mmmm, hurry, Douglas," Sandy beckoned. "Just don't kick over my wine glass."

Segui shed his clothes and wrestled into the bag with her, the heat of her nude body vitalizing all his senses. They entwined, kissing lushly, hands roving over flesh.

"Oh, my cupid, I can feel your quiver," Sandy whispered as Segui pressed against her thigh and inched his fingers between her legs.

Despite the night the spyglass revealed the United States flag hanging limply from the *Cynthia Lee*'s stern.

"Yank ship all right. Flying the colors and marked from Delaware. No sentries or lookouts to be seen. Prepare to attack, gentlemen. Two hundred yards and we have her."

Sandy Madison straddled Segui. She had partially unzipped the sleeping bag so that she could sit up and was now astride him like a horny Lady Godiva.

Segui's eyes rolled back and his head jerked from side to side. Above him Sandy savored the primitive pleasure, humping him as if there would be no tomorrow. Their moans punctuated each down thrust.

As she bounced, a faint movement and the slightest shimmer of a reflection drew her eyes aft. She sat on his legs and squinted into the night.

"Doug, something is moving out there."

"Where, honey? What are you talking about?" Segui was flustered. Still pinned beneath her, he looked in the direction she pointed. "Damn it, Sandy, there's nothing out there but a dolphin or sea turtle playing around."

At that second the moon peered from among the clouds as if looking in on a condemned prisoner. It's sallow light unmasked an object shaped like a candy bar churning through the water at a very slow speed but aiming directly at the schooner's broadside. They both saw it now, thirty yards away and closing.

"There it is, Douglas!"

"I see it! Let me—"

Time blew up around them in a haze of hissing ocean and steam, whirling splinters, and chunks of wood, steel, canvas, and Plexiglas.

The underwater eruption ripped a twenty-foot hole in the *Cynthia Lee*, sending her to the seabed like a bubbling aquarium toy.

Sandy was hurled into the cold water, last seeing Segui being hit in the throat by a can of tuna from the galley, flying into him at slap-shot speed.

She surfaced, spitting and coughing, into a tattered portion of the spinnaker that had been flung into the sea. Frantically she tried to claw from under it, but the canvas was too wide and weighted by some pieces of rigging and a chunk of the bed frame from the main stateroom. All began to sink.

Fighting to free herself, Sandy became tangled in the rigging and was dragged into the depths. Her last panicked screams burbled to the surface with the end of her death struggle.

Ashby's awareness of the *Hunley*'s anniversary prompted him to reread the newspaper clippings about Iceman Turner's killing and the sinking of the *Sea Lynx*. There just had to be something there, but he scanned the articles in vain. With no other avenues, he decided to renew his one-man harbor patrols, which had been curtailed temporarily by the demands of the *Yorktown* investigation. After all, what better chance would there be than the date, much less the location, of the submarine's finest hour? If ever her crew would be stirring, this should be a prime opportunity to contact it.

Friday night, February 17, was the witching time, when the *Hunley* might once again do battle with the Union fleet off Rattlesnake Shoal. Yet he wasn't about to waste Thursday night either—too many attacks had occurred on other dates for him to take anything for granted. Weather forecasts called for calm conditions and outgoing tides just after dark both nights. And just as on the night that the *Housatonic* met her doom, a full moon was due on Friday evening.

Ashby planned to put in at a public boat landing on the south end of the Isle of Palms. From there he could troll the waters off Breach Inlet and Sullivan's Island. It had been almost a month since he was face to face with these devils, but it somehow seemed as though it had been centuries, so much had occurred in the meantime. He knew that if he actually did contact them again the chances were great that he would pay with his life.

With this in mind, he spent much of Wednesday night writing a farewell letter to his parents. Several times before he finished he had to stop, choking back tears as he remembered the good times with his family. They had to know that he was doing his duty if anything happened to him. He had had a living will prepared shortly after the Chesapeake Bay rescue. The letter done, he placed it and several personal photos in an envelope with Starnes's name on the outside. He then put the envelope in his footlocker. If he didn't return, Rod would know what to do with it.

❦

Ashby attended to his regular duties on Thursday. It was a routine day, and he couldn't help thinking about what lay ahead. His truck, boat, and trailer were ready so that he could leave as soon as he came off duty at 5 P.M., barring any further catastrophes.

Late in the afternoon he called Starnes and asked if he had a few minutes to talk. Shortly afterward he was in the captain's office, where he laid out his idea and plans.

"Rod, with all the evidence I have and everything else that's happened, I still believe the *Hunley* is responsible for these attacks. Now I haven't figured out how, when, or if it surfaces, but I am gonna try to bring them in."

"Bring them in. How do you propose to do that, Eric?"

Ashby showed him a copy of Dantzler's report about the lantern communications with the *Hunley*.

"On the night of their last mission, they left their berth at Battery Marshall on Sullivan's Island and went out Breach Inlet to sink a Union warship. Obviously they accomplished this with the destruction of the *Housatonic*, but she never got back to port.

"Rod, this Friday is the 131st anniversary of the *Hunley*'s sinking of the *Housatonic*."

"Wow, the 131st, I bet the 130th was a real blowout."

"You tell me, Rod. That was before my time here. Got here in April, remember?"

"So what are you proposing, lieutenant?"

"I am proposing to use a lantern tonight and Friday night to signal the *Hunley* back to its harbor and end this killing. Signal her off Breach Inlet, where her captain expects to see the light and bring her in. Just like in Dantzler's report."

"So you are going to just wave around a Coleman camp lantern on the beach out there and attract a ghost submarine that you think is responsible for torpedoing civilian pleasure craft."

"No, sir. I'm going out in my johnboat. Rod, you got to understand, I've met these people or things or whatever they are, before, whether you believe me or not. Maybe I can reason with them. What have you got to lose in letting me do this?"

"Maybe a good man, that's all. Eric, what you do in your spare time is your own business certainly. And you can't argue that I've been more than lenient with you over the past months."

"Are you telling me that I can't try this, captain?"

"Not at all, Ashby. You can go floating around the harbor all you want when you are off duty. Eric, I'm in the dark about all this stuff just like you are. The difference is that I am looking for concrete answers, not playing trick or treat on the ocean."

Ashby felt the red anger rising, but held his calm.

"Is that all, captain?"

"Not quite, lieutenant. I put you on administrative leave a few weeks ago and only brought you back because I needed you— and still need you. But I'm telling you, Eric, I am seriously considering ordering you to get some psychological counseling. We've talked about it before."

"Of course I will obey orders, captain."

Starnes leaned back in his chair and rubbed his face. "I wish I knew what was going on around here, Eric. Almost fifteen years in the Guard and I ain't never seen anything to beat all this."

Ashby's eyes narrowed.

"Rod, you're talking like there is something new."

"There is."

Starnes showed a folder across his desk in Ashby's direction.

"Another overdue boat and two more people missing."

Ashby read the brief incident report about the *Cynthia Lee*.

"This is the first I've heard about this. Is there a search underway by anybody?"

"You didn't hear about it before now because I just got this information within the half hour. I was about to send for you when you called me. This guy Segui and his girlfriend were on their way to Florida from Delaware. They were supposed to call a friend in Jacksonville last night to let them know about their arrival time. Nobody heard from them by early this afternoon so the friend calls Coast Guard Jacksonville. They notified us.

"There is no active search. They are listed as overdue at this point, that's all. You know the procedure. Hell they could be anywhere on the Intracoastal from Norfolk to Jekyll Island. We have no reason to believe they are in the Charleston sector."

"Sounds like you're trying to convince yourself about that, Rod."

"In a way I guess I am, Ashby."

Nothing new came in about the *Cynthia Lee* before Ashby's shift ended. Quickly going back to his quarters to change into civilian clothes, he was off to the islands by about 5:15 P.M. Despite rush-hour traffic downtown, he still made it to the boat landing in about thirty minutes, just as night settled over the Isle of Palms.

In the rapidly fading light Ashby checked his duffel bag of supplies: emergency flares, two flashlights, survival knife, binoculars, rain cape, blanket, waterproof matches, extra pair of heavy socks, first aid kit, a change of clothes, two canteens of fresh water, and some freeze-dried rations. In addition to topping off the Evinrude's fuel tank, he also brought along two extra ten-gallon gas cans.

Ashby also carried what he considered his most vital equipment: a green Coleman lantern, navigational map, and his 9-millimeter Glock.

He backed the trailer to the water's edge and cranked his boat into the shallows. Anchoring her, he drove his truck to the parking lot, walked back to the dock, and climbed aboard. Easing the fifteen-footer away from the landing, he opened up the throttle and nosed toward the open ocean.

The sea mist flying up from the bow and the night's temperatures in the thirties caused him to raise the hood on his Army-issue camouflage parka as the craft knifed over the sable waves. Behind him, Breach Inlet eternally separated the narrow fingers of Sullivan's Island and the Isle of Palms.

Ashby imagined the skipper of the *Hunley* looking back at the outlined coast from this ocean point and setting his bearings before diving to engage the hulking *Housatonic*. Ashby slowed his motor and by flashlight checked his map. He was close to Rattlesnake Shoal, a notable sandbank about two miles off the Isle of Palms.

Somewhere in these waters in 1862, the Union navy sank a fleet of old whaling ships filled with rocks and boulders. This "Stone Fleet," one of two, was supposed to obstruct Confederate vessels leaving or entering Charleston.

Somewhere in these waters the *Hunley* and the *Housatonic*

met in epic combat. And somewhere in these waters Ashby believed the *Hunley* still lurked.

Blue signal from Dixon, return white beacon light from Battery Marshall. That's how Dantzler had described it.

Ashby turned on the lantern, its intensity searing the night. He winced like a vampire in a lighthouse before his eyes adjusted to the effulgence.

He checked his wristwatch. Just short of 9 P.M. The *Hunley* would have attacked by now, shoving her payload into the belly of the *Housatonic*. Even if he was a day early for the anniversary, Ashby sensed the guests were already present.

He cut the engine and placed the lantern securely on the seat closest to the bow. Nothing to do now but wait. If this didn't work he would spend some hours Friday night walking the Breach Inlet beach with the lantern. He had not done this first because he believed there were enough lights emanating from the homes on the islands to attract the Rebel firefly. Better to try to make contact on the ocean.

Huddled in the cold, he relaxed with the lullaby of the water. Before him the Coleman hissed in its brightness, illuminating a crescent of restless sea around the bow. Miles offshore he could see the lights of a freighter waiting for suitable tidal conditions to enter the harbor.

Suddenly he realized he had company.

Something big broke the surface about twenty yards off his stern. Startled, Ashby at first thought it was a trophy-sized game fish showing off its magnificence. Then he realized the fish was manmade.

Its studded black hull came up nose first and leveled off with seawater running down its sides. Two turrets jutted a few feet above the hull. Ashby judged the vessel to be more than twice as long as his boat.

Through his numb terror he knew he had again found the *Hunley*. The more terrifying thought was that it had found him. Déjà vu with only Peter Mueller's cotton-white corpse absent from Satan's latest hoe-down.

Almost in the same instant the hatch covers atop both turrets whined open. A head appeared in the aft turret, and a hand gripped the rim of the fore hatch. Ashby could hear faint talk from the craft's interior, but couldn't make out the words.

He was about to face the keepers of Castle Pinckney from whom he had escaped. He could only guess at the savagery of their wrath.

Now there was a man in each hatch, both peering toward him through the dimness.

Ashby kept his eyes on them while reaching down for some reassurance from the Glock tucked in his waistband.

From across the way he felt the deadeye stares of the silent mariners boring into him like coffin nails. If they recognized him, there was no immediate reaction. He decided to take the initiative.

Ashby swallowed hard and tried hard to instill confidence in his words as he spoke.

"My compliments, sir. I am Lieutenant Eric Ashby of the United States Coast Guard."

"Coast Guard? What the hell is that? Why don't you just say you're assigned to the blockade, bluebelly?" jeered the man in the aft hatch.

"That's enough, Carlson. You're wearing a mighty strange-looking outfit for a Yank," replied the other. "You best know that soldiers or sailors caught in civilian clothes are considered spies. You want to feel the grip of some hemp around your neck? We can make it happen real quick."

"Sir, I know you are Lieutenant George Dixon, late of the Alabama volunteer infantry and that your command is the CSS *H. L. Hunley*, named after one of the boat's inventors. You and your crew have served the Confederacy admirably for many years, and your courage is unquestioned. What I must tell you is that the war is over and that peace has been declared."

For a full minute there was hush while Ashby waited for some answer. The sound of the water slapping at his boat seemed loud enough to wake the world.

"Friend, only the fact that you seem to know so much keeps me from putting a ball between your eyes right now. We have received no word that the Yankees have surrendered, although you may rest assured that it will happen."

"No, sir, you don't understand. The South lost the war. Lee surrendered in Virginia, and General Joe Johnston capitulated in North Carolina about two weeks later."

Ashby hesitated, knowing his next words might herald his death.

"The Confederacy no longer exists. This is 1995. The war has been over for almost 130 years."

"Listen you blue-tailed piss ant! It is not out of the realm of possibility that our armies have suffered a setback, but submission is not an option. My crew and myself should be sufficient evidence of that."

"You are Lieutenant Dixon, aren't you?"

"You are obviously a spy, Mr. Ashby, or whatever your real name is. I am not familiar with you, and only a Yankee operative would have access to much of the intelligence you have offered."

"I am aware of the *Hunley*'s brave exploits as is everyone in Charleston." Ashby tried to speak calmly although he felt his hands and knees shaking. He knew what he wanted to say and gathered himself for a moment in fear before blurting it out.

"They have already erected a monument to you and your men. Please let me show you, lieutenant."

There was a pause.

"Mr. Ashby, I will have no qualms about slicing your throat if you lie to me. It would be a proud moment for me and the crew of this craft if what you say is true. It will be an equally terrible experience for you if what you are saying is a falsehood. Are we clear on that matter?"

"Yes, sir. I won't disappoint you. Will you follow me into Charleston?"

"You just get yourself there. Don't worry about anything else. And, sir, you are to consider yourself a prisoner of war released on temporary parole, is that also clear?"

"I understand, but lieutenant . . ."

Before he could finish the sentence, both men disappeared in the hatchways and the covers clanged shut. The vessel churned away, barely disturbing the water, and soon was gone.

Ashby slouched onto the boat seat, breathing heavily, adrenaline racing. The encounter had lasted no more than two or three minutes, but he was exhausted. His mind boiled with emotions and sensations—hundred-proof fright, exhilaration, ear-to-ear anxiety, and the urge to soil himself being the most prominent.

Then he realized that he had accomplished what he wanted— he was bringing in the *Hunley!* Dixon wanted to see the monument!

Ashby knew that a granite memorial to the *Hunley*'s crews stood in White Point Gardens at The Battery. He would go there now, as Dixon instructed, and see if the Confederates would follow. Starting the Evinrude, he turned toward shore.

Finally it looked as though he had something marvelous, possibly astounding, to show for his hard work and pluck. He knew that he could communicate with the crewmen; they had responded to his words. Perhaps he could reason with Dixon, find out about the world in which the *Hunley* existed to punish vessels more than a century after her death. He might even have the chance to negotiate for the release of the Castle Pinckney prisoners.

Ultimately, if seeing the monument to their achievements would make them rest in peace then his mission would be accomplished.

It seemed to take a lifetime before he finally reached the landing. Ashby reeled his boat on the trailer and headed back toward Charleston. Was the *Hunley* gliding into the harbor at that very moment, en route to meet him at The Battery? The thought of this possibility elated him. He toyed with the idea of phoning Starnes but decided against it. What would he tell him anyway, at least at this point? Be patient and take care of business.

With difficulty, Ashby tried not to speed. All he needed was to be stopped by a cop and possibly miss his rendezvous. Weaving his way downtown, he passed the crowded bars on Bay Street—not even eleven yet, the night was young for the partiers. A few of the houses along Rainbow Row still had lights on as he passed, turning onto South Battery Street beside White Point Gardens.

The *Hunley* monument stood in the park where South Battery and Meeting Street intersected. Taller than a man, it was shaped like a large tombstone with gurgling ornate fish spouting slow streams of water on either side.

Ashby stood on the yellow sand by the memorial and waited. In one direction he could look north down the throat of Meeting Street, past a number of darkened colonial masterpieces, flushed in the mascara of the street lamps. To the south was a bandstand-sized white gazebo with a green-shingled roof. Beyond, through the trees, the Ashley drawled toward the sea.

A cutting wind bustled in off the ocean, and Ashby grimaced into it to see the pancake of Fort Sumter more than a mile away in the harbor mouth.

Nearby was a marker at the site where the infamous pirate Stede Bonnett and twenty-nine other buccaneers had been hanged in the 1700's.

From a dark corner of the park a figure emerged and approached Ashby, staying in the shadows to seemingly avoid contact with the street light's glow.

Ashby was transfixed—until he saw that the newcomer was an exquisitely dressed black drag queen.

"You looking for something warm on this chilly evening, honey?" the man asked, sashaying up to him.

"No, thanks, I'm waiting for a friend."

"Oh I see. Not in the market for some brown sugar tonight?"

"Nope."

"Well I guess that's clear enough. Y'all have a good time, all right?"

"Be seeing you."

"Night, honey buns."

In a swish of gold sequins and blonde curls, the hooker wheeled and strutted back down the path toward the gazebo, darkness soon enveloping him.

A church bell tolled midnight and still Ashby waited, for what he wasn't sure. Passing cars became scarcer, and he saw that there was no one else on the streets. He shifted on his feet, trying to stay warm as the deepening night dropped the temperature.

A police car came down South Battery and slowed near him. Ashby gave the two officers a wave and the cruiser eased away, leaving him to his vigil. In his boredom he read the plaques attached to each side of the marker, learning that the Daughters of the Confederacy and a group called the Memorial Association of Charleston had erected it in 1899. On the other side were listed the names of the *Hunley* crews, including Dixon and his men, who gave their lives for the South. Missing was any mention of the five sailors killed in the first sinking.

The wind gusted higher through the bare tree limbs, clattering them like an anatomy class skeleton being shaken. As he listened to the moaning of the branches, Ashby suddenly was aware that he was not alone.

From the trees came another figure, but this was not the previous meddler. Walking deliberately toward him was a pale man in the dirty uniform of a Confederate infantry officer.

Lieutenant George Dixon of the *Hunley* had finally returned to Charleston. Without a word Dixon stopped at Ashby's side, his eyes roaming to take in the monument, the park, and the surrounding cityscape.

Ashby stood motionless for a minute and then turned slightly to study Dixon. His antagonist was little more than a boy really. His short light-brown hair looked matted, and the slight Vandyke was sparse. Dixon's gray jacket appeared to be stained with oil, sweat, or both, standing out against his blanched skin. His trousers were tucked into knee-high, muddy black boots and looped around his waist was a thick belt with a burnished gold buckle and a flapped pistol holster.

Ashby was the bigger of the two and couldn't help thinking that if they had crossed paths on the lacrosse field he would have blocked this guy into next week. But this wasn't lacrosse, and he could only guess at how many ways Dixon could beat him if he pulled any funny business. Yet he had nothing to lose in his boldness now. He had somehow coaxed Dixon ashore and was still alive, at least to this point. Convince him that the war was over and maybe the attacks would cease.

"Lieutenant, this monument was dedicated in 1899; that was thirty-five years after you and your men sank the *Housatonic*. You can see that it gives the exact date of your mission, the names of your crew and yours as well."

Dixon now stared at the inscription on the memorial, and Ashby realized that he was watching a man read his own epitaph long after he had any mortal right to walk the earth. The Confederate stared for a full five minutes without moving or changing expression; and Ashby followed suit, partially out of respect, but primarily because he did not know what to do next. Nothing in his Coast Guard experience had prepared him for this occasion.

Dixon slowly began to read aloud from one of the plaques:

"In memory of the supreme devotion of those heroic men of the Confederate army and navy—first in marine warfare to employ torpedo boats for the enterprise of extreme peril in the defense of Charleston Harbor."

Ashby now lost his patience.

"The war's over, lieutenant," he blurted. "It's been finished for a damned long time, and whenever you blow up a ship bearing the United States flag you are killing innocent civilians.

"Charleston and the rest of South Carolina are back in the Union—as is Alabama, Georgia, and the rest of what used to be the Confederacy. The war is over!"

"It won't ever be over as long as my men can fight," Dixon snapped. "Now you must excuse me, there is much work to be done."

Dixon whirled and took a few steps before pausing.

"By the way, Coast Guard Lieutenant Ashby, you will find your friend over there. Dress like a spy, expect to die like a spy."

He pointed to a clump of camellia bushes near the gazebo.

"The only reason you have been spared is because you have been of some service to me."

"Friend? What friend?"

Ashby knew he was losing his chance and his cool with it.

He glanced at the bushes and then back, but Dixon had vanished, leaving nothing but his diehard words to further ice the wind chill.

Ashby trotted toward the camellias and was a few feet from them when something glinting on the path caught his attention. Scattered on the sand and reflecting in the partial moonlight were seven or eight gold sequins. From the underbrush he heard a gurgling sound and stepped through the bushes to investigate.

What he found doubled him over, retching in horror as his senses screamed in anguish. Twisted on the grass before him was the drag queen, lying on his back with one leg bent backward beneath his body. The wig was askew on his head, and sightless wide eyes bore into the sky. His dress looked to have been torn open from the waist up, baring his chest. Sequins littered the grass like fish scales.

Even in the dimness Ashby could see how the hooker had been killed—a bloody slash ran from the tip of his chin vertically down the center of his throat to the larynx.

Ashby staggered back into the open, stumbling over one of the man's high heels. There was nothing he could do for the poor bastard. He wiped his mouth with his coat sleeve and stood for a moment, thinking and catching his breath.

If he called the police they might hold him for questioning and jeopardize his chances to contact the *Hunley* again on Friday night, the anniversary. Besides, no one would believe his story anyway. Hell, in all likelihood he might be charged with the guy's murder!

Ashby looked around but saw no one. Shaken but still thinking clearly, he made his decision—don't call the cops. In the grand scheme of his world, the death of a $20-a-trick transvestite couldn't interfere with stopping the *Hunley*. And anyway, he was already hot on the trail of the hooker's killers, something the authorities would never be able to do.

In twenty minutes Ashby had returned to base, secured his truck and boat, and flopped on his bed. The clock read 2:25 A.M.

Had 'em on the hook and let 'em get away. For a second he delved into a memory of his grandfather, who trolled the beautiful Finger Lakes of central New York and always had a tale about the one that got away.

He recalled the old man's favorite joke about the one-armed fisherman describing his biggest catch of the day: "It was this long," the angler said, holding out his only arm.

Although one rotund haddock was worthy of being mounted on the den wall, his granddad had never netted anything re-motely as large or significant as the *Hunley*. Who had?

There was still Friday night. The fact that he had made a breakthrough was encouraging for better results. Forget the dead drag queen.

14

SHOWERED, SHAVED, AND IN uniform, Ashby was in Starnes's office at 7:30 A.M.

"I made contact last night."

Starnes stirred two packets of sugar into a cup of coffee and suppressed a yawn.

"Tell me."

Ashby laid out the night's events, other than the hooker's death, while Starnes watched him, not changing expression. Cut the orders for a psychiatric evaluation as soon as he leaves. Recommend inpatient treatment. This crap has gotta stop, but humor him for now.

"So you plan on going back out tonight, Eric?"

"Absolutely. Last night was only the beginning. Rod, I fully believe I can reason with Dixon and stop these attacks."

"So then what? They move in with you? Eric, we ain't got the space."

Ashby studied him for a few seconds. He knew Rod didn't believe him, but he didn't want to hear the painful words. He just needed a little more time to prove all of them wrong.

"So have you been talking to Alison?" he said, changing the subject.

"Yeah, she called earlier in the week. So why am I talking to your girlfriend more than you are?"

"Number one, I've been too busy chasing bogeymen to have any time for girls, which I greatly regret. Number two, I know that you remain a pencil dick and therefore are no threat to me."

They laughed together and forgot, for a moment, the woes of the planet.

"You really should call her, Eric. No accounting for taste, but I know for a fact that she has a lot of deep feelings for you."

"I'll get around to it. Bigger fish to fry right now."

"Eric, why don't I go with you tonight, just to keep you company? Hell, who knows, we might even scare up a ghost or two."

"Try nine."

Ashby knew that Starnes was more concerned about his mental well-being than he was about the eventuality of locating some unearthly killers.

"Rod, you don't have to worry about me. I've been going out in that old bass boat so much that I pretty much know this harbor like the back of my hand, not to mention the islands. Every time I go out I figure it's a hit-or-miss deal. Last night I came close to the bull's-eye. Tonight . . ."

"Tonight I'll help you throw the darts," Starnes interrupted. "Meet you at your truck about 5:30."

On his lunch break that afternoon, Ashby went back to his room and went through a folder containing his notes and photocopied documents about the *Hunley.* At sea the night before, Dixon had called the other Confederate by the name of Carlson and Ashby checked his list of the sub's crews. Sure enough there was a Corporal C. F. Carlson in Dixon's last squad. Some sources identified him as a member of a unit called the German Artillery while others said he was a South Carolina light artillerist.

In all the excitement he had forgotten seeing Carlson's name on the *Hunley* monument the previous evening.

He remembered that the dying victim from the *Sea Lynx* gasped the word "Carlson" and wondered if Snapper Gould knew of this possible connection with the *Hunley*. With no time to spare Ashby decided to call Gould Saturday morning.

Starnes meanwhile told Mike Green of his plans to go out with Ashby. He wanted someone to know of their whereabouts in case of—anything.

"So speaking of girls."

Ashby switched on his headlights as his pickup descended the Cooper River bridge on the outskirts of Mount Pleasant.

"Who was speaking of girls? I didn't say anything," Starnes answered. "I'm looking at the *Yorktown* down there and thanking God that she wasn't blown up."

"Anything from the Navy about those mines?"

"Not yet. Talked to Patterson yesterday. Still waiting for forensics results. Seems like we're not the only ones who can't catch a break."

"So what happened with the roses? You sent them to Melanie Potemkin, right?"

"Oh that's right, Eric. You've been so busy busting your goblins that you haven't heard."

"Heard what, that she called the police on you for being a Peeping Tom or something?"

"No, pervert, she got the roses and we are stepping out on the town Saturday night. She called me and said she was very flattered that I would think of her."

"Think of her? Did you tell her you have been dreaming about getting in her skirt for months?"

"Nope, that didn't come up. Taking her to dinner tomorrow night, so get me back from this boat ride in time to get some shut-eye."

"I'm not making any promises."

"So what exactly are you expecting to find out there tonight, Eric?" A few hours earlier Starnes had filled out the documents to place Ashby on administrative leave with pay while he underwent psychiatric testing. He planned to break the news to him on Monday. No need to spoil the weekend.

"Rod, I learned a long time ago, well just in this last year, that just when you think you've got everything pegged into neat little holes something comes along that defies anything you've ever experienced. That's what I've been dealing with."

"So you gonna answer my question?"

"I don't know what to expect tonight to tell you the truth, Rod. I'm still wired about last night. Think about it. On this night 131 years ago the *Hunley* embarked from Sullivan's Island to attack a United States warship. These nine guys were braver than you or me can ever imagine. They knew that two other crews went to horrible deaths in that same submarine, yet they were willing to climb aboard, submerge, and go on the offensive. They achieved something that revolutionized warfare. And we'll be in the same waters where it all happened."

"So maybe I can get an autograph or two."

"You laugh now, Rod, but I'm planning on getting you that close. Hope you brought a pen."

Less than an hour later they were shoving off from the Isle of Palms boat landing. Ashby had his usual equipment while Starnes brought his own tote bag.

A full moon reigned over the Atlantic, a glinting monarch over the stars that surrounded it. Ashby's boat plowed away from the coast with Starnes on the bow seat. Ashby had marked last night's coordinates on his map and wanted to again anchor as close to that spot as possible.

"So anything else I should know, other than we're on a ghost hunt?" Starnes shouted back at him. "You on a first-name basis with these guys?"

"No rules, that's what makes it so interesting. And I enforce strict formality with Dixon and his crew. I'm still alive so I must be doing something right."

"Just let me know if I get out of line and violate some code of hobgoblin etiquette—never clear on what to do."

"You better know that I will, Rod."

Checking his map by flashlight, Ashby changed course slightly for five minutes and then shut off the motor. They drifted in silence as the outgoing tide shuttled them further to sea.

"This is the place, more or less, where I met them last night. We'll just float around here a little bit and see what happens."

"You're the captain. Pass up that thermos of coffee, will ya."

Ashby fired up his lantern and passed it to Starnes, who placed it in the bow. The waiting game had started and the time for idle talk had passed. They sat, each in his own world, listening to the water and watching the dancing moon and stars mirrored on the ripples.

Starnes knew he was primarily there because a buddy and a fellow officer needed him. He certainly didn't buy Ashby's story, although he could not come up with any legitimate answers of his own. He would stick by Ashby no matter what happened with the psychiatrist. He recalled the sight of Ashby digging madly in the Castle Pinckney sand, looking for his "dungeon." Damned shame that such a good officer and a decent guy should have problems like this. Get him the help he needs and go from there.

What he had not told Ashby and what he couldn't rationalize was the information he had received Thursday afternoon. A detective in Perth Amboy had called to tell him that the hand-writing on the note Ashby had given him was indeed that of Majorie Wagner. The cop had pressed him hard for more details about how the note turned up, but Rod had put him off, saying that he would call in a couple of days. As they rode the waves, he still was trying to plot his best strategy to handle this stunning revelation. Still, he didn't believe in ghosts. Never would. There had to be a logical answer to all of this.

Ashby thought of all that had occurred in the past eleven months. It certainly had been the most intriguing time of his life, a runaway roller coaster ride of fantastic reality and unbridled insanity. He tried not to put himself in Rod's head, but it was hard not to wonder what his friend was thinking.

He decided to call Alison sometime over the weekend, he owed her that much. Maybe they could still salvage something of their relationship. He was willing to give it a shot if she was interested.

Ashby glanced at his watch—8:40 P.M. In another time the *Hunley* was making its final thrust at the *Housatonic*'s unprotected broadside. Where the johnboat bobbed at anchor all had been a chaos of a stifled explosion, screaming, yelling sailors, and snapping, tortured timbers as the warship crashed to the sea bed. Must have been one hell of a scene.

He remembered Starnes was going out with Melanie Potemkin.

"Hey, Rod, you need a couple of bucks?" he said quietly.

"No. Why?"

"I just bet Melanie is high maintenance, buddy. No hamburger and shake for her, you gotta spring for one of the four-stars if you're gonna get anywhere with her. And don't go Dutch."

"Eric, do I look like I need coaching to handle women? I think not. Rest assured Miss Melanie will be treated like the princess she is. In fact, I already have reservations at . . ."

"You off the bow! Identify yourself real quick or we'll open fire!"

The call came from the blackness seaward. Ashby and Starnes strained to penetrate the night, the moon glow revealing nothing but toiling water.

"Who the hell is challenging us?" Starnes whispered, groping for a flashlight in his bag.

"No, Rod, not right now. You might spook them or worse if you shine that thing on them. Douse the lantern."

Starnes complied and they scanned the indigo ocean around them.

A sheer fog seemed to have wafted from the deep in the direction of the voice. For a full minute they did not see anything else. Then it began to materialize in the mist, at first a low-slung silhouette slowly carving the waves.

Ashby watched in awe as the *Hunley*, riding on the surface, her turret hatches open, approached them, a mailed monster from the depths of another age. She swung in a slow arc and came parallel to his boat about ten yards distant. Beside him Starnes deliberately stood, wordlessly watching the odd-looking contraption. Both saw the long iron spar, tipped with what appeared to be a metal barrel attached to the vessel's bow.

Men emerged at each turret, and Ashby recognized Dixon climbing out of the fore hatchway.

"My God," Starnes muttered, staring at the submarine and the two crewmen.

Ashby ignored him. He had to continue his talks begun the night before. Cupping his hands around his mouth, he yelled. "Lieutenant Dixon, I am Lieutenant Ashby of the United States Coast Guard. You will recall that we met last night. With me is my commander, Captain Rod Starnes."

Dixon and the other man, both in Confederate gray, were standing atop the *Hunley*, their every step made gingerly as they inspected the exposed portion of her hull. Dixon knelt to examine the spar fittings before turning to the Guardsmen.

"Mr. Ashby, I don't give a damn about your allegiances or your fancy talk right now. Most of my boys are exhausted, and I need a fresh man or two to take a post cranking the propeller shaft. You look capable enough. We are in the midst of a major mission here."

"The hell with this." Starnes was angry.

"No, Rod."

"I don't know who you clowns are, but we are officers of the United States Coast Guard and it would be in your best interests not to make any threatening movements against us," Starnes shouted.

"Rod, you're trying to reason with aberrations," Ashby said, trying to humor and calm him. "They aren't real, that's what you said, remember?"

Even as he spoke he realized he had made a bad mistake.

In the shifting haze Ashby heard the unmistakably metallic click of a revolver being cocked.

"You don't think we're here? Well here's a little show for you. Pay for your sass bluebelly."

The white spit of flame and a deafening blast sheared the night. At point-blank range Starnes had no chance. His arms flayed the air as his chest spewed a red spray. His brief scream of agony was smothered by the gunshot before he fell backward into the boat like a discarded marionette.

Ashby almost lost his footing and grabbed the engine rudder to keep from falling overboard. Regaining his balance, he looked down at Starnes's jerking body splayed before him. He knew there was nothing he could do for Rod. His friend's lifeless eyes and the blood spouting from his mouth told the story.

"I got five left in the chambers, Yank. You want the next one? Guess your friend will hold his tongue now—for a really long time don't you think?"

Enraged Ashby whipped around, intent on ripping Starnes's murderer to pieces. But he found himself looking into the maw of a revolver less than five feet from his face as the *Hunley* had drifted closer to them.

"Just give me the reason, Yank. Just give me the reason."

"Now that we have completed that unpleasant business perhaps you will join us," Dixon called to Ashby.

"Carlson, he makes a wrong move, you put him out of his misery."

"Yes sir, lieutenant. Shed that jacket, Yank. You ain't gonna need it and we ain't got the room. You'll be sweatin' up a storm in a few minutes anyway."

Ashby slipped out of his coat and let it fall behind him, partially draping the Evinrude. Carlson stood almost on top of him, the revolver trained at his forehead.

The Rebel's leer was accented by his pallid features, his wan complexion almost radiant in the dark. Carlson wore a brownish-gray tunic with red piping, unbuttoned to reveal his white chest and stomach.

He looked to be a boyish corpse of about twenty years old and sported a short sword that hung from a belted sheath at his waist. Ashby noted that his belt buckle bore a "U.S.," and his pants appeared to be blue. If these were indeed Confederate soldiers and sailors, the belt and trousers likely were equipment captured from the Federals.

Without his coat the Glock tucked into the front of his jeans was exposed and Carlson saw it.

"I'll take that fancy piece there too. Give it to me grip first, the barrel pointed toward you."

Slowly Ashby pulled out the automatic, thinking of any chance, any trick. He reached out with the gun and Carlson grabbed it. Their hands touched briefly, and Ashby felt as if he had thrust his into a bag of ice. He recoiled and again almost toppled.

By now Dixon had gone back down the hatch, and Ashby contemplated making a lunge at Carlson. Knock him over the side and maybe grab one of the guns. Too far to swim in, but maybe he could restart his boat and make it back to shore. He'd escaped from these cracker cadavers once before, and there was no reason that he couldn't do it again.

"Now that is one fine-looking weapon," Carlson said, examining Ashby's Glock. "Must be a French or English make. Never seen one like this."

Ashby tensed to spring. He would hit the man low and hard, body-blocking him into the water.

But Dixon suddenly reappeared in the hatchway.

"Mr. Ashby, I will kill you myself if you do not obey my orders immediately. I have no more time to spare. Please get below."

"You heard him, bluebelly. Plant your ass down this hole." Carlson motioned toward the aft turret with his pistol.

There were no options for Ashby at this point. Under Carlson's hawk eye, he jumped onto the *Hunley*'s hull, his feet thudding on the solid iron beneath him when he landed.

Ashby edged along until he stood over the aft turret and looked down into the vessel. Two dirty faces bathed in dim orange light stared back at him.

"Down you go, Yank. Time to meet the boys," Carlson said with a jagged grin.

Bracing himself with his hands, Ashby swung his body into the abyss, trying to get a foothold. He almost retched from the foul air issuing from the interior. He glimpsed Dixon's head vanishing in the fore turret.

Slowly Ashby eased through the hatch and Carlson followed him, slamming shut the heavy cover. A minute later the *Hunley* churned forward and slid into the fathoms.

A commercial shrimper discovered Starnes spread-eagled in his own blood in the johnboat just after daylight Saturday about four miles off the southern tip of the Isle of Palms. Eric Ashby was nowhere to be found.

The startling news of Starnes's death and the missing Ashby rocked Coast Guard Station Charleston like a sledgehammer blow. Grieving station personnel were issued black armbands, some worn over uniforms while they searched the harbor and outlying waters for Ashby.

His pickup and boat trailer were found at the landing with Ashby's undisturbed wallet in the glove compartment.

Grizzly Vandencomp immediately flew back to Charleston upon hearing of the tragedy, but there was very little anyone could do other than pray that the massive air and sea hunt paid off with Ashby's being found alive.

The rescuers' optimism dwindled by the minute, the winter water temperature in the thirties meaning that a person adrift had little chance of surviving even a few hours. Late Sunday afternoon, Vandencomp issued the grim order: the search-and-rescue operation was changed to a recovery mission—Ashby was now considered to be missing and presumed drowned. The search was scaled back. His body may or may not surface, depending on the whims of the Atlantic. No one could do any more.

Starnes's autopsy showed only that he was killed by a large-caliber gunshot to the chest, the bullet exiting through his left shoulder blade and not recovered. Powder burns on his clothing indicated the death shot was fired at close range.

Starnes's body was returned to Mississippi and buried with full military honors in the cemetery of his family's Baptist church near Biloxi. Cliff Okai, Snapper Gould, and Mike Green were among the pallbearers.

Some two weeks later a similar memorial service was held in the hills of western Maryland. In an Episcopal chapel in Rohrersville near Frederick, Eric Ashby was eulogized, Vandencomp solemnly presenting the folded U.S. flag that had shrouded an empty casket to Ashby's shattered parents.

As the mourners departed, Vandencomp, resplendent in his

dress whites, strode into the churchyard. He watched the Ashbys get into the funeral home limousine.

Winter still hexed Maryland in early March, and a raw wind gusted among the valleys and hollows hugging the Potomac River. Vandencomp drew a lean brown cigar from his inside coat pocket. Behind the church was a graveyard dating to the 1700's where a headstone to Ashby would be placed.

Vandencomp walked among the tombstones, striking a match on the cheek of a marble cherub guarding an infant's grave to fire up his stogie. He pulled an envelope from another pocket and flipped open a five-page letter—Ashby's last words to his parents. He had found it in Ashby's personal effects. Everything else had been sent home to his family, but Vandencomp had held onto this after reading it.

Grizzly scanned down the pages and stopped at a particular passage. He read loud:

> As strange as it may seem, Mom and Dad, I feel that the Civil War submarine *Hunley* has been responsible for some of the unexplained attacks that have occurred around Charleston during my time here. I have contacted her crew and am trying to reason with their captain to stop this murderous violence against innocent civilians. I know this sounds like pure insanity and it has been a total nightmare but please, please believe me. You know that I have always done what I believe was the right thing and never looked back.

Vandencomp stopped and looked up to watch a pair of gray squirrels racing through the gravestones and up the trunk of a sycamore tree.

"Ashby, you were one messed-up kid," he said under his breath. "Not gonna burden your folks with this lunatic drivel."

Grizzly pressed the cigar against the paper, which began to smolder. Walking to the back fence of the cemetery, he found a long-discarded flowerpot and stuffed the letter into it. A flame shimmied through the stationery, crisping it to withered cinders in less than two minutes.

Vandencomp picked up the smoking pot and hurled it long

and hard into the woods. It splintered in all directions when it whacked into the waist-high stump of a titanic oak.

"Burial at sea. There's another one for Beauregard—and me."

Grizzly chomped into the end of his cigar, wheeled, and patted a few of the memorials as he headed out of the cemetery's deepening gloom.

"See y'all in hell."

15

The Future

TOURISTS AND NEWS CREWS from as far away as Australia and Japan had been streaming into Charleston for days. Six years after an archaeological team discovered the *Hunley* hulk on the ocean floor, she was to be raised!

Only three months after Starnes's death and Ashby's vanishing, a search team using a magnetometer located an unidentified metal object on the seabed off Sullivan's Island. Could this finally be the *Hunley*, which had eluded so many other search-and-salvage operations in the decades since her last mission?

In about thirty feet of water, divers had to use air blowers to remove three to four feet of silt to get to their find. They realized they had found the *Hunley* when they uncovered one of her turrets. Further inspection of the wreck proved they were correct. Resting on her starboard side, the submarine was pointed toward Sullivan's, four miles and an eternity away from her base.

Now, after years of examining the site and digging away the sand, the researchers were ready to bring the *Hunley* back to port.

The unexplained disappearances had continued, sporadically as always, after the Starnes and Ashby tragedy. The *Adirondack Star* from Lido Beach, New York, and the *Chelsea II* out of Portsmouth, New Hampshire, with a total of six people were lost on the Intracoastal within a two-month span in 1996. The two-master *Connecticut Yankee Doodle* and the *Salem Sea Witch* went down with all hands in the winter of 1997–1998. The Boston-based sloop *Whistler's Brother* never made Florida in 1999—she and her family of five were last seen off the coast of Charleston.

All of the murders that Ashby had worked on remained unsolved, as did the explosion that damaged the carrier *Yorktown*. Ella Solomon passed on peacefully in her bed on a steamy June night in 1996, finally putting to rest the fiends that had pranced through her mind since that awful night when Iceman Turner was slaughtered.

Among the jewelry, cosmetics, and other personal effects her relatives found on her vanity was a newspaper clipping that chronicled the Starnes and Ashby incident.

Snapper Gould and his "lovely Rita" were less fortunate. Fire engulfed their home in the dead of a March night in 1998, burning it to the ground like so much kindling. Snapper and Rita didn't escape the inferno. Islanders used garden hoses and pulled pails of water from the bay before the volunteer firefighters arrived, but it was like trying to quench the flames of Hades itself. A state fire marshal sifted through the charred rubble and deemed the fire "of suspicious origin" in his report. That was as far as the investigation progressed.

Jeremy Lord didn't live to read Gould's obituary. The haunting pressures of not being able to nab the killers of Hal Frye, Gwen Lagrange, or Charles Hoyle eroded his sensibilities. The biggest cases of his law enforcement career and he couldn't pry up a clue. He ignored the fact that state and federal authorities had not been able to do any better.

Nightly he sank into his couch and spread the homicide photos in a ghastly montage on his coffee table, leaving room for the half-liter bottle of cheap Kentucky whiskey and a tall glass of water. On Labor Day evening 1996, Lord surveyed the photos, poured a long slug of the rot gut down the barrel of a Smith and Wesson revolver, and ran his tongue into the pistol before squeezing the trigger.

Commander Hugh Vandencomp retired from the Coast Guard in June 1998 with very little fanfare. Reclusive and with no family, his refuge was a seafront home on Catawba Island, an exclusive community about twenty miles south of Charleston. Vandencomp immediately had a six-foot-tall lighthouse erected on his expanse of shoreline, its white light glaring nonstop day and night. The neighbors chattered about the ever-glowing beacon, but didn't dare to knock on Vandencomp's door.

The sole intruder, a white French poodle named Ivan the Terrible, nuzzled through the high thick hedges walling Vandencomp's back yard. Grizzly sent the dog home—cartwheeling over the hedge with a fatal pellet gun wound in the head.

For several weeks a team composed of underwater archaeologists and marine salvage experts readied the *Hunley* for her return to the surface. Dr. Lawrence Brookerbanks, a noted scientist with the U.S. Institute of Oceanographic Studies, had been sent in by the federal government to head the project.

The sand around the hulk was excavated to a depth of about four feet and in a hundred-by-forty-foot area. A steel frame was then secured over the top of the sub and a series of belts was run beneath it, anchoring it to the frame. From the *Corinthian*, a specially outfitted 180-foot research craft, the team would use a large crane to hoist the *Hunley* from her grave.

Helicopters whirred overhead, and dozens of assorted boats filled with news crews, city and state dignitaries, and the curious waited beyond a Coast Guard cordon as the crane winched its load from the bottom. Several boaters displayed various Confederate flags. Tourists watched from the parapets of forts Sumter and Moultrie. Other onlookers, some using binoculars or telescopes, lined the beaches of Sullivan's Island and the Isle of Palms and enjoyed the spectacle.

The slender dark mass in the green sea sharpened in detail as it rose, and excitement electrified those afloat. Hundreds of thousands of dollars had been raised through the federal government, state legislature, private donations, and fund-raisers to make this moment possible. All the hard work would mean that the *Hunley* would be raised, restored, her long-lost last crew buried with military honors, and the submarine put on display at a Charleston museum.

Finally the *Hunley* emerged, her brownish-white hull partially encrusted with oysters, mussels, and corals, but glistening in the twenty-first century sun. The white patches on her were calcium deposits left by the sea. Rusty water cascaded down her sides, and clumps of mud slid off, splashing back into the brine.

Despite the ocean's ravages, there was no mistaking the unique shape of the submarine. Rebel soldier and amateur artist Conrad Wise Chapman had been stationed in Charleston during the war and painted several illustrations of the *Hunley*. Watching her swing over the water in the crane's cradle, the jubilant researchers popped corks on bottles of icy champagne and toasted the little vessel and her valiant crew. It was as if one of Chapman's paintings had come to life.

She returned as a revered warrior, a prodigal Amazon who really had never left the battlefield, but had been buried under the waves where she fell almost 140 years earlier.

Onlookers applauded and shouted as the crane lifted the submarine and gently placed her aboard a platform on the deck of the *Corinthian*. She was laid on her starboard side as she had been on the seabed so that the recovery team did not shift the position of any remains or artifacts where they had rested inside the hull through the years.

Sprinkled among the living were the ghosts of Confederate Charleston. They did not cheer; they had witnessed the craft being pulled from the depths on two other occasions in 1863. Like this time, the *Hunley* had been a tomb then as well.

The porthole glass in the fore hatch was missing, meaning that silt that had covered the wreck had also filled at least the greatest part of her interior.

Certainly no one expected to find the bodies of Dixon and his men draped over the crankshaft. The length of time underwater and sea scavengers had seen to that. But the researchers did hope to find some skeletal remains—long bones, at least portions of skulls and teeth, and maybe some soft tissue from internal organs. From any cranium fragments they hoped to find bits of brain tissue.

A skull segment could be the first piece in a puzzle for a facial reconstruction to determine what that crewman looked like. The only known photo of any of the *Hunley* mariners was one believed to be that of Dixon. A molar or long bone could be a stepping stone for DNA analyses to try to identify some of the remains.

Then there likely would be the artifacts, probably only metal items carried or worn by the sailors—weapons, buttons, belt buckles, and coins, perhaps even the twenty-dollar gold piece given to Dixon by his sweetheart.

The *Corinthian* brought the *Hunley* home, docking at the old Charleston Navy Yard, where the sub, still in its protective crib, was transferred to a flatbed tractor trailer and driven to a specially constructed restoration facility nearby. It was here that the painstaking project of preserving, surveying, and excavating the shipwreck would take place, the experts estimating it would take ten years before the *Hunley* was ready to be put on public display at the museum.

Still resting on her starboard side, the sub was lowered into a tank of cold fresh water to protect her from oxidation. Brookerbanks held a news conference, jammed with journalists from around the nation and other countries as well, to discuss the significance of the salvage effort and plans for the *Hunley*.

Weeks after being raised, all was in readiness for the beginning of the internal excavation. The researchers prepared to enter the *Hunley* as if they were embarking on an archaeological dig. Since the hull was intact, they would go in through the turrets, extracting and mapping the silt layer by layer while uncovering the secrets within. This meant team members equipped with hand tools and suction hoses would actually crawl into the sub's entryways to flush out the dirt and reveal what, if anything, was left of the *Hunley* crew.

The team found that the fore hatch was not bolted from the inside, likely meaning that it had been open and that the sub was sunk by swells, possibly at the very moment when Dixon was signaling Battery Marshall. The only other explanation was that the *Hunley* sank on account of some other problem and that the crew had unbolted the hatch cover to try to escape. The outside sea pressure would have been too much to allow them to open it. The aft hatch was secured from the interior.

The researchers decided to go in through the fore hatchway. The wreck was pulled out of its tank and placed in an area where cold flowing water would inundate it during the excavation.

At last the long-awaited moment had arrived. The hatch was finally pried open and the molecules of air from a past age wafted into the building—the long-trapped atmosphere of the Confederacy unleashed after well over a century, along with the putrid odor of decayed sea life and the lost cause of long-dead heroes.

A young archaeologist looked into the mouth of the turret, her flashlight probing the pea soup inside. The sub was filled with muddy silt. This would be a very long process.

For three days the hull was excavated inch by inch, the team members taking shifts working in the hatchway. They used trowels, toothbrushes, and jets of water to remove the silt, always a bit further in the submarine. Not until the fourth day was anything found—but it was a discovery that was to shake the foundations not only of the entire project, but also of history itself.

"Somebody want to explain this?"

The voice of the archaeologist on excavation duty boomed through his radio from the sub's interior.

"Unfucking real. Is this a joke?"

"What do you have, Gilchrist?" Brookerbanks called down the hatchway.

"I'm coming out with it."

Gilchrist shimmied backwards, his feet, calves, and torso sliding out of the maw like a man wriggling from the throat of an anaconda. Some of his colleagues grabbed his lower body and helped pull him out. His arms, stretched over his head, were last to appear.

The archaeological team gasped and cursed in a chorus when they saw what he had found.

Starting to hyperventilate, Gilchrist held his find over his head —a crumpled, dripping pair of faded blue jeans.

"Levis," he panted between gulps of air. "Look like they've been in the water a day or so." All began to babble at once.

"Obviously someone's been in here before us, and I'm not talking about the crew."

"There is absolutely no way anyone could have gotten inside this hull. It was firmly sealed!"

"The Navy and Coast Guard have had the wreck site under 24/7 observation since she was found. The satellite surveillance didn't work? Come on! Nobody could have gotten in or out. Impossible!"

As Gilchrist held them aloft, the jeans unfurled and two metal objects dropped from the folds, clinking to the concrete floor.

One flashed gold as it fell, the other silver.

Brookerbanks' people scrambled to retrieve the items.

"Let me see them."

The team leader held out both hands, and the treasures were given to him.

Brookerbanks opened one fist and stared at a gold button. The capital letters CSN, a cannon, and anchor were on the face. In tiny script on the back was "Courtney & Tennent/Charleston/S.C."

Deliberately he unclasped the beaded chain and little metal plate in his other hand. They appeared to be dog tags or some other type of identification necklace.

"Doc Brook, we got car keys and some others on a ring in the front left pocket of these jeans. Definitely twentieth century."

Brookerbanks didn't reply. He rubbed the water and grime away with his thumb and read the tag's inscription. Without a word he let both finds slip from his fingers and hit the floor again, his team standing in a sullen stupor.

Then, like a man reeling into a coma, he mumbled the words he had just read.

"Eric Franklin Ashby, Lieutenant. United States Coast Guard."